BEAR ME SAFELY OVER

BEAR ME
SAFELY OVER

Sheri Joseph

Atlantic Monthly Press
New York

Published simultaneously in Canada
Printed in the United States of America

FIRST EDITION

Library of Congress Cataloging-in-Publication Data

Joseph, Sheri.
    Bear me safely over / by Sheri Joseph.
        p. cm.
    ISBN 0-87113-841-7
    1. Stepbrothers—Fiction. 2. Homophobia—Fiction. 3. Gay youth—Fiction.
4. Georgia—Fiction. I. Title.
PS3610.O67 B43 2002
813'.6—dc21   2001056080

Atlantic Monthly Press
841 Broadway
New York, NY 10003

02 03 04 05   10 9 8 7 6 5 4 3 2 1

for Trinity, who kicked me in the back to start this book

The reasonable hymn of angels rises from the ship of salvation: it is divine love.—Two loves! I can die of earthly love, die of devoutness. I have left souls behind whose grief will grow at my departure. You choose me from among the shipwrecked; those who remain, are they not my friends?
Save them!

—Arthur Rimbaud, *A Season in Hell*
translated by J. S. Watson, Jr.

He will keep me till the river
Rolls its waters at my feet
Then He'll bear me safely over
Where the loved ones I shall meet.

—"I Will Sing the Wondrous Story,"
a Baptist hymn

contents

hindsight

Sidra wore her hair up, twisted in the jaws of a fierce toothed clip. Curtis, wedging a pocket with his nose, found it still damp on the inside, fragrant with her apple shampoo. Though she'd been mucking stalls for an hour, heaping horseshit into a wheelbarrow, the sweat along her earlobe tasted as clean as her hair—apples and salt—maybe saved by the clip from the smell of horses. Curtis didn't know whether to be thankful, since he loved the look of her hair loose. Without it long and shining over her shoulders, she seemed to be missing something, to be only partly there.

"You're in a mood," she said. He backed her into a corner of the stall, hands pushing under her shirt where she was slicked with sweat.

"I missed you last night, is all." His hands traveled over her backside, the tight-muscled ass of a rider, and upward over the knobs of her hipbones, the soft-skinned rails of her ribs. So thin, this girl— *bony as Faggot-boy*. His stomach lurched at the thought, touched the back of his throat with the taste of last night's beer. Now *why*, with his hands on Sidra, would he go and think up a comparison like that, his fairy of a teenage stepbrother? It was definitely time to break up with her. He rummaged for her breasts, but she was wearing an exercise bra that made her flatter than usual. She might as well have taped herself down with an Ace bandage.

She grabbed his hands through the shirt. "Curtis, you know Mama could walk in here any minute."

Curtis was pretty sure that Sidra's mother could catch them buck naked and not say anything more than "Excuse me." But Sidra liked her dramas arranged her way. His fingers laced into her ribs, burrowed against her skin; he had to force himself to turn her loose, to step back, palms out. "Now, Sid, that is exactly the kind of shit I'm talking about."

She lolled her head. "Poor baby. If you're not getting enough, why don't you just pick up one of those girls that hang around Slocum's?"

Maybe I will, he wanted to say, but she had beaten him again. He had been thinking of that very thing just the night before. Girls followed the band he played with, leaned at him across tables with breasts mounding out the scoop necks of their tiny T-shirts. There was *real* action, offered, his for the taking. But she emptied the threat straight out by speaking it like that, as if it were her smallest concern. How in the hell was he supposed to break up with a woman who would say such things?

He had intended not to miss her the night before, not to think of her, though he dimly recalled driving away from Slocum's in some dark hour of the morning, and then, jump-cut, he was staggering drunk up her mother's driveway. Had it really been him, or a dream, that moony puppy outside Sidra's bedroom window?

"I'm just saying—" It was too late, now, to keep the whine out of his voice. "Why'd you have to move home anyway? If you were at all thinkin' about me—"

"We've been over this, Curtis. If my horses are here, I gotta be here. And Mama needs me with her."

He snorted—the biggest crock he'd ever heard, and she knew it. That Florie Ballard would need anyone. Sidra was home purely to piss her mother off. And maybe to piss him off in the bargain. He had thought of that before when he tried to imagine what went on in her head. But it wasn't logical. She fell into pieces whenever he tried to tell himself *this* or *that* was the true Sidra, the reason and the answer.

"Baby, it's not like *you* don't have a place. And a car." She grinned, stroking his belly, and he tensed the muscles against her touch. "What's your problem, anyway?"

⌒

All the way out to the back field, alone, he listed her pros and cons. They were going to go riding. Sidra's own horses were an oddball collection of half-broke babies, too spooky for strangers. But in the various weedy, barbed-wire fields and leaning sheds where she had managed to board her horses in the past, there had always been someone else's horse he could ride. Now that she was back home, he had several to choose from. "You can take my old show horse," she had said. "Name's Simon. He's out in the back with Mama's mares, seal brown, you can't miss him." She had put a halter in his hand then, and pointed.

He did enjoy having a horsy girlfriend. He liked to ride. It was something he felt he could do with a reasonable appearance of skill. Sidra called him a natural cowboy. He liked to see himself that way, straight in the saddle—even if it was an English saddle—halfway to Marlboro man. Horses looked tricky, but they were easy once you knew what buttons to push.

So the horses were one of her pros. But making him trudge half a mile all by himself to catch one was pure Sidra. A girlfriend ought to think ahead about catching a horse, say, so it would be waiting at the barn. Or she might even want to walk out with him, spend a little

time. But horses, he suspected, were all that Sidra truly needed. Her
own were cozy in the barn and she was with them, and that was that.
He ranked second and was on his own.

The sex was good; another pro. He was addicted to her skin and
all the angles of her body, the secret spots he understood the work-
ings of. He knew where to kiss her—inside the elbow, back of the
neck—to make her toes curl. Something in that reaction, such a little
thing, made him happy in a way he couldn't account for. He knew
where there were dimples in her lower back that even she had never
seen. More than anything, he loved the look and feel of all that blond
hair against his thighs when she went down on him. Even though
now it seemed they were beginning to fall into routines, the newness worn off of everything between them, he couldn't tell himself
he was tired of her. Not in bed, maybe never. When he broke up with
her, he thought, she would still belong to him. And when she was
with someone else—he tried to picture it and struck a closed door.
Not Sidra with anyone else.

But it was time to move on. He could see that look in the eyes of
the band when they asked, full knowing the answer, "Now, *how* long
have you two been together?" It was going on two years, incredibly; he
had never meant it to last so long. They somehow just kept going. It
was like his job at Athens Walls and Windows, where he had been
since college graduation: nothing impressive, but it paid the bills, and
he could think of worse places to be stuck. He knew what to do with
paint and wallpaper and Venetian blinds. The work was reliable.

He came to a fence, found the gate. The horses were grazing at the
back of the weedy field along a stand of scrub trees and brush. On the
rise beyond the fence was a bizarre landscape—a whole neighborhood
of fresh new two-story houses. No lawns yet, only scrubbed red dirt.
The few that faced him had the dollhouse look of wide factory-new
windows looking in on nothing but another window at the back, the

view unobstructed straight through. They made him feel vaguely watched, though no one lived there yet. It was Sunday, no workers around. He and Sidra could ride the horses over there and explore.

He counted four horses in the field and picked out the one that looked most like a seal—Sidra's former show horse, now a retired old nag. One day, he thought, maybe I'll be good enough to ride one of her precious babies. He pictured Sidra's shock if he were to lope her black stud colt in circles around her, bareback, the horse full of fire but not bucking, halting at his command. "No big deal," he would say. "We understand each other." But something like that would take time—he and Sidra could be broken up tomorrow, for all he knew.

The dark horse grazed a little apart from the others. Curtis felt in his pockets for a carrot, but he had forgotten one. He held out his hand, faking carrot. The mares down the field raised their heads, looked at him with interest. The gelding, sweet-faced, stood still and stretched out its nose toward Curtis's hand. "Whoa there," he said, looping the lead shank around the horse's neck.

With the other hand, he straightened the halter to go over the gelding's head. He was thinking, for some reason, of Sidra's hands on the halter, on the head of this horse that she had ridden for so many years. How many years? He looked at the eyes of the horse as if it could answer, and he saw that something was wrong. The gelding raised its head, took a step backward. Something in the eyes was no longer what he thought it had been, sweet old pet after a carrot and a good scratch. "Whoa—" Curtis tightened his grip on the rope. The muscles of the animal's neck flared suddenly against the restraint, and Curtis knew then he was no match, but he set his heels, gripped down. "Whoa, you bastard."

The horse sat back on its haunches, spun away into a bolt, and not thinking to let go, Curtis felt his body jerked around like a doll, then a sudden shock of impact in the center of his back. He hit the ground on his knees, the horse long gone, and he knew he had seen the rear hooves airborne in his peripheral vision. The bastard mule had kicked him!

The blow had slammed all the air from his lungs. He went to his hands, sucking for air. When he looked up again, the three other horses were directly above with their muzzles in his face, ears pricked. "Jesus!" He scrambled away, thinking they could trample him in an instant. With loud snorts, they shied back, but at once they were calm again, ears pointed like raised eyebrows, as if he were the most interesting creature ever to appear in their field. One mare glanced at her companion and back at him, so that he had to wonder what the old ladies were saying. "Mildred, what do you make of this?" Or perhaps, "Whaddya know, ole Simon got one right in the back! Will you look at that!" On the ground, so vulnerable, he knew they must be capable of thinking such things, as if he had stumbled into the frequency for their thoughts. The culprit stood cropping grass, unconcerned, several yards off.

⤺

When he'd first laid eyes on Sidra, it had been from behind—long blond hair and her beautiful ass rounding under a miniskirt. That night, from the stage, she'd been the best-looking thing at Slocum's. Even Kim Fisher—who ran their lights and sometimes, if drunk, went home with him, to the head-shaking envy of the other band members—turned forgettable. He tracked Sidra's movements in the crowd by the flash of colored lights off her pale hair, and Kim seemed to spin the colors wilder and wilder until Curtis thought he was falling, forgot his place in the song.

But her face proved a sore disappointment. He couldn't decide— still couldn't—if her nose was too long, her lips too thin, her eyes too small, too strange, if it was the mole on her chin, the reddish crescents beside her nose, or the mere fact that she wouldn't wear makeup. All those things and more contributed to a face that was not unattractive, at times strangely attractive, at times just plain strange. He didn't dare think *ugly*. Not after the way she drew him to her as if she were the only true female thing he had ever run across.

Oddly, when he faced her, when she spoke, she hardly seemed like a girl at all—at least not like the girls he was used to. She had none of their aloofness. Her games were all her own. She thumb-wrestled him for drinks, and won; he couldn't be sure that he had let her. She taught him a curse word he had never heard before—*chordee*—straight from the Middle Ages and dirtier than anything he knew. She downed tequila shots in a single deft motion: lick of salt, roll of the hand over the glass and done, glass clunked on the table. Nothing dainty about it. Those reckless movements, the narrow, laughing eyes. He knew he would have to see her again, if only to talk himself out of her.

Before she left Slocum's that night, she had taken hold of his wrist, unbuttoned the flannel sleeve, and rolled it slowly, painstakingly, back to the elbow; then, in black ballpoint pen, she'd written SIDRA and her phone number over the blank expanse of his forearm. For days after the ink faded, he felt the bite where the pen tip had furrowed his flesh, as if she had meant to leave a permanent mark.

⌒

Horseless, Curtis walked back from the pasture. He couldn't risk another failed attempt at Simon, and besides, he no longer felt like riding. Sidra, he knew, had somehow planned this fate for him, this humiliation—she was a conspirator, after all, with horses. She was probably laughing already. This was the end of them. The horse's hoof was like a proclamation of God and a stamp slammed out of heaven to seal Curtis's decision. Even he couldn't argue with a thing like that. He tried to light on the right words to say to her, so that she would know how deeply she had injured him, the degree of her blame. "Your goddamn horse," he mumbled, but already it sounded childish, petty. He revised. "Good-bye, Sidra. Don't call me."

The trail from the field led up beside the house before descending to the barn. The house, blue clapboard, was half shaded by a massive, gnarled oak and set about with roof-high sprays of hot-pink flower bushes. The back porch was a deep one, dark and cool and inviting, studded with white wicker rockers. In one of these sat Florie Ballard, Sidra's mother. Curtis shouldn't have looked over, but he did, and she waved. Then her terriers were suddenly colliding under his feet in a white-and-brown-spotted fury.

"Here! Gertie! Zeus!" The dogs rolled off, paying him little mind but snapping at each other, spinning circles around him. He could see Florie's solid form in her wide-brimmed hat at the wall of the porch, insistently waving him up. He had no choice. Sidra, brushing Gumby, her spotted four-year-old, was darkly visible down in the barn hall.

"Look at this good-looking young man! How's the music business?" Florie held out her hands, downturned. Though not especially tall or fat, she always struck Curtis as being twice the size of her daughter. Without softness, she carried an ease of flesh that seemed definite, somehow intentional.

"Can't complain, Florie." He smiled, gave her his hands to squeeze. She made him forget all his anger in an instant, even the swelling ache of his back. The porch seemed like neutral ground, a place where he could put everything on hold for as long as he felt inclined. He did like talking to Florie.

"You been working on any new songs?"

"A few. One I like a little."

"Well, you bring that guitar over and premiere them for us. We want to be the first to hear them, so later on we'll have that claim to fame." By "we" she meant Sidra and herself and her elderly mother-in-law, who was mostly deaf. Curtis played bass for his band, Fried Baloney, shy of the spotlight that followed singers and guitars. When he brought out his old guitar, played his own songs, it was almost always locked in his room alone and singing half in whispers. Only once had he played aloud and for an audience, one night on Florie Ballard's back porch.

"Sidra won't mind if I make you sit awhile," she said, with a wink that meant she cared little what her daughter minded. "I haven't seen you in so long. Now that she's moved home, though, I expect we'll see more of you." Florie sat in her accustomed place, and the dogs fell panting at her feet. Sidra's mother—he couldn't help adding her to the pro side of his list, even with his mind already settled.

Mr. Ballard was gone, like Curtis's own father. But as Sidra liked to point out, he hadn't left by his own choice—Florie had kicked him out. And not for running around or hitting her or any of the usual reasons, but for buying Sidra too many horses. At least that was how Sidra put it, eyes flashing fury. Curtis figured there was probably more to the story. But Florie shrugged it all off, Sidra's anger along with the whole notion of the man who had been her husband. "Pish, him? What was he ever good for? Doesn't the place look nice? I keep it up fine without him, just like I always did." She had said this, he remembered distinctly, over the body of a stray dog she had just shot for running the horses. That kind of woman had no need of a man.

His own mother had finally remarried. But for most of his growing up, since he was ten, they had been on their own, and he still wasn't sure how his mother had survived it. She was no Florie Ballard. She hardly seemed strong enough to carry herself, let alone a son, through a single day. In the midst of preparations for some errand—a doctor's visit, a trip to the store—she would sit down in despair.

They would never make it in time, or the store would be closed, the prices too high, and who knew if a certain item might be found cheaper at Rigby's across town? It was no use. He might tell her, carefully, that the supper she fixed tasted good. She would flick her fearful eyes over him—he couldn't bear her eyes—say no, she should have put in more onions, she shouldn't have cooked it so long. She would collapse in tears, wailing about the proportion of spices, what should have been done to avoid this ruin. "No, Mom, it's fine," he would insist, helpless. "It tastes real good."

Eventually he lived with his grandmother close by, never knowing for sure who decided the matter, except that it wasn't him and he had no say. In his iron bed under the sloping roof of his grandmother's attic, he wondered where his mother was and if he would know it if she needed him. He dreamed up fires, wild animals, solid threats from which he could rescue her. He dreamed of his father's return, ragged and starved, begging to be taken back into the house, and Curtis would bar the door with his body. "We don't need you," he would say. "It's too late to be sorry now."

Halfway into a rocker beside Florie, Curtis grimaced. His back was seizing into an angry, hoof-sized knot. It hadn't bothered him much until he tried to put it in a chair. He finished sitting, released his breath.

Florie stared with her mouth open, and he explained, "I, uh, had a little run-in with a horse out back—"

"What, get bucked off?"

"Got kicked. Right in the back." Speaking it made him feel injured and pitiable all over again. His face felt hot.

"Who did that? Not Simon!"

"Yeah, Simon. I caught him fair and square, you know, had the rope on his neck. Then I guess he just decided he didn't want to be caught after all."

"And he kicked you? That little jerk! He's an old jerk, actually. Too old to be behaving that way."

Sidra was headed up the hill from the barn, looking put out. "What's going on, Curtis? Are we riding or not?"

By then Florie was beside his chair, coaxing him to lean forward so she could raise his shirt. "Not today, you're not!" she shouted. "Come and see what your evil horse has done to this boy! He's got a *hoofprint* on his back."

"Really?" he asked, straining his head back over his shoulder as if he might be able to see. "A whole hoofprint?" He was pleased to have such dramatic proof for Sidra, who was otherwise bound to side with the horse.

"Don't you move." Florie turned his head back where it had been.

"God, Curtis." Sidra was behind him now, opposite her mother. "How did you manage that?"

Their fingers trailed lightly over his skin, so light he could barely feel or tell how many fingers, who was touching. It felt like when Sidra would curl against his back after they made love and write silly messages with a finger on his skin, forcing him to guess the words. *I love Curtis. Sidra is great. Sidra loves Gumby.* Now he stretched his own hand to feel his back, and there were three hands reading the braille of his skin, a perfect U raised in ridges of flesh.

"Wow," he said. "It didn't really hurt that much. It doesn't."

"Son, you need to go to the emergency room," Florie said firmly.

"No, I'm—"

"These things can be more serious than you think. You don't mess around with a back."

"Like when I broke my back," Sidra said. He looked up at her, surprised.

"Yes, this same thing," Florie said.

"I was riding, well, Simon, actually. Back in high school. Took a big, solid cross-country fence, and he was used to those little show ring fences that knock down—"

"They went ass over teakettle, both of them!"

"But I was fine, you know, a little sore. Got back up and everything. Rode some more fences, just to—"

"But the next day!"

"The next day, I went to get on my horse, put a foot in the stirrup and I thought someone had shot me in the back—"

"Turned out she had cracked two vertebrae and never knew it!"

"So you never know about these things. You should go."

"You should take him, Sidra. Right away."

"Yes. Of course."

He looked up at Sidra, feeling the heat return to his face. The afternoon sun was in his eyes, and Sidra was a haze of gold, close enough that he could smell her skin lotion even under a day's layer of horses. She touched his hair. "I'm sorry this happened, sweetie. I should have gone out there with you."

He looked away, swallowing back a sudden emotion. "I shoulda taken a carrot."

⌐

He was in Sidra's car before he thought to notice he was being put there, and then she was carting him to the hospital. Somehow he had let a couple of women turn a little bruise into a medical event. He wondered what Sidra would do if he got out at a stoplight and said he had places to be, no time for this silly shit. "Good-bye, Sidra. Just don't call me for a while, okay?"

But she would never let him go, not injured. Not when he hadn't even planned well enough to pick a fight with her, make her mad enough to send him off with such epithets as she was fully capable of. Maybe the horse had delivered not a final blow but only another delay, and perhaps that was the plan all along. Somehow, he would believe, Sidra was still moving the pieces in this game as easily as she drove the car, with him stuck in the passenger seat like an invalid.

He thought of a teenaged Sidra with her back broken, never suspecting. He imagined that he would have known it. Maybe, having unhooked her bra, he would have felt the bones through her skin, their edges made unfamiliar. He saw himself carrying her through the halls of the hospital, her head slumped at his shoulder and later, a doctor who would say something like, "Good job, young man. You've saved her. God knows what would have happened if not for your efforts."

In the emergency room, Sidra put him in a chair and went to the front desk. It was far across the waiting room, an acre away, and he thought that was a ridiculous way to design a hospital. In the glare of fluorescent lights, he found it hard to focus on her distant back, her dirty cutoffs and T-shirt, thin legs browned with sun and stable dirt, the clip that still fastened her hair like the bite of a persistent animal—one of those lizards that go on biting after their heads are severed from their bodies. But all day, strands of blond had been escaping. He wanted to call out to her, but she was speaking with a nurse now, so far away. Pure Sidra, she wouldn't have heard.

⌒

Because of a horse, she had refused to come out to Slocum's the night before. Gumby, the last of her little herd, was being trailered over from his former home, a dirt lot rented by her father. She wanted to settle the horse in. "All night?" Curtis asked, incredulous. "How long does it take?"

He spent the evening in a sullen rage, drank too much beer, spoke to no one. "You got it rough with her," said Lyle, the band's drummer and his friend. "Even she couldn't blame you now for having a good time—one night. Look at all that." And Curtis couldn't have missed the new blood, for it circled him, drawn to his brooding, all curves and shining eyes. Count on women to have the cure-all for anything that ailed you, simple as their bodies.

Drunk, he had driven home alone and turned without his knowing to the Ballard farm. He left his car in the road and stumbled over the long drive, between fences draped in honeysuckle that exhaled a thick summer breath into the night. Approaching this house always felt to him like entering a room walled in flowers, a secret pocket in the center of bulldozed dirt and the suburbs that had come up on all sides faster than kudzu. Only the Ballard land had not been sold to the developers. There were no lights on in the house and it was a darker shape against the sky, under the black limbs of the oak. He found her window up in the second story in the back. There was only a faint shine of starlight to distinguish the glass from the wall—he couldn't tell if it was open or closed, shade drawn or not. Sidra's new place, he thought of it, where they could not make love for fear of Florie's hearing them. But really it was the oldest of rooms. She had slept there as a child, through nearly her whole life before him. It stunned him to think of a girl before him, a green stick ten years old, looking out that very window at nothing but horses.

Then he shuddered into a more sober awareness, noticed for the first time where he had come to. What the hell was she doing to him? He had to get control. Worse, she was not at the window to meet him, hair streaming moonlight like Rapunzel, which meant she must be somewhere else. If only in a dream behind the window, she was else-

where, without him. The dew was turning cold at his shoes. His own
father had walked out across a lawn like this one, past midnight, gone
without even a note. What would the man have said, Curtis always
wondered, if he had stopped to say goodbye? Would there have been
any last advice, something dramatic and final that would fix him sol-
idly in Curtis's memory? All that remained was the man's hard-jawed
profile as he watched TV, voiceless, as if he had never spoken a word.

His mother's new husband was nice enough. Curtis didn't mind
talking to him, but then again, it was obvious the man's influence
had done nothing for his own son. Curtis was half afraid if he listened
too closely, he might be infected with whatever had made Faggot-
boy the way he was. Closed in his room, Curtis strummed out a Lynyrd
Skynyrd song that he thought of as his father's song, sung not to his
mother but to him. Last advice. If he sang the words, it was only in
whispers: "I'm as free as a bird now, and this bird you cannot change."
It was the first song he'd ever learned, the one any crowd was bound
to yell for after a few sets. It was the one song that Curtis, on stage,
absolutely refused to play.

He sat on an exam table with his shirt off, waiting. Beside the door,
Sidra thumbed a magazine she had brought from the waiting room,
checked her watch. The article open across her knees said, "Fifty
ways," and he couldn't make out the rest. Fifty Ways to Catch a Man,
probably. It was one of those magazines. Then he thought, *Fifty Ways
to Leave Your Lover*.

"You'll be glad you did this," she said, glancing out the door, down
the long hall. "It's probably nothing, but you'll just feel better, I promise. You won't be wondering at every little twinge if you're gonna be
crippled for life or something."

You, you, you. What about her? What was she in this, the chauffeur? She went out into the hall, beyond the doorway, and he felt tethered to the table. "Sid?" he called, heard his voice crack like some terminal case.

In a few seconds she returned. "How long could it take to read an x-ray? Well, I suppose we've got nowhere better to go." She found a box full of rubber gloves on a shelf. They were thin as membranes, and she plucked out a pair, pushed her hands into them. "Now vee must examine the patient." She sidled toward him, snapping the rubber. "Please to remove the pants and bend over."

"God, Sid." His laugh ratcheted over the battered muscles of his back.

"Please not to laugh. Laughing can be very dangerous to the condition."

"Then don't make me laugh. It hurts."

Her voice became her own again. "Now how could I make you do anything? If it hurts, that's your own lookout." She stood before him with her gloved hands on his knees, pushed them apart and eased her body up between his thighs. "I can't help it if I'm a comic genius."

He reached behind her head and took the alligator clip. Her hair uncoiled behind her, and she shook it out dramatically, tipping her head forward so a wild swath fell over one eye. "I bet that looks gorgeous, doesn't it?"

"Yeah, as a matter of fact."

"Let me fix it or something."

And before he could stop her, she was gone, down the hall. He could hardly believe she was gone so fast, and he had thought of nothing to say in time. It was only because the hospital made him nervous, that her leaving seemed so final. He still held the clip, a spring-set pincer of hard plastic. He opened and closed it, set its teeth into the skin of his arm, and was surprised how strong the grip was.

"Is that better?" She was back, minus the gloves but otherwise looking not at all changed. Again she leaned out to the hall. "The doctor hasn't come yet?"

"Sid."

"Hmm?" She stared off down the hall.

"Sid, come here."

"What?" Her eyes seemed bored or sleepy, he couldn't tell.

"Come here." He held out his hand until she gave hers over. He felt the echo of every motion toward her ripple through his back, which lent him an odd confidence. "Sid, listen. Are you listening?"

"Yeah," she said with a touch of impatience.

"Sid. Marry me."

She paused a beat, then scoffed. "Please. Did you get kicked in the head?"

But her voice had fallen a shade in confidence, and he saw he had struck a blow after all, made contact. She had felt it. He smiled, and she shrank up against him as if she were cold, pushed her lips up to his, arms winding around his neck. Her hands fluttering off and on his bare shoulders, as though she could hardly stand to be careful. They were kissing when the doctor came in the room.

"Ah, young love," he said with a smirk. "I promise he's not dying yet. You can save some of that for later."

He snapped a pair of x-rays up into the lightbox. The light flickered on, and there were the bones of Curtis's chest, the shadows of his organs, the hollow bend of his neck in profile looking as delicate and fossilized as the remains of a prehistoric animal. It could have been anyone's insides, but the doctor insisted it was him, proceeded to point out all the places he had not been damaged.

wrestling at the gates

When that man calls me Angel, I swear I never felt so high. "Angel of God," he says, my face like a crystal cup between the heels of his hands. I don't know what to call him, except what he tells me, which is Mack. It's not his real name. I'm told never to look him in the face, as if angel eyes could burn him, so I look past his shoulder, his hip, out the Thunderbird's window where the view is solid brick on one side, a wall close enough to block the door. On the other, a few feet away, a hurricane fence rises before great broken slabs of concrete, cantilevered against each other at impossible angles. His breathing is the only sound, and while his big blunt hands move over my body, my eyes try to stay on the diamond weave of the fence—try to follow the wire that loops up and up until it's interrupted by a red-on-white construction sign.

Because he says, "Look up, over there," and directs my chin with a fingertip. I smell the sweet, stale smoke on his breath. "Your eyes are full of light," he tells me, and his voice is amazed, though there can't be much light getting past the tinted windows.

Mar-Co Construction, No Trespassing. A phone number. Up again, up and up as I sink lower, to an angled triple row of barbed wire. Higher, beyond the teeth of the wire, sky, a small, irregular gap torn between buildings. Atlanta. I want my eyes back inside the car, with him, but I can only steal quick glimpses now and then.

With this man, I never wonder where to be. He shows me, turns me and folds me beneath him so there are no choices, and sometimes I fight a little, pretend to, just to show us both his strength. He likes that. He laughs if I resist, a soft, thrilling, wicked chuckle against my ear. Mack Daddy is what I call him secretly, mouth it to myself, face crushed into the armrest or against the door, next to that silver handle that cranks the window. The black knob of the handle is sometimes all I see, and my head knocks the glass. Knock knock knock—not hard, just like, *I'm in here*. Like if there was anyone standing in that erupted earth beyond the fence, they might turn and squint and recognize me, maybe wave.

This is the only place I understand anymore, the rank, scarred velour of the seat under me and this man above, always above. When did angels ever stoop so low? But I swear, it doesn't feel low. He comes dressed in glory, suit and tie most times, rarely bothers to disrobe. I take everything off, the way he likes me, though I feel clothed in his clothes, serge stroking my skin.

After it's over, he pays me. I don't exactly know why he does this, since I've never once asked for his money. Maybe I look hungry or something. I know I'll be even thinner as he leaves, thinner in my clothes. I pull on my cutoffs, and he tucks the folded bills into my back pocket like it's a secret. When he lets me out, two blocks west of where he found me, I can barely stand. My skin is all one fine vibration, as though serge has rubbed every surface and only just this moment stopped. The hollow above my right collarbone is still wet and stung with the suction of his mouth, the scrape of his teeth. I touch the spot—there will be a mark—slide along the spit and taste my fingertips. I can adjust my shirt to cover it later. The Thunderbird, gold and leviathan, drives off, and I watch until it's gone, until I'm sure I'm alone on the side of the road—that this is me, and my own legs hold me up, and even if the car doesn't turn back again, which it won't, I will go on breathing.

It's Thursday afternoon, always. Thursday's child, says the rhyme, has far to go, and I can't ever decide if that's criticism or prophecy, or maybe just the actual distance traveled.

ᔕ

It's easy to get here, to the city where Mack finds me. Much harder to get home. Where I come from is country, and I mean *kuntry*. I don't know anyone else in Greene County like me, though I guess there are plenty enough who watch the trucks rolling over the Lake Oconee Bridge and think they'd like to go somewhere too in such a gigantic way. Log trucks and semis and cattle trucks and big flatbeds hauling fertilizer, machine parts—there must be a reason for all these trucks to pass through the middle of nowhere. Don't ask me to explain. But I know this: stand in the pull-off just beyond the bridge and sooner or later a truck will stop. Down to the Interstate, I-20, is not much farther, and there it's the simplest thing to catch a ride. I'm forever amazed how many cars are streaming to Atlanta, always more going that way than coming.

Once, a couple of years back when I was riding in a car over the bridge with my dad and my stepmom, I caught sight of a black boy named Leon Sharp, who was in my grade at school, getting into one of those trucks. Leon was never someone I knew or paid any mind to, but I did after that. I thought about him, and I wondered too where a boy might go in a truck. Later on, when I started taking walks over the bridge, past the black men who fished all day under the darting swallows, I'd pass Leon as well. Slender body the color of oak bark, usually shirtless and tucked into the shade of the woods beside the pull-off. He'd be whistling a song in his teeth and I'd look and he'd look, and even though we'd never actually meet each other's eyes I could feel the way our glances struck each other, lower in the body, electric.

After I had passed him three separate times in three weeks, passed the pull-off too and never went anywhere but back home again, he said he had something to show me. "Back in the woods," he said, husky. I had heard his loud, wisecracking voice in the school halls, and this wasn't it, this low offering like he might have gone on his knees to speak the words. I went.

He had set a plank bench back there in the thick of the woods, close to the lake. The water was just visible through a gap in the black-berry, and I remember how a towhee scrabbled at the dirt under the thicket, paused each minute to call, "Drink yer tea." We sat on Leon's bench and kissed. It was one kiss, really—a long, slow, sweet burn all the way down and back like a double shot of Everclear, his long-fingered hand resting on my jeans. I was sixteen, old enough to want more, and to know what. Too old to be out here testing my mouth for the first time on another human person. But I took off running for home, before our lips found even a second purchase. I still won-der why. Maybe because Leon was black. Or because he was a boy, my own age, and my head was all full of men. Or because even in that private cove of dogwood and wisteria bloom, so deep the mos-quitoes nipped us from all sides and sang in our ears, it was still Greene County and too close to home.

When I say there is no one at home like me, I'm neglecting Leon. I could say there is no one white like me, if you don't count the men whose wives and girlfriends won't do for diamonds what Leon and I do gladly, for free. For a ride. Conyers, Atlanta, just about anywhere past the county line will do. But those hometown men who stop for us from time to time are only answering a need, which is different than wanting it. They are not what I am. I'm an abomination in the eyes of the Lord, same as Leon—black or white makes no difference. But then, I haven't seen Leon in a year, and I expect by now he's long gone.

⌒

Sometimes I get home only by spending Mack's money down to the last bill. I'll take a cab if I have to, just to avoid the wounded look I'll get from my stepmom if I'm late to supper. To Muriel, supper's a big deal.

I have the cab drop me over the bridge so no one will see, and then I cut across the neighbor's pasture for home the back way. The unsheltered grass is brittle from the sun, rocky with old dried cow chips. I pick my way through. Down the little slope, I can see someone out on the back porch—Muriel's blood son, Curtis. I almost stop there in the middle of the field, like I have an option, before I go on with more deliberate steps, duck through the barbed wire fence, walk into the yard.

I keep my eye on Curtis, who won't look back. He's around twenty-five now, the stormiest blond I ever saw. Eyes like shadowed water, this color I can feel ripple in my gut. A smile tries to flinch onto my face, but I swallow it back and say, "Hi, Curtis." It comes out a whisper.

He mutters something that sounds like, "Out playing in shit again," but I am past him too quick to hear, up the steps and through the screen door.

Muriel's turning pork chops at the stove. Through the open window, I can see the white wooden back of Curtis's rocker, the tension in it that reveals his body's presence even though he's out of view. I sneak up behind Muriel and kiss her just above the mole on her cheek.

She cries out with a jump. "Lord, Paul!" She turns with one of her frowning smiles and touches my face as if to make sure I'm real. "Now, why you have to scare the bejesus out of a person?"

She has on a sheer, melon-colored blouse over white shorts and a bikini top. Against those clothes and her yellow-dyed hair, her skin is a dark contrast. "You went to the tanning bed." I wrinkle my nose, thumb her cheek like the brown might rub off. "Why you have to do that?"

She pats the spot I rubbed back into place. "You can tell a difference? Dennis says it does a worlda good, takes off ten years. Says I look like a girl on the beach."

"Of course, Dennis says! He owns the place." My voice is so loud it rings down the hall. I try to talk quieter, end up talking faster. "You don't see him crawling into one of those death traps, now, do you? I can just imagine him trying to fit! He'd need the jaws of life to get loose again."

She bubbles over in giggles, and a snort escapes her nose. "Oh, Lord! Darlin', you do crack me up."

"I can't understand why you'd have the first thing to do with Dennis Corrigan, that bloated joke . . . that—"

Past the window screen, Curtis is listening. I can tell by the way his chair is poised, not rocking. I can't see his head. Muriel covers her mouth, glances that way too. I know she's about to explain him, apologize in a hushed voice, but he would hear even a whisper. He's that close.

Before she speaks, I turn and cross the kitchen, pivot at five paces to face her like it's high noon in Laredo. "You realize the man is unethical, he's an aesthetic disgrace. He's an inveterate liar!" I can feel my voice climbing again, over her laughter, past my control. "He's leaving beautifully tanned corpses and motherless children all over town!"

She laces her hands into a ball against her mouth to stopper the giggles, like another sound could crack us both to pieces. We feel Curtis not rocking outside. She looks like she's praying now, brown forehead creased with distress. But she's looking straight at me, and I meet her eyes, let out a breath, take another. Breathe.

"You're through with Dennis, darlin'," I say, quieter. "Pork chops are burning."

⌇

Here's a midsummer night's resolution of mine: try always to tell the truth, no matter what it costs. I said *try*. So when I pass through the den and Dad, from his recliner, lowers the edge of the *Journal-Constitution* to ask if I had a good day, I stop to consider, then give the same answer that serves most other days of the week: "Yeah." The truth, after all.

I ask about his day and he says, "Oh, same as usual."

I nod. I would keep nodding until it's been long enough and I can go, but today I add, improv, "Curtis is over for supper, I see."

"Well, he's staying for a bit, I think." Dad cocks his head like a curious, sympathetic dog. "Muriel didn't tell you? He and his buddies got kicked out of that apartment in Athens."

"They did, huh?" I try to say this with cool nonchalance. I look at the sunburst clock on the wall and count its gold rays. "That's okay. I mean, it's—"

Muriel appears in the kitchen doorway, a pleading look in her eye and a glass of sweet tea in each hand. She's had an inspiration. I'm already shaking my head no.

"*Just* take him—yes—take him out a glass of tea. Y'all can have a chat on the porch, make better friends."

"I was about to, uh, grab a shower." What I almost said: *Shove bamboo sticks under my fingernails*.

"No time for that—we're eating soon. You be the one to make the effort. He'll come around." She pushes the glasses into my hands. Behind me, Dad's gone back behind the paper. "He's really a good boy, underneath it all. You'll see."

I give her a martyred look, but Muriel knows I'm her patsy and errand boy. She sends, I go. Plus, I actually want to believe her. Every time, it comes to this.

Shoulder to the screen door, I sight down to Curtis's chair, his clean, square jaw in profile, crossed with a pulsing band of muscle like he's working something in his teeth. I go out, take a few steps, and he throws a corner-of-the-eye look that could be a warning. *Get your goddamn eyes off me*, is what he usually says, what I wait for now. *What are you looking at, Faggot-boy?*—a glance of mine almost as painful to him as an accidental brush of skin in the narrow hall just before I am slammed back, head smacked to the wall and I can only wait for the next blow with open eyes. But he almost never strikes again. More likely he'll see his own hands on me like two traitors and snatch them back, stalk off in a hurry. I can't remember a time he has ever said my name. Now I'm holding the two glasses, and I see, too late, that he has a beer bottle pinched by the neck in his fingers.

"Oh. I—" I turn wistfully half back to the screen door.

He looks at me, nostrils twitching. My eyes going anywhere else. "Just set it down," he says finally and shakes his head at the cows. "Pathetic."

I do as he says. Then I step off a safe distance and lean my back to the wall, my own glass between my hands, look where he looks: black and white mosaic of cows strung along the fence, headed home.

Muriel went through a rough time after her first husband left, so Curtis got raised mostly by his grandmother. He was starting college by the time Dad and I were on the scene, but he still came around, has been coming around for years. From the beginning, I think, he knew the truth—me no more than ten and without the smallest idea of it myself. He saw something. Honestly, I don't know what it was. Maybe I've always held my body like I do now, arms close to the ribs, crossed in front, chin to shoulder; when I sit it's knees together and tucked to the side, folded over and over myself like that Japanese paper. *Pansy*, he used to say. *Sit normal, for God's sake!* He no longer offers instruction.

It's Muriel's sorrow that she lost Curtis, for a time, when he was still growing. She would like it if I could be this lost son reincarnated, and so I do my best—try to be Curtis for her, the last thing I'd know how to be. But she barely tells the difference. She loves me, sometimes I think better than she loves her own sullen boy. Sometimes I tell myself it's for this alone that Curtis hates me, this, the true reason we have nothing to say.

"How's Sidra?" I ask after a while. All around us, cicadas scream in the trees.

"Fine," he says.

I sip my tea and count cows. Each one is such a solid thing, and I admire the massive, slow, inevitable way that one step rolls into the next without the hope of variation. "She coming over?" I ask.

He pretends not to hear. But then he shoots a glance at the window screen and mutters, "How should I know?" His eyes return to the field though the cows are gone.

Just beyond him is another rocking chair, but I won't try to pass. Our conversation is about used up anyway. I watch the lowering sun and think about Leon Sharp, while my head taps a rhythm on the whitewashed boards behind me. *Leon, when you leave, where do you go?* I will stand here in silence until it's been long enough and then go back into the house.

⌐

Really, if you ignore Curtis, I have so little to run from. Home cooking, a roof and a bed, a family that honestly loves me. My life is like a code they pretend they can't crack, and here I mean not just Muriel and Dad but grandparents, aunts and uncles, family and stepfamily from around the state. At picnics I get, "What a sweet, good-looking boy!" and then they ask why I don't have a girlfriend yet. My Grandma Trish pinches my chin and says, "Look at this face!" She turns my head, eyes grazing the empty hole in my right earlobe so that the glance shadows with concern, turns down my body, and she adds, "You should eat more, is your problem." Only Curtis's grandmother will say aloud, "That boy's a mite funny, ain't he?" and everyone in the vicinity will shush her, as if I'll overhear this assessment and be hurt—or worse, influenced. To the gathered relations I am an always-expected event they pretend to wait on, breathless, as if they haven't already blinked and missed my incarnation, the splitting of cocoon walls, spirit made flesh.

Dad sells insurance, travels a lot. He's so quiet and steady, or he's been at the job so long, that he can grow his hair to his shoulders and no one blinks. Because of his height he always stoops a few degrees, dark-bearded, dark spaniel eyes. I favor my mother, I've been told, small and fair. "But none of her temperament," Grandma Trish adds quick, not to miss a warning against this mother I never knew, who ran away.

Dad and I used to be close. When I was younger, before Muriel, I could hardly separate my movements from his. *What shall we eat? What do we like?* I remember him once asking, "Do you think we like Muriel enough to marry her?" (We did.) I couldn't say exactly when it changed, what moment sparked it, though I know whatever happened is my fault.

"Paul, you used to read so much," he'll say now, dove-voiced, the softest note of lament. "Why don't you read anymore?"

There are times on my way out the back door to hit the bridge, wait for a truck, I am stopped by the sight of my father at the kitchen table, half lost under a gold shaft of light. "Paul," he says, only that. *Paul when you leave, where do you go?* I count my breaths and inch along the wall, as if I am no more than a blind instinct, an animal fear, a sense of direction. I know I can't speak to him. I will never be able to make a sound, if only because he sits there looking like Jesus Christ and would never strike a blow and would try, try so hard, to understand.

⌐

Dinner is a strained geometry, four of us at the square table and speaking only in triangles, as if Curtis and I are not aware of each other. Soft, brief, tentative sentences, question and answer, one triangle then the other. As soon as I can, I excuse myself, escape to my room at the end of the long hall, the one with the Yield sign mounted on the door.

Lights off, blinds closed, I switch on the globe that rotates colored spots of light along the walls and over the ceiling, and I punch up my CD player—Depeche Mode's "Behind the Wheel" on continuous repeat. Then I sit cross-legged in the middle of my bed with my stuffed bear in my lap and my father's old college dictionary spread open before me, where I look up the word "sylph." Besides what I expected, it turns out to mean "mortal and soulless." I'm thinking Mack is going to boost my SAT score in a big way, always sending me for the dictionary. He speaks these words in the simplest of sentences—*You are*—each one a small revelation and all I'm ever given to keep. If you overlook the money.

The last one was "sybarite," which means you're from one of those Biblical cities where everyone is guilty of the same sin—the Sybarites, I guess, being pretty close neighbors to the Sodomites. I've always thought it was sad those cities died with Biblical times. It'd be comforting just to move to a new town and never have to wonder again what to call yourself or how to greet the people around you.

I run my yellow highlighter over "sylph." There are others I didn't have to look up—"prodigy" was one—but I've highlighted them all anyway. None of these words can be read now except in flashes, in the instants when a colored light grazes the page, speeding on. *Sylph,* I think, rides a blue light flying along the edges of my room to the dark echo of the music: *Get your kicks on Route 66.* Sylph is only a column away from sybarite in this massive book, which must mean something. All of this, everything, must mean something, and maybe one day I'll figure it out.

I stay in my room for the rest of the night. The next night is about the same, and Sidra still hasn't appeared. I have the idea she'll come and we'll pull out the Monopoly board and play—me, her, and Curtis. I'd never dream it except this once, a while back, she came to my door and said, "Paul, we need a third for Hearts." I didn't know how to play but she taught me, patient, laughing at my mistakes so I laughed too and all the while Curtis sat docile as a daisy and took it. Not even a sneer. Somehow Sidra did this to him, mesmerized him, like those guys who flip full-grown gators belly up and stroke them into a trance. It was fascinating, the chance to sit so close to those teeth.

But so far, no Sidra, just him, slouched before the TV with a beer. He works during the day up in Athens, where he's got friends, so there's no telling why he's here now, evenings and weekends. I think he's gone and done something stupid—like, ditched Sidra, the one person who might could turn him into a decent human being.

In my room with Mack's words circling me, I start to hear his mocking voice too: *Grow up, little boy. Get a hold of yourself. No tears in my car.* Would he tell me how to handle Curtis? I wish it was Thursday but it's barely half through Saturday and the Braves are on in the living room. Muriel and Dad are out for the afternoon. Well, honey, I say to myself, why keep *all this* under wraps? Can't the beautiful people watch baseball too? I go get one of Curtis's beers from the fridge and stroll in, perch on the arm of the sofa opposite him. In a gutsy mood, I'll even swish a little around Curtis, the one person in my family who will name me to my face. A little swishing, I figure, is probably good for his character, even if it's unlikely to do much for me.

"So, what's the score?" I ask. Grissom takes a strike.

Curtis rubs his eyes, looks askance at the beer in my hand. "Can't you just disappear or something?"

"You know, I live here. This is my father's house."

Curtis's hand comes off his face stiff like he's made a mask of his features and it's going to harden that way. "Do you know you make me physically fuckin' ill?"

His eyes are slits, dumb-ass spit-shiny mouth hanging slack like he's actually about to puke. *Stick something down your throat, Curtis, you'll feel better,* I want to say, but I know I'd choke on the words. He shuts his mouth and turns back to the TV. He drinks his beer. I stare at the set, blind and deaf inside a buzzing, purple cloud of rage and humiliation.

After a while my eyes clear and travel back to the spot where his jaw intersects his throat, a clean valley that pulses as he swallows— sharp flare of muscle but underneath it, something softer, sinking, that brings me to the edge of tears. Here's this boy I'd be happy to crush under my shoe, and at the same time I'm wondering if it would be possible to touch just this one square inch of him. To separate it, somehow, from the rest. Would he ever let me have that much? Never, and no telling that I wouldn't shred his smallest offering—I know him too well by now to love him more than I hate him. But still, I can't help this wild urge to wrestle him into submission, make him look at me once without disgust, make him say brother, say my name . . . *There are things I could do to you, boy,* I think, smile flickering. *You'd like it too.*

"What in the shit-fire are you looking at?" His shout bounces back to us from the end of the hall.

I raise an eyebrow, defensively. The eyebrow thing, by the way, is all I had to do that first day to bring the gold Thunderbird to a shrieking halt. But subtlety is bound to be lost on Curtis, so I switch to offense—drop my mouth elaborately slack and roll my tongue up to the edges of my teeth. The fact that he doesn't react with more than a flinch and a groan, hand back to his face, tells me Sidra is still around, at least in spirit, that she's stroked a promise from him to *play nice with Paul.* Blauser knocks a homer and two men come in—three-nothing.

"You don't mind if I have another beer, do you, bro?" I ask.

Curtis is on his fourth. He follows me into the kitchen, and as I'm sliding a bottle from the case in the refrigerator, he slaps my arm away. The bottle smacks against the floor, spins unbroken across the linoleum. He shoves me back against the kitchen counter and there before me I have as much as I will ever get from Curtis. But here's the surprise: it's enough. Over fistful of my shirt, he stares me full in the face. Drunk, but it's almost better this way—he's less guarded, couldn't pull away to save his life, and I've got him in my laser-beam gaze. I will burn him. At least I have this, this one moment, before he shatters it. I'll burn his eyes open so that he sees himself as clearly as he sees me, and when that fist comes flying, I know he has.

It's not that I want to be hit. But when a thing can't be avoided, I figure you might as well take what you can from it. For a long time I've watched Curtis making me over into his most colossal fear, and maybe I half enjoy that transformation. There are many ways, I have to believe, to be born again.

⌒

Off both sides of the Lake Oconee Bridge, the water shimmers blue, then silver, then blurs to gold. A water-cooled breeze whips up from the shadows below where the swallows nest, dries my damp face, blood and tears. Tears I can't help. *Grow up, little boy.* Once along the banks below I saw a drowned swallow, its splayed body held just under the skin of the water, arrow wings outspread, drifting, white throat bared to the sky. Still so white, so soft-looking, so close to the air. I'd never seen such a thing, and now when I cross the lake I think how there could be hundreds down there, caught while skimming between two states of matter, their bodies never seen.

I'm too angry to stop crying. Long ago I gave up on Curtis, turned the rage on myself, and now it's Mack I can't stop working over and over in my head like a bone. Red-eyed and miserable, I catch an easy ride—woman in a pickup, bound for Atlanta. She's a henna redhead, fifties, puts me in mind of Muriel, and for half a second I wonder if it's one of her ladies from church. But it doesn't matter now. I get in. I tell her a partial truth to get her foot off the brake: my brother beat me up, I'm going to my grandmother's in the city. Little Red Riding Hood's on board, lady, so hit the gas, speed past the wolves to safety. Good that it's a woman, since half of all men want at least a blow job before they let you go, and I am not in the mood. I lean my head to the window, calming. She turns up the radio, AM, All-Country-All-the-Time.

I realize now I know nothing about where Mack lives, except that it's beautiful: a white mansion, landscaped terraces descending behind to a pool. This pool, he once told me—his one moment of candor—is like other pools, clean and chlorinated, but its irregular edges are set about with ginkgoes and the bottom is tiled black instead of blue. It's strange, he said, and lovely, dark as a natural pond. "I'd like to see you swimming in that water," he said, stroking my hair as I leaned against his chest, the only time he ever allowed it. Something was different that day, something had upset him, so that he had first pulled me into his lap and kissed me for a long time and then opened my jeans with his own hand and took me into his mouth. I almost passed out before it was over, too fast, and he laughed and said, "Such an innocent, Paul?" Then he lifted me back against his body and told me about the pool where he wanted to see me swimming, lean white body breaking the surface of black water.

"Let's go there now," I whispered, because I thought everything must have changed. I'd never held many illusions about this man and his made-up name, wedding band slipped from his finger, who wouldn't even get a hotel room because somehow his wife, whom he never once mentioned, would catch on. Too many tracks, too much evidence. All this I knew without being told and so I should have known too that he would flash with anger, fist suddenly full of my hair, and say it would never, never happen. You got that, little fuck? Remember it.

"You're gonna have a shiner, son," the woman beside me says. I nod without looking at her. My lip is swelling too, and I push back a sheen of tears and picture the look on Curtis's face when he saw he had split his own knuckles on my teeth when he split my lip, opened the blood between us. *Good, you prick,* I think, *Asshole. I hope you stay awake for a week wondering.*

I smile at that and close my eyes, zeroing in now on Mack. I don't know where or how I'll begin to look for him. He's never given me a thing I could use, and I've never thought to steal it. But I'll find him anyway. I know I will. He thinks I'm a child, I'll show him how I can grow up clean before his eyes.

I see him in a lounge chair at the edge of a dark pool under a white, sunless sky. His wife brings lemonade on a tray, his children gaze into the water. Does he have children? I don't know, but I see them flitting along the concrete edge, small, pallid, sexless. They are laughing and so is the wife and then so is Mack. Behind them, the white house, a deep green of hedges, a white-coated gardener trimming the hedges into shapes of animals. As soon as I imagine this place, I know that the gold Thunderbird, a boat-like hulk circa '79 with badly tinted windows, is not even his car. It never was.

From the pool, underwater, I see their wavering images high above me. I never was a strong swimmer, but in this dream I am, hold my breath with ease, open my eyes in the chemical sting, all light from above. But still no sun—no matter where I look, there is nothing but this sourceless light. Mack has imagined me here. Even now he sees me just this way, teases my limbs through the water and watches, voluptuous. But the skin over my shoulders is no longer winter white; it's tanned with the sun, dusted with freckles—I want to tell him. I want to say *look again*. But even as he watches me, he's smiling with his family, laughing soundlessly. They are all laughing, all so happy and I can't break the surface.

Jesus is staring at me from the center of the dashboard. He's four inches tall and plastic, his painted eyes enormous, his unpierced hands outstretched with offered blessings. Above him, a square cardboard of air freshener printed with a leaping whitetail turns lazily from the rear view mirror. The woman is talking, something about city driving, a trip out west with her husband, crossing twenty state lines. She's been talking all this time and I haven't heard a word. Around us, lanes have multiplied to ten across, filling with cars.

"This ain't nothing to bother me," the woman says, flipping a hand at the road, "since I've driven in Los Angeles. Now that's traffic."

"I'd like to go there." I say this though the idea has never crossed my mind until now. "City of Angels."

She snorts. "I didn't see no angels, I tell you. Crazy people out there pulling guns on you, driving right down the Interstate! Crazies all over." She gives me a sidelong, motherly glance. "You shouldn't oughtta hitchhike."

In the dewy sight of tiny Jesus, I can't help feeling guilty for breaking the promise to myself, for lying even to this stranger. I have the sudden urge to say, "Guess what. I'm a fag, a queer, a homo, a sodomite—take your pick. My grandmother lives in *Dahlonega*, okay, and I'm going to meet my lover right now, a man, and since you've carried me this far I thought you should know." What would she do? Slam on her brakes and kick me out? She doesn't seem the type. More likely, she'd try her everlasting best to talk me out of it. Love the sinner, hate the sin, and never suspecting that I am no longer the sinner but the sin made flesh. That we will not be separated.

So I am on the verge of speaking these very words when I pull out my wallet, remove the creased picture of a girl—a white-bordered school photo of Sidra's sister. "Her name was Marcy," Sidra told me. "She died a few years ago of AIDS. I want you to put that in your pocket. Keep it with you." Marcy is thirteen in this photo but she passes for older because of her thin, ironic smile, her straight brown hair pulled back smooth behind her head. She has wide, unblinking blue eyes under a level brow. I have spent a lot of time staring at the girl in this picture until I feel like I know her, like she's as close to me as Sidra wanted her to be.

"Pretty girl," the woman says.

"That's my girlfriend," I tell her. "She lives in Los Angeles."

⌒

The woman lets me out near the park, in front of a house I tell her is my grandmother's. I thank her for the ride. She touches my hand and says, "You take care, Paul," though I can't recall ever telling her my name.

In the last of daylight, the city gives off a little airborne charge. Like a promise, like always. But I still have far to go, don't know which direction. It will be night soon. I need to be there now, wherever *there* is—I'll take anywhere that I can lie down and just absorb his shock, feel his hands on my skin, this one man. Before I can think of a plan, I've walked to the Thursday place where the gold Thunderbird turns off the road and the door unlocks for me. The shadows are pulling long off the buildings downtown. I am tucked below that lengthening wing, the shadow that will stretch from here to Greene County, from here to the ocean, that in a matter of hours will cover this half of the world.

Cars roll past, catching light in their polished surfaces. Down a hill and away from the buildings, along the park woods, I can see aimless-looking boys, two or three at the road's edge, waiting. I wander toward them, thinking Mack will come before I get that far. But suddenly I know two things for certain: he's not coming and it's because he's already with someone else. Some other boy, whichever one is Saturday's child. The thought makes me dizzy. I have to grab a post. For half a minute I feel like I could kill somebody. In my head I'm counting bills, Mack's money, trying to think of a good place to buy a big knife. I think I could cut the man's eyes out of his head and put them in my pocket like a pair of pearly marbles, for keeps, and then I think I must be going flat out of my mind and what am I doing here anyway? I have no idea what I'm doing.

A gleaming dark car is at the curb beside me. Window scrolls down. For a stupid instant I believe it must be Mack, come for me now in his real car. But the man inside is older, fat and balding, the seat belt slicing him across the belly as he leans toward me. "You lost, honey?"

I put both hands on the passenger window frame to steady myself, shake my head, no. This one simple thing I know the answer to. He motions for me to get in, and my first impulse is to do exactly this as quick as I hop a ride off the shoulder of I-20. Fate brings the car, baby, your job is to take the ride. Take it like a man, boy. What more do you want? What else is there for you in your little short shorts, wandering the shoulder of the world with your thumb sticking out? So it turns out you're all that, face smacked half to mush but who gives a shit when that tight little ass is hot enough to stop traffic—well, traffic is stopped. Now what are you going to do with it? But I shake my head again, tell the man I'm looking for someone, guy named Mack in a gold Thunderbird.

He just grins. "Oh yeah, well, I'm Pete. I'm better than a guy named Mack."

I'm getting a whopper headache. I want this loser to take off, but he can't very well when I'm holding myself up on his window, and now I'm looking at the hand that's stretched across the back of the velour seat, the dry, blunt fingers.

"How do I know that?" I ask.

"I won't smack you around, for one." He says this rushed, glancing back over his shoulder. "Come on, get in. We'll see if we might can figure out what you're looking for, but we gotta get off this curb first."

I step back, regain my hold on the post. He's rolling forward off the brake, hissing, "Come on!" Then, "Fuck it!" and he squeals away.

Marcy, I think, *are you here? Is this where you've been?* My hands feel like hers, her fingers gripping the post of some warning sign in another city, New York, Chicago, Los Angeles—wherever she went in those years before she crawled home again to die. But I'm not her, won't give up so easy. The night's just coming on and I know what I want. Maybe I have no image for his face, nothing more than a freakish collage of stolen glimpses. But I feel him, even now, rippling through me like wind on water, his breath on my neck. My head knocks the glass softly, softer than one caress after another, and I see . . . black knob, door handle, rubber floor mat, condom wrappers, and a single word. *Paradiso,* white script on a black background. A matchbook.

A police car comes cruising into my peripheral vision and I jump a little. I take my hands off the pole and start walking in the opposite direction. The car passes slowly, the windows down and the two men inside with their eyes on me. Over my shoulder I watch them cruise the three boys in the culvert below. Then they're gone again, too slow for comfort. The boys look up my way. One takes a few running steps and flings a rock, which can't cover half the distance between us. I tuck my chin and glare back. But I recognize the stone-thrower—this Mexican kid I met once called Rio.

Hands pocketed deep, I amble down the hill toward them. Rio comes bluffing for a fight but drops the act when I keep walking, twitch him half a smile. He grins back. "Hey! Greene County!" I go past him and drop onto the banked grass of the shoulder. Glad to sit, I draw my knees up and rest my chin, push my fingers into my hair.

"You got any weed, man?" one asks me, the tallest. He's dark-haired and bone white, his face scarred with acne. He toes me in the hip. "You hear me? What you got on you?"

"Leave him be, man. He ain't got shit." Rio walks a wide half-circle on the pavement below. "Can't you see that's a sad boy? Tricks ain't treating you so good, Greene County. I thought I told you to wise up."

Silent, I comb through the damp, waxy grass under the arc of my knees. It feels almost safe here. A cardinal back in the woods calls, "What, cheer, cheer, cheer," and a nighthawk hunting overhead goes "zzzeerp" every few seconds like a bug zapper. All around us the park is velvet green with summer, cooling into twilight. Slowly I catch the eyes of these boys one by one, first Rio's black-lined ones, then the tall kid's slitted blues, then the round, dark eyes of the third—another Mexican-looking kid, couldn't be more than twelve or thirteen.

"What, I got to look out for everyone's ass around here?" Rio rants, hands on his hips. "You missing 'em too, boy. Let one get away up there. If you ain't fucking around on my corner, now, he'd be mine. Wouldn't he?"

"I ain't a hustler," I tell him.

"Listen at you!" He laughs. "Shit, boy, who you fooling?"

"I'm just looking for a guy, is all. This guy Mack. You ever see him?"

"Whaddya know," the tall one joins in—I decide he's at least twenty. "I'm looking for a guy named Mack myself!"

"That's Midway." Rio jerks a thumb for an introduction, then crosses his arms and studies me. "Oh yeah, you're all about love or some shit, ain't you? Lover boy. Think that makes you so much better than us, like you don't walk the earth! Is that right? Least I ain't no faggot!"

I crack a laugh at that, and he rants on, waving a hand at his little band. "Ain't none of us faggots. We just do it for money. Who's crawling on his belly now, Greene County? Who's lower than who?" He's trying to sound pissed, but he's starting to amuse himself.

The little one comes over and sits by me, close. "How come he calls you Greene County?"

"Guess that's my name."

He's got a feathering of dark baby-down above his mouth and these wide-open eyes, not a guard in the world between him and me. It's almost scary to look at. The rest of him is made of contradictions: he's alert, but has tracks on his arms. Clothes dirty, but he's so clean inside them he smells of Ivory soap.

"That's Angel," says Rio, narrowing his eyes at the kid. "Another little shit-ass that don't know jack."

"You need a better name," Angel informs me.

"There's an idea."

"You gonna hang out with us?" He leans his head against my arm, and the hair looks freshly cut, a little damp. I kiss his neck. The hair bristles soft against my lips. Under the soap he smells of park grass and something buttery, sweet, like cookie dough.

"So who's this Mack anyway?" Rio wants to know. "What's so special about him?" Midway goes wandering up the road toward a slow-moving car.

"I'm a faggot," Angel confides, whispering it in my ear like it's his secret favorite word.

I pet his head distractedly. Then I remember the matchbook and ask Rio, "What's Paradiso? Is that a place?"

"Paradiso's a bar, baby. Like a club, you know. Where the big boys play."

"Where?"

"What's the difference? You can't get in there."

"Let's go back in the woods," Angel whispers.

He catches me off guard and I laugh. "Me?"

"I'll do it for free. I don't care." He puts a warm little hand on my crotch. I pick it up by the wrist and give it back to him.

"Go sit over there, darlin'." I push on his shoulder until he scoots his bottom over a few inches, lower lip poking out resentfully.

"Jesus Christ," Rio mutters. "Angel, you need management. You're the fucking reason for pimps." He starts scanning for cars again.

I stand up. "I'm going to the Paradiso. Where is it?"

"North, like. Buckhead." Rio sneers as I go past him. "You can't walk there."

I turn and meet his glossy-hard eyes, hands to hips. "Honey, I don't intend to."

"Oh, yeah? Like it's so easy for you!" He mutters something under his breath as I'm walking away. A minute later he calls out, "Hey, Greene County. You see a guy in a blue Chrysler, youngish guy with a mustache, that's your man. He'll take you where you need to go." I smile a thanks and Rio salutes, two fingers off his forehead. Angel sits bleakly on the slope where I left him.

I'm up the hill—the way Midway went, but he's vanished now—when I hear Angel's voice, his shoes slapping the road behind me. He comes around into my path and stops me with his hands, panting, bright-eyed, only half a head shorter than me now that we're standing together. I wonder if it's possible I look that young.

"I gotta tell you something." He's grinning, trying to catch his breath. "It's important. But if I tell you, you gotta take me with you."

I shake him off. "Boy, I don't got to do anything. Now make some sense."

He frowns, scuffs the asphalt with his sneaker. "You really have a lover? That's where you're going, isn't it?" Like I've answered the question already and he's thinking on what I've said, he doesn't look up. What would I have answered? Tell the truth. *Yes. No. I haven't the faintest idea in hell.* But even if the road is rough, if the door will most likely be barred to me, at least for now I have a destination. At least the pale hint of one.

He meets my eyes again. "I just had to tell you. Don't go with that guy Rio said. He's trying to set you up with a cop."

"What?" I look back down the hill behind me, where Rio pays us no mind. He has a live one on the hook, leans against the open window of a car.

Shaking, I turn and walk, try to walk out of the shaking. But this little thing seems sharp enough to split the sky open, leave me so exposed that it would no longer matter which direction I went, how far or fast. I am that dumb. I can't tell which is worse—that I never suspected Rio could set me up so casually, for nothing? That it never crossed my mind that there might be cops in unmarked cars? That I might do something, offer something, that would get me in trouble? Even Angel knows this much. *What they beat you for, they will arrest you for, they will kill you for. Wise up, boy. Nothing, no one, is safe to you.* "What'd you say?" Angel asks, beside me.

"I ain't talking. I'm walking."

So, fine, I'll walk it, if I have to hike to kingdom come. I'm not about to let anyone stop me. Not even Mack, drawing his lines to hold me off, when I want so little, not even love. If he insists, I'll even renounce his shifty face. Body alone will serve. Is it so shallow to crave nothing but flesh? To me it feels fathoms deep, this longing, deeper than I can measure, more than I can hold. But watch me. I do. I'll follow where it leads, forever amen. I never had a choice but to keep going, though I can see that just beyond the trees ahead, even the city rises like a wall.

◦⌐

I'm past the west end of the park, thumb out for a ride, and Angel paces me doggedly. As soon as I stop, he's up close again, his face in front of mine so that I lay my hands to his jaw, both sides of his neck, just to brace the distance between us. His bones feel soft, eyes melting off the heat of my face—he's way too young. Too young to be out of doors in the first place. I have one urge to swat him off like a bug, fighting another to offer him something, can't think of what.

"Thanks for telling me," I say. "About the cop and all. I owe you."

"Rio's a bastard sometimes." He shrugs, blinking mournfully. "He's my brother, so I know."

He's far too close already, touching. I can feel the pulse in his neck and I accidentally breathe, relax, slip closer. My mouth is on his mouth. Cars fly past us, strobe us with headlights, and I can't find a way to stop now. I forget the reason. For a minute, we're nothing but flesh, undesignated, any two mouths—the soothing of contact. Then I push him away, half-disgusted. Above us, the city sky is cobalt with twilight, and even here, the cicadas drone without mercy, like voices of home.

He's back at me in an instant, like he's attached with a rubber band. "You'll take me with you?" he whispers.

I grip his shoulders and step him back, pin his eyes. His lower lip sneaks fearfully between his teeth. But those eyes never move.

"I'm sorry," I say, trying to sound stern. "I shouldn't have done that."

"It's okay."

"I'm not actually interested in little boys."

"I know. That's okay. Just let me come with you."

"Listen to me." I shake him once, but I can't do it hard enough. "What the hell's the matter with you anyway? You shouldn't be out here. You don't belong out here, a place like this."

"So you tell me." His soft face goes stony, defiant. "Tell me where I belong."

absolute sway

Have thine own way, Lord, have thine own way.
Hold o'er my being absolute sway.
Fill with thy Spirit till all shall see
Christ only, always, living in me.

I kept my eye on Joelle Hunnicutt. From under my lashes I watched her toeing the asphalt right next to Gary's sneaker, Gary my almost-boyfriend, thank you. Gary the only decent guy who ever showed up for Sabbath Outreach. Twelve of us had piled into the van on a Sunday afternoon, plus Rob, the new youth minister, who had then driven us on a slow, aimless route into a tangled maze of neighborhoods where none of us lived, up one street and down another, until the Lord said stop.

We made a quick prayer circle in the street. There was no good reason I should be stuck holding hands with Rob on one side and Tamara Fisher on the other except that Joelle had probably arranged it that way, just like she probably had something to do with the fact that Gary wasn't looking toward me, catching my eye the way he used to or even sitting next to me in the van. Technically, he hadn't sat next to Joelle either, but she hung over the seat back in front of him;

I couldn't hear what they were saying. They both had solos in the spring musical, which was going to be this super jazzy version of *Pilgrim's Progress* called *Pilgrim!* I didn't get picked because, supposedly, I flatted all the high notes. Joelle sang through her nose, but no one seemed to notice that.

Rob prayed, "Dear Lord, I'm so grateful, so very grateful to see you working in the hearts of these young people." His hand in mine was warm and dry and big, all in contrast to Gary's, and without looking up I pictured the way a wing of dark hair fell just to the edge of Rob's forehead. Rob was full of the love, we said—brimming. The love of Jesus shone out of his eyes and struck us all straight in the heart like a spray of bullets. Though he had been with us only a few months, it was hard to remember a time before him, as if there had never really been a youth group before he came along.

"And I ask that you bless us, dear Lord," he prayed, "in our mission as we seek to spread Your Word to these precious souls. In Your Name, Jesus, we pray, Amen." I thought I would add a quick, silent prayer of my own (*Please Lord, make Gary look at me; make Joelle trip and bust her freaky little flared-out nose on the curb*), but holding Rob's hand, I felt pumped so full of love and peace and good will that I just let it all go and said Amen.

Rob checked to be sure we all had plenty of literature as he parceled us out through the neighborhood. It was a north-side Athens neighborhood I didn't know, the houses all two-story and square. I watched Joelle and Gary head off, not together so much as in the same general direction. Surely, I thought, they wouldn't try anything underhanded in the middle of Outreach, in the very face of the Lord. Outreach was supposed to be a solitary mission anyway—no partners.

Rob pointed me to the top of the next street over, which was called Pepper Lane, the opposite direction from the way Gary and Joelle went. I fixed my eye on the first house, your basic white vinyl siding number, rows of hedges leading up the walk—my first errand of the day for Christ. But it was hard to hear Him calling me there. I hooked Rob's elbow and drew him around the front of the van. The others had spread out to hit their doors.

"What's up, Loretta?" He put a hand on my shoulder, bending a little to look in my eyes though he wasn't very tall. Kind of compact, a compressed strength. Unlike the last youth minister, Rob would hug you just to say hello, and he was the perfect size to get his arms all the way around you.

"Would you pray with me again?" I asked. "I just don't feel right yet. I've been having some un-Christian thoughts."

"You want to talk about it?" He sounded just a touch worried, like now was not the time to talk.

"No, I just want to clear out my heart so I can do the Lord's work."

"Good girl! You're always right to stop, Loretta, take a time-out, take it to the Lord in prayer." He took my hands and squeezed them. "You have a special gift. I can see that the Lord will do great things through you."

I looked straight into his eyes, and they were like rays aimed back at me, so intense that I felt tears welling up. Those eyes looked capable of seeing every black sin in my heart, seeing too the *great things* that waited beyond, in my future.

He wadded my hands together between his and spoke the prayer about me alone, said *her sweet spirit,* and *cleanse her heart, O Lord,* and I prayed that his words would take and I could walk away purified. We said Amen together, and I brushed off the tears and smiled. I could almost feel all that clean, heavenly light shining out.

Which is the way you want to look walking alone up the front steps of a stranger's house. You never know who will come to the door, what will be hiding or maybe hurting, lost and searching, hidden deep in that person's heart. Rob never called us children. He called us "young people," and he let us in on a secret: while Adult Outreach fizzled every Sunday, the youth ministry was going off like firecrackers in the hearts of the community. Every week we tallied souls—six, eight, twelve saved. Amazing. Rob praised us, Christ-in-us, without ever dipping below the heavens to touch on earthly reasons. But he didn't need to. We knew that a soul unaware of its condition would put up defenses against an adult, but that the walls came tumbling down in the face of an earnest child.

A fortyish man with tousled hair came to the door of the white house, looked at me sleepily through the storm glass. I just smiled until he opened it and set one foot out on the top step. "Hi," I said, looking straight into his clouded eyes, his hell-bound soul. "I'm Loretta Moss and I'm here from King's Way Baptist Church to ask you one simple question: Do you know the Lord Jesus Christ as your personal savior?"

⤺

"You have to say it all in one sentence like that," I explained. "Straight to the point. Don't go asking people if they have a church home, 'cause then they just make stuff up and close the door."

I was the celebrity of Wednesday night Fellowship on account of my record Sunday saves: two authentic souls. The first man had hardened his heart against me, but the next one was a keeper and then, five houses down, I came upon a woman who actually broke down in tears and kept me in her living room for an hour. Rob and the others eventually had to come to my rescue. So at potluck supper I was famous. Some of the kids I called the Serious Christians—Brad Waller, Tamara Fisher, Jennifer Hayes, and Susan Peralta—were clustered around me at the table to talk shop.

Or maybe the five of us were gathered around the new girl, Sidra Ballard, so that she would have the benefit of overhearing. It was strange to have someone like Sidra in our midst, a middle-schooler like us, but one who showed up for church without her parents, whose parents didn't even belong. The rest of us had been together our whole lives, and we had never been offered much choice about church. Sidra had started hitching a ride to services with a neighbor, since I guess her own folks couldn't be bothered about her soul. We thought she was precious. We all wanted the honor of bringing Sidra to the Lord.

"And people will tell you they're Lutherans or Episcopalians or something," Jennifer added, her plastic-rimmed glasses perched on her nose in a slick of sweat. "That doesn't mean saved anyhow."

Gary sat at the next table over with Joelle and Andrew Gordon and these other girls who didn't do much but choir. The Backsliders' Club, I called them. The whole *Pilgrim!* cast. It hurt to look at them over there, laughing together, Gary leaning to brush his shoulder against Joelle's.

I turned to Sidra and pinched her pink sleeve. "Cute polo!"

"Thanks." She smiled and looked back down at her plate.

Sidra was a natural blond, acres of this gorgeous straight blond hair. It was the first thing I noticed about her, because my own hair was such a dull, thin brown. I figured that anybody with hair like Sidra's must have been touched by God, even if she wasn't saved. At school I had seen her spoil it by tying a bandanna around her head and then wearing some hideous heavy-metal-concert jersey besides. Way back in fourth grade, she and I had been friends for a while—went to each other's slumber parties, and once she had invited me out to her farm to ride her horses. That was long ago, before God meant much in my life other than the routine Sundays and Wednesdays. In recent years at school she had tended to hang out with headbangers and burnouts, but I knew it was only because she was looking for meaning in all the wrong places. Now she dressed like us.

She lingered after the rest had dumped their plates and gone on to the Fellowship Hall for youth group. "So how do you like our church?" I asked her. She had been coming to services for a couple of months now, but she had not yet made the big walk to the front during the Invitation.

"I like it," she said shyly. "It makes me a little nervous. Like that—" she pointed at the banner that stretched across one wall of the dining hall—"makes me nervous."

In big purple letters, the banner read, *If being a Christian were a crime, would there be enough evidence to convict you?*

"Isn't that a horrible thought?" I agreed. "But the day is coming, you know. Christians are already persecuted everywhere, and one day we probably *will* be thrown in jail."

"No," Sidra said, "I mean the evidence part scares me. I don't know if there would be enough evidence against me. Like what Rob was saying last week, brushing your teeth for the Lord. I don't know if I can do *everything* for the Lord."

I considered that. "I think when you have Jesus in your heart, it's just kind of automatic."

"Really?" She looked at the banner like it was God himself tacked up on the wall. I tried to picture her in her bathroom, a room of a house I vaguely remembered from years before, agonizing over how to brush her teeth.

"How come your folks don't come to church?"

"My mother, she grew up a Baptist, but she gave it up before I was born. She hates all kinds of religion but especially Baptist, and Daddy's never been much of any kind of faith, I don't think. That's probably why she married him."

My mouth fell open. "Your mom has turned against her religion?"

"She's never once took me to church." Her jaw hardened over the last of her brownie. She folded the plate and stood. "I guess I came to see what I was missing."

⌣

I decided to adopt Sidra. She was a better ally than most of the Serious Christians, who tended to be afflicted with acne or fatness, and I was starting to imagine a line drawn down the future of our youth group, the possibility that I could fall on the wrong side of attractive. So far, there was no real line, and maybe there never would be, what with all of us together since we were babies, together for at least the next four years—no remedy for that. Even Joelle and I could still act chummy and gush over each other's outfits.

Sidra, if not gorgeous, at least had the hair going for her. She was neutral, and she gave me a project. From the way she started inviting me home, I figured she needed me too. I started going to her house some days after school. The first time, Sidra made a big deal out of introducing me to her mother, even though I had met her years before. The instant we set foot in the house, Sidra went calling through every room for her mother, and when she didn't find her, we went straight down to the horse barn. Mrs. Ballard, a wide-hipped woman in overalls and a straw hat, was stacking sacks of feed.

"Mama, this is Loretta," Sidra announced. She stood feet apart, chin tipped up like she'd brought home someone unsavory and half expected a fight. "My friend from church."

Mrs. Ballard straightened from bending for a sack and nodded at me with a big smile. "Pleased to meet you, Loretta."

"Likewise, Mrs. Ballard." I figured if this was Sidra's game, I could play along. "Sidra tells me you're a church member."

Her face fell a bit, and she cut her eyes at her daughter. "Once upon a time, I was."

I came back fast before she could tell her sad story. "We would sure love to see you on Sunday. I hope you'll think of coming with Sidra."

She gave me one of those ironic looks that adults will give you at doors when they think they know more than you do. Rob always said that was just the devil's lie to harden their hearts. Never back down, he said. They might be adults, but all the worldly experience there is can't compare to the experience of God.

Sidra and I went up to her room to play records. She had some K-tels and Amy Grants, but almost everything else was heavy metal. I pulled one out of the rack. "You listen to Ozzy Osbourne?"

"He's so great," she said, gazing at this gross-out picture of him on the cover, black paint around his crazed-looking eyes. "I've seen him twice in concert. My dad took me."

"He's a Satan worshipper!" I had heard other kids say this, which was all I knew about him—that, and he supposedly got rabies once from eating the head off a live bat, which sounded to me like more than enough proof in itself.

"That's a misconception." Her eyes sparkled with sudden light. "His music is so beautiful. Listen, this is the best song." She put the record on the turntable, set the needle down carefully. "I just love him."

I grimaced at the cover. "He's fat and ugly." A strained wailing came out of the speakers, kind of haunting, hypnotic. I couldn't help listening.

"Maybe," she said, "but he has a beautiful soul. His *music* . . . I saw him in concert right after his guitarist Randy Rhoads was killed in a plane crash—it was so sad. His voice was all cracked and awful and he was so grief-stricken he couldn't even finish!" She flopped to her back on the floor, hugging the album cover to her chest.

"I guess it's kind of pretty," I admitted. "It doesn't sound like I thought it would."

"I wish I could sing. Don't you ever wish that? I sit up here and sing along with all my albums and pretend like it's me giving a concert. Isn't that stupid?" Then she added, "Gary's got a nice voice."

I scowled, then stretched onto my elbows beside her. "Wanna know a secret?" She raised her eyebrows, and I hid behind my hands. "I think I have a crush on Rob!"

"*Rob*? He's, like, thirty!"

"He is not! He's only twenty-four. It's not like I'd do anything about it. I just think about him. He has the sweetest spirit. I wish I was older, that's all."

"Thirteen is so annoying." Sidra curled on her side, plucked tan fibers from the carpet. "You can't do anything or know anything and nobody listens to you. I want to be in love with a guitarist who dies in a plane crash, and then sing about it so everyone bursts into tears." She giggled, grinning half into the carpet. "I want to have a *great passion*."

I knew what she was hinting at. I smiled and let a little silence fall before I said, "Being saved is kind of like that."

"Really? I hope it happens soon."

Her response stopped me—I'd thought we were on the same page, but I wasn't prepared for her notion that being saved was something that happened to you, like getting asked to the prom. All you have to do is ask Jesus Christ into your heart and there He is. It's not an astral event. *Say the words*—that's what I told people who invited me into their living rooms. *Confess that you are a sinner and your sins will be washed away. He died for you. He's waiting now.*

But she went on. "I'm waiting to feel it, you know, like Rob was saying on Wednesday, that sermon about *E. T.*—how God is the Great Extra-Terrestrial. How he reaches out with his glowing fingertip to touch you and heal all your pain? You ever think what that would feel like?—the actual touch of God!" Her face was flushed a faint pink, gazing up at the ceiling as if looking for something bigger than I had ever imagined. My own offering felt strangely small, and for once I didn't know what to say.

Of course I could have kicked myself later—missing an opportunity like that. I should have taken her hands, prayed with her. But that kind of thing was easier with strangers than with people you actually knew. Rob always said how our lives could be a witness, but that wasn't enough. "You must speak it aloud," he said, "witness aloud, shout it out. You must witness to your friends at school, to your teachers, you must tell everyone the Good News. Even your own family, your parents who sit in our pews every Sunday—even *they* need to hear your testimony." I would look at my parents all dressed for services, my little brothers combed and subdued—what could I possibly say to them? Didn't they already know? "At the end of every day," Rob said, "think over all the opportunities that you missed to witness. Count them up. Jesus Christ sees those lost souls. He cries for every one."

I dealt souls to Jesus like cards. It was enough, I protested, knowing all along I held these few back, tucked up my sleeve because I didn't know what else to do with them. A tiny voice whispered to me *this* was the reason, not my age, why I could never be with Rob. *You, Loretta Moss, you will never be good enough for him.*

⌐

On Sunday, salvation was the sermon topic. Sidra was ready; I could sense it. She sat in a pale green dress with the youth group, her gold hair brushed smooth and the top layer gathered in a darker green bow, all of it clean and glowing over her shoulders. I swear I almost watched it happen to her, as if the ceiling of the church slid open so the light of God could strike her full in the face. Reverend Gaines made the Invitation to come forward, and when Sidra rose I thought she was going to keep on rising, straight up through the air on that column of holy light like a tractor beam to the mother ship. Everyone watched it. I sat between my parents, across the aisle and two rows behind her, wiping my sweat-slick palms on my skirt.

The pastor's eyes went wide. He was a warm, charismatic speaker, a man with an appetite for the gospel, a man who loved his Invitations. Every Sunday, he knew, we all knew, his heartfelt words would call a few nervous people to step forward from the bowl-shaped coliseum of the sanctuary. Sometimes there were more, five or six—during Revival week, ten, twelve, fourteen—and they would stand in line with blank and sober faces to answer yes as he prayed with them, one by one, and a few of the emotional ones might blink back tears in embarrassed silence before he presented them to the congregation as newborn souls, washed in the blood. But hardly ever was there a soul like the one that approached him now.

No one else rose. No one else was called that day. Only Sidra, streaming tears, sobbing—a single choked breath that rang the still air to the back of the sanctuary before the pastor caught her hands. The pastor's face seemed to pull apart, eyebrows and mouth stretching out from a still center as if he fought to hold them together; suddenly he went down on his knees and Sidra went with him. The church gasped, one breath caught in a thousand mouths. We weren't used to this drama of sobbing and kneeling. They prayed on the floor, the pastor's voice barely audible, their hands joined into a single fist between their faces. Then they rose and Sidra smiled out at the crowds, her face glossy wet and broken and shining, beatific and beyond control, as if she had just been crowned Miss America.

The whole youth group was crying. The service ended with the call to welcome the new child of Christ, and I pushed past my mother and brothers, pushed to the front where Sidra was already engulfed. But she searched me out of the crowd, held onto me so hard that I didn't even notice I was sobbing too. I got the honor of the longest hug, at least that, and then she was passed on to other arms. Wiping my eyes, I saw Tamara and Jennifer beside me, both watching Sidra's progress down the line with that sort of desolate, miserable joy you see at weddings. "Oh, isn't it wonderful," we said and hugged each other, the thinnest substitute.

◦

I waited for the glow to wear off Sidra, but it didn't. People wanted to touch her like she was some kind of saint. She spoke about her conversion as if it was the very physical thing she'd expected all along. "It was like being touched by the fingertip of God," she told her audiences. "Like I was no more than an eggshell for the Lord to tap on, just crack me open. I could feel Him all around me, warm light, perfect love and safety." The more I watched people trailing after her agape, swallowing her words like they should have been written down in red ink, the more I couldn't help thinking it—*fake*. I felt guilty for thinking that way, she was so sweet and sincere, but come on! This was taking the whole sanctified thing a little far. I mean, this was the Baptist church, not the damned Catholics. We preferred miracles of the everyday variety.

At night I prayed for Christ to forgive my doubting thoughts. Who was I to judge? Maybe it had happened, after all, just as she said. God moves in mysterious ways, and I wouldn't put it past Him to reach down from heaven, His closed hand just the size of the sanctuary of

King's Way Baptist Church, to reach forward with a finger as long as three joined train cars and point straight at the upturned face of a single young girl. But the flesh I tried to see on the hand of God turned woody, stretched as thin and delicate as E. T.'s finger, tipped in electric light. The tip touched Sidra and candled her whole body so that she gasped and shook, went phosphorescent, remained caught inside that glow. Maybe it had been that way. But this was not the God I knew. And surely it was a sin, had to be, for me to invent such a warped picture of God, but I couldn't escape it.

Wednesday afternoon when I arrived for choir practice, Sidra was sitting on the hallway floor talking to Gary. They were almost hidden beside the rack of hanging robes, their backs against the wall but faces leaned close together. Gary was so intent on what Sidra was saying that he didn't even look up as I passed, though Sidra paused and said, "Hi, Loretta." I thought of stopping to chat but instead ducked quickly into the choir room and started thumbing through the music for *Pilgrim!* My heart was racing, stumbling—*Sidra and Gary.* The others came in, practice started, but I couldn't concentrate and Mr. Duffy, the choir master, barked into my daydream, "Loretta Moss, you're an alto. Stop singing the soprano part!"

My face flushed hot. Everyone looked at me, twitters of laughter here and there. But Mr. Duffy went on, and I realized that we were all terrible—he was calling us out one by one, reciting our names and our failings. After dressing down the choir from one end to the other, he started in on the leads. Even Joelle was terrible. Even Gary. We faltered through another song, mangled it so badly that Mr. Duffy dismissed us all in disgust.

After the disaster of choir, we moved on to Youth Fellowship, where we sat stunned under the tireless whip of Rob's voice. That night he urged us to shut off the outside world, to associate only with other born-again Christians. Witnessing was one thing, he said; allowing ourselves to become tainted by the devil's offerings was quite another. "Even as you speak for Christ," he said, "your friends at school, your teachers, are witnesses for the devil. You know what they have planted in your hearts to fester, what festers there even at this moment. It is their worldly influence. How will you cleanse your heart now? How will you keep Christ's temple clean?" Gary sat in the front row beside Sidra. We all sat rapt and nodding; sparked here and there around me were sudden sobs, broken breathing and tears. We hugged each other, kept our arms around each other for comfort.

"You think you've got tickets for that heavenly train," Rob cried. "What will you do when you find your ticket was counterfeit? The train is leaving the station!" In his words, I could feel a test coming, the impending call to some unknown but decisive, heroic action— like a leap into a moving railcar. Not everyone would make it. In our desperation we would push and trample each other, scramble over each other's bodies. One thing was clear though: Sidra was already aboard. She and Rob shone together like angels from the rear of the train, disinterested, waiting to see who among us would have the strength to join them.

～

Two weeks after Sidra's conversion, at Reverend Gaines's Invitation, Joelle Hunnicutt rose and went forward. We watched, astounded. The pastor didn't kneel with her, but her sobbing was almost more heartbreaking than Sidra's had been because it was so loud, so inconsolable. Only a year before we had all watched Joelle baptized in the new sunken pool in the middle of the sanctuary, watched her rise again under the pastor's hand, streaming water from her choir robe.

"What, it didn't *take* the first time?" Jennifer Hayes sneered. "It's 'born again,' period. Not again and again!" But she joined the crowd surrounding Joelle as I did, Sidra too, all of us hugging her while she tried through tears to explain. She had never been saved, never truly felt it happen until this very moment, when the Lord called her to step forward and accept Him before the eyes of the congregation—this time for real. How could she hold back, knowing she was lost?

The next Sunday I sat beside Sidra, while Reverend Gaines shouted, "Look to your own heart!" and clutched his chest as if he were having an attack. I looked to my own heart and saw what I had come to suspect I would find there, a hollow yearning, an empty God-forsaken place. I needed to be filled with that light too, touched and filled. Perhaps that was all it took for others to see into your heart—that candle glow of God's love to light you from within, mark you with fire. "Touch me, Lord," I prayed, "fill me." And not knowing what to pray next, I lit on the words of the one song I never flatted: *Mold me and make me after thy will, while I am waiting, yielded and still.* Then the church flooded with white light.

I wobbled and Sidra took my arm, whispered something I didn't hear. My vision went purple and green and the church slowly returned, the backs of a hundred heads and Reverend Gaines halfway through the Invitation. Flanking him I recognized two girls from the Backsliders' Club, and then, from the left, there was Tamara Fisher walking up between the pews. It was almost over, the train was leaving the station. *Wait,* I thought. Almost falling, I staggered forward. Faces turned toward me, their mouths forming O's of surprise.

Then I was at the front with the others—five of us, all members of the youth group. We waited quietly for the pastor to make his way from one to the next, and the many-faced bowl of the sanctuary stared in silence. The pastor was on the third of us, and his murmured prayer seemed to me threaded with suspicion or annoyance. My cheeks burned; I wanted to crawl back to my pew. I tried to think of a way to look more authentic—but how could I, three Sundays too late and fifth in line? But I *was* authentic! I had really felt something. The congregation murmured faintly and here and there checked watches, thinking about lunch.

⌒

A few weeks later, Sidra was gone. No one could have been more stunned, though by then the fervor of her conversion had already begun to die down. Maybe we should have known that an outsider, with such a sudden faith, wouldn't be strong enough to last. She had us duped. Even I had stopped doubting altogether when she went door to door with us. She witnessed to her parents and her little sister. She witnessed in school. But it took nothing more than a single sermon to end it. It was Rob who struck the blow, by preaching on the evils of heavy metal music. To most of us, the topic seemed a welcome break in the heat, but Sidra waited until he finished and then she walked out of Wednesday fellowship without a word. I can't say for sure if that was the very moment when the flame was snuffed, if she had carried it until then. Maybe all along it had been dimming, flickering.

I tried to reason with her at school, but she wouldn't listen. If Rob was wrong about heavy metal, she told me, he must be wrong about other things—the whole church must have gotten it wrong. "Rob's just a person, you know," she said, leaning against her locker. "A person with ideas."

"So that means you think whatever you want?" I couldn't believe what I was hearing. "What about the Bible? What about Jesus—is He 'just a person'?"

"I don't know." She shrugged, looking bored.

I was shaking with indignation, but I was oddly happy too, more thrilled with the revelation than I was angry at her. "You faked the whole thing, didn't you? Was it just for attention?"

"I had something real, a real experience." Her subtle emphasis seemed to accuse the rest of us, though she gazed off blandly down the hall; she might have been talking to herself. "I don't think Jesus is who I thought he was."

She shifted her books, looked me in the eye. "Look, I can't explain it to you. You wouldn't understand. All I can say is the God I met wouldn't pitch a fuss about what kind of music I listen to."

With a flip of her hair, she turned and walked off. Blazing fury, I yelled after her, "That's because your god is Satan!" Passing students turned and paused to watch our show.

Nearly the end of the hall, she shouted back. "Loretta, you idiot! You just swallow everything, don't you? They've got you brainwashed. All of you!"

So much for Saint Sidra, marching away through the school halls and back into the devil's clutches forever. But did it mean that she had never really left him? It soon became impossible, I found, to look back and know anything for certain about the brief, strange time she was with us, because the quiet returned in her wake as if she had never been. Even Rob softened, the fierce light in his eyes turned back to love. We all breathed easy and remembered we were friends; when Gary began dating Tamara, I agreed with everyone that they made a cute couple. We all got back to the routine of choir practice and Fellowship and Sunday sermons.

But for those few weeks, our youth group had suffered from a kind of collective brain fever. Maybe it was the devil's confusion. I can't bring myself to call it that, though, because I remember the bright, hard edges of everything, a clarity of vision so sharp it hurt. Our lives had importance, potential, the urgency of a quest. When it was over, we had lost something we would never have again, and we could only be relieved to lose it. We returned exhausted to the soothing arms of the church.

say the magic word

For the modest ranch house it supported, Dan Foster's yard was a large one—a sloped acre of winter rye, bordered in cow pasture, kudzu-tangled scrub, and a gray curve of rural Georgia highway. Halfway up the slope between the road and the house grew a single mature water oak. With only one tree of any size, the yard wouldn't take much work to rake, Dan had decided, especially for two. His son was eight years old and a handful—a lonely boy without friends nearby to help him take the edge off his energy. A little yard work, Dan reasoned, would be good for him and fun as well, a father-son activity.

Except that raking day arrived, and Paul chose not to participate. Politely declined. He'd rather not. So Dan raked alone, the heap of oak leaves and fallen twigs growing taller beside the tree, and from time to time he looked up the hill to where the boy sat fixedly on the front stoop of the house, as if engaged in a sit-down strike. There appeared to be a blue blanket over his head.

Something in the boy's demeanor, the calm satisfaction of this rebellion, perplexed Dan. Eight was plenty old to be a help—even if Dan's mother acted as though the boy were constitutionally afflicted somehow, in perpetual danger of collapse. Paul had no mother, only this grandmother who visited once a week from out

of town to lend their bachelor home the woman's voice it otherwise lacked.

"He's a perfectly normal boy," Dan would argue. He felt himself
arguing again as he raked, but as if they were all in the kitchen—his
mother perhaps squinting gravely at one of the boy's small, translucent hands, spread before a late afternoon window light. Paul enjoyed
demonstrating how the sun could erase the borders of his fingers to a
white brilliance around five slender stems, candled red. "See the
blood?" he would ask, earnest and awed.

"I raised three boys," Dan's mother announced. "Don't tell me
about normal." She stroked the pale hair from Paul's face, and the
backs of her fingers assessed his forehead, cheeks, and throat for vital
signs. Paul smiled dreamily. Otherwise a blur of hyperactivity, he
turned passive and silent under her touch.

"Mother, don't do that." He wanted to peel her off the boy, but
he restrained himself. "You make everything so dramatic. He's got
more energy than he needs." Dan chaffed in the knowledge that her
judgment somehow reflected on him, as did all judgment concern-
ing Paul—the opinions of teachers and preachers and county women
in the grocery store who, just because a boy was motherless, couldn't
help casting a critical eye. "His teachers want him on drugs, for
Christ's sake! He runs them ragged."

Like the others, his mother barely listened. He extracted Paul
firmly from her grasp and said to the boy, "You're hell on wheels, right?
Tell Grandma all the trouble you make."

Paul nodded in solemn confirmation. "I need drugs."

"Paul—" Dan exhaled with a sharp, disgusted sound. "You don't
either. You're normal like you are." At which point, Paul began to
giggle and repeat the word "drugs," until Dan sent him out to play.

Despite the snag in his plan, Dan was glad to be working outdoors,
to breathe the fall air. He recalled raking as a child with his older

brothers, the satisfaction of raising the brown carpet into a mound nearly big enough to hide them all. His brothers would not let the burning begin until they had buried him, the youngest, in leaves, and he would lie as still as he could, choking back giggles, while Gerald and Frank called their mother from the house: "He's gone! We don't know, honest. We can't find him." Dan still looked forward to the work, the dusky smell of leaves he had once breathed while waiting to leap out of hiding with a shout of surprise. What boy could resist a leaf pile, enticing as a magician's dropped cape?

Paul remained rooted to the stoop. From under the blue blanket, which he wore like a hood, he watched Dan's efforts with unwavering, interested eyes. Dan was about to call him down, put a stop to this nonsense, but Paul called first. "*Jonathan!*" he shouted, shrill as a peacock.

Dan stared at the boy's face, which was unchanged, small with distance and draped in blue. *Jonathan?* Making a casual turn, Dan checked behind him in case someone named Jonathan might be lurking nearby. A car fired past at the bottom of the hill, but otherwise he and the boy were alone.

"*Jonathan!*" The boy hollered again, before Dan could think of a response. It was not a voice to be ignored: richer than his normal voice, more nasal, with an odd inflection—was that British?—that made Dan think of a duchess summoning a servant, an aristocratic old mother calling her son.

He crossed the yard to the stoop, where the boy sat demurely blinking up at him, hands clasped around his crossed knees. The blue satin edge of the blanket framed his face. The rest fell over his shoulders and into a whorl on the concrete behind him, as carefully arranged as a bridal train.

"Paul." Dan shaped his son's name with care because there was something eerily transformative, Madonna-like, in the blue veil, the placid eyes beneath it. "Come help your old man with the leaves."

"Now, Jonathan," the boy chided, face stretched long and comical between a pursed mouth and raised eyebrows. "Is that any way to talk to *moi*? You should address me as Miss Pritchett." He drew his fingertips along the soft border of his face, one side and then the other, leisurely, precise.

Dan tried to smile, though his stomach did a nervous flip. More and more, this child seemed determined to unsettle him with a new trick, sent him searching for the correct response. He could hear it now—his mother and all the neighbor women taking him to task. He was doing *something* wrong, obviously.

"I look divine. Simply . . . glorious," Miss Pritchett announced. One hand slipped a curl of blanket back from a shoulder, and the blue head canted to the left with a frown, as if musing for another adjective. "Jonathan, you should say how I look."

Dan felt himself wanting to oblige, searching a flurry of words for something descriptive. But nothing seemed to apply. "Miss Pritchett," he pronounced instead, carefully. "How about putting the blanket back on the bed?"

Miss Pritchett rolled round eyes heavenward, but under her dour frown the boy's own spritish grin flickered. "Don't be silly, Jonathan. You silly thing. You're such a trial to me."

Dan laughed in an exhaled breath—he couldn't help it. Where was all this coming from? The boy was inventing, riffing, maybe copying something he had seen on TV. More wonders turned through that brain every day. How was a grown man to keep up?

Paul's eyes were fixed on him as if he were the one watching the show, and Dan dropped the smile, turned away. He went to the black shutter that was pinned against the white clapboard of the house, the paint beginning to lift and shed like scales. "Lot of work to do out here," he said, picking at the paint.

"Oh, but first we must have tea!" The boy rose, careful not to disturb the drape of the blanket, and approached. His smile was an effort of restraint, Mona Lisa, arms crossed to stroke the satin border that fell along each elbow. "It's definitely certainly time for tea."

The week before, the boy had used words like these. Tea time. They had been at the Dairy Queen, where they went nearly every Saturday for a cone. But on the last trip, the boy had selected a Mister Misty so that he could sip, awkward pinkie in the air. When the drink sloshed onto the table, Dan had asked him to hold the cup with all his fingers, both hands, please.

So he realized with some fear that the boy wanted to go to the Dairy Queen now. Did he want to go with the blanket on his head? Dan could imagine the looks they would get, the comments that would trail them around Greene County to bolster the already common opinion that Dan Foster didn't know what he was up against with this child.

"*What* do you say, Jonathan?" Miss Pritchett's tone carried a note of demand, as if coaxing a child's tutored politeness, some *Please* or *Thank you* or *I'm sorry*.

Under the long blue fall—so clearly, undeniably, it was hair—the boy wore a white Georgia Bulldogs T-shirt and blue jeans, gray sneakers that were fraying and pulling up along the rubber seams. His lightly freckled face was clean. No other decoration, nothing more than a plain blue blanket for a child's bed, a normal thing. What else could he have found in that house, the closets and drawers, to aid the game? Hadn't Dan thrown it all away, all Nina's clothes and every beaded necklace, the costume jewelry with faux pearls she had kept in a sleek black music box and never worn, her old hairbrushes and clasps and the dingy tray of makeup she had left under the sink? He had boxed it all for the dump, her sheer scarves that had shaded the lamps, the feathers she collected straight from the ground to tuck into her long hair, all boxed with her books, her letters, pictures, every trace she had left behind.

There had been so much of it. He thought he would never be through with the boxes, but he packed it all away the same day she left and smoothed clear tape across the seams. Nina had always been like a spirit to him, a blond waif more of the air than earth, and it baffled him when and how she had managed to accumulate all these things—so many boxes, so much weight. But she walked out telling him that none of it was hers at all, that it had never been hers. She dismissed it with a wave of her hand that included him and the house and the state of Georgia and their five-month-old baby, asleep in the back room. With her backpack hitched over her shoulders then, she was exactly the girl he'd first seen two years before, returned as if untouched to the side of a road, thumb out on an effortless westward glide.

He told himself that Paul had never been her child. But nevertheless, here was that child on the stoop before him, still waiting for his response. The blue crown of his head was level with Dan's collarbones. Dan touched the blanket lightly, brushed his hands over both trailing edges to cup the boy's ears hidden beneath. The boy gazed up at him with trust and open wonder and his wife's sharded crystal eyes just as they had looked so often when she'd stood before him as a pale supplicant, waiting to be kissed.

Along the Oconee River, a mile to the west, a bank of clouds crossed the sun, dropping a light shadow over them. A breeze touched the blanket, moved it under Dan's fingers. He had intended to kiss his son's forehead. But it wasn't his son, and almost against his will he drew the blanket back, lowered it until he was faced with a boy again—a boy like any other, wrapped in a plain bed blanket as if against a chill.

The glow of the boy's face dimmed and he stood for a moment, the blanket along his shoulders. Not waiting for a kiss, he turned away. He walked entirely out of the blanket, down the steps and into the yard.

Walking away, he was a normal-looking boy, ears protruding, slender neck. Under the clouds, his close-trimmed hair shone gold; perhaps it was sudden exposure that made it seem brighter than usual. With measured, somnambulant steps, he passed the pile of leaves and never turned his head. Beyond the leaves, the yard sloped more sharply into a curve of the highway, two thinly traveled lanes. But the few cars that passed were always speeding, blind drivers intent on far-off destinations that were never Greene County.

"Paul!" Dan called. The boy knew his limits, knew he wasn't allowed to cross the ditch that fronted the road. But his legs looked skittery as a fawn's, ready to tumble him into traffic, and Dan called again, more sharply.

At the ditch, Paul turned and walked along the edge, head down and deaf. His slight form, white shirt against the deepening green, passed behind the water oak so that for an instant he was lost from view, an instant later returned.

Dan picked up the blanket from the step. It was full of the smell of the boy, the dense, sweet way he smelled in his sleep. He flipped it open like a cape and drew it over his head, along the edges of his face. The weight of it surprised him, how it tugged his scalp as if taking root there.

He called again—"*Jonathan!*"—the voice no longer his own. Paul's head jerked up in response. For a moment he stood motionless, mouth agape. Then, even across the distance between them, Dan could see the boy's slow, expanding smile like another sun emerging. *My son.* He thought, *you look radiant*—that word that had eluded him appearing now, without effort.

mercy

I notice what shines. Standing in the line for school pictures that stretches behind me out the library door—I'm next—I see her, passing beyond the photographer. Like a star in the dark room. She lingers with cool, sadistic interest to watch as the students fall alphabetically, one by one, into the photographer's chair, as he forces their heads by rigid degrees left, up, down, and back. She's one of those Jennifers—you know the ones—come in a ten-pack like gum, all in matching foil wrappers. But this one, maybe because she's alone, I notice.

I never did shine that way. Most days, I'm who nobody would notice. But at this moment the photographer's silver disk is throwing so much light in my face I can barely hold my eyes open, like there's never been more light caught and turned to strike so small a space, a frozen instant before the pop, and the room falls to black.

"You didn't show your teeth," she says, after. The breath of her words comes from about two feet behind my right ear. Milky cereal and Doublemint gum. Underneath that is some drugstore impostor perfume like "If you like Charlie, you'll love CHUCK."

There's no reason for her to talk to me, unless it's a trick. Maybe she knows I hate Jennifers—Katies and Kimberlys too, along with the odd Mitzi or Marlo, Cathi with an *i*, those names you see sewn into the bloomers under cheerleader uniforms. This one's not a cheerleading Jennifer, just secretly wants to be. When she offers that comment on my teeth, I'm handing in my printed form at the table so they'll get my name right in the yearbook. Marcy with a Y, V period, Ballard. My middle name is actually Lynn, like everyone else's if it's not Ann.

I turn and curl my lip at her, snarl and snap—teeth click. At least I think it's her—she's no more than a voice, a smell, the blue nimbus of my own blindness from the flash. Then I grin, disarming, into the light.

This is when the girls of her tribe usually sneer, their faces twisted in disgust. They call me dog. Little bitch. Excuse me! But this one waits a beat and I hear her laugh, startled. The sound of it breaks and shimmers around me, like a mirror that I still can't see.

⌒

I sing in the chorale. It's the only thing that I like in the world. It's the only time I am erased, drifting through some pleasant middle range of consciousness. Checked out. Instead of me, there's sound—music, I guess, though I'm not listening enough to judge. Notes—the usual kind—rising and falling, but to me each one seems higher than the last, each one reached only in climbing. The song is a thin rope dangling from the sky and I climb it. The other end, attached to nothing, is up there somewhere like a charmed thing, doesn't matter if you can't see it. What counts is the next note, then the next. You climb. Nothing else makes that much sense.

I've had solos before, but I like best singing in a group. There are twelve of us. I'm the only freshman. We wear red choir robes, red for the Red Devil school colors with white trim. No one thinks it's funny that devils dress in choir robes, then go about singing church songs under the banner of a public school. Sometimes we sing Michael Bolton. You have to mix it up a little for the contests.

It's never occurred to me that singing in the chorale could be uncool. I never had the urge to wonder.

Here's what Jennifer says in the Girls': "That's cool." But she says it slowly, elaborately, no gasp of disgust but something that teeters more precariously on the beam of judgment. Which way will it fall? You wait for it—the fall that's coming—with a kind of sickening dread. It doesn't matter how long it's poised there, wobbling, because you know that once balance is lost you'll never get it back again. Your whole life can change that quick.

I tell Jennifer the story of too many Jennifers, which has never occurred to her. "You can't be that anymore," I tell her. "Be something different."

She bares her teeth to the bathroom mirror, rubs coral lipstick off one incisor with a fingertip. With the rolled-out lipstick tube, she applies another layer to her mouth, then she presses her lips together and pokes them out pettishly at her reflection. "I'm so fucking gorgeous I could die of myself." She lifts and twists her hair; it falls back in a cloud around her face.

"Who cares?" I say, from my post against the mirror between the two sinks. It's halfway through freshman year and this is, literally, my first time in the Girls'. I've trained myself to hold it all day so I'll never have to venture through those doors, ever, but now here I am with a Jennifer. A sophomore, no less.

"Grow warts," I say. "Shave your head. Get a skull tattoo on your left cheek."

She takes my chin between her fingers and makes the fish lips, a command. Holding the lipstick like a pen, she draws my mouth, then nods in approval. "Now you're gorgeous too. That was easy." She turns my jaw savagely toward the mirror, then like an afterthought she turns it back and plants her coral lips on my forehead: "There's a tattoo for you."

In the mirror now I have two perfect mouths, one mobile and familiar under paint, the other like a coral lesion or the mark of two fingers rough enough to raise a bruise. It looks more permanent than my own lips. Like an apocalyptic sign, a way that armies of angels might know me from the others.

"I won't say your name anymore," I tell her. "We'll have to think of something new."

"You know—my friend Donny at the Physical Plant has some pot," she offers. "If you're gonna keep up this shit, let's do it stoned."

Meanwhile, at this precise moment across campus, eleven members of the chorale are waiting to have their picture taken for the yearbook. Robes cleaned and pressed, all alike, they stand in two tiers, shoulders angled inward and faces turned to the light like so many moons. O, their mouths will say, perhaps, angelic cartoon of a choir, as if the camera has caught them in the act. Or they will smile as simply as the Key Club on the next page, the Junior Thespians, the 4-H'ers and the National Honor Society. Perhaps there will be a shot each way, the singing and the smiling, but first someone will say, "Wait! Where's Marcy? Wait for Marcy, wait, we can't take the picture with Marcy missing. We're only eleven, unbalanced, unfinished, without Marcy. A few minutes. Wait." Or maybe there would be no delay at all, only the assumption that some must go missing, some bound to be absent or otherwise unaccounted for on picture day and there are so many pictures that must be taken, so many clubs, and only one harried photographer to cover it all. No time. Move along. Snap the shutter, done.

⌐

At home, an old woman's shadow is over everything that used to be mine. She arrived in June. We thought, Mama thought, she would not be long for this world but she is long after all, a thing that won't die, will never leave.

She's my father's mother. You can tell she is at least partly how my father got to be the blight on my life that he is. He calls me Pal. When he does this, I have to make a retching sound, so that he turns nervous and leaves. Truthfully, he's nervous before he ever says "Pal," hesitating in every doorway. He'd rather be facing Sidra on her worst day. Sidra he calls Star.

Now I know my father better, knowing he came from this old woman. It's the stroke, Mama says to explain her behavior—maybe the old woman has had two or three little ones, living on her own after grandpa died. A *little stroke* is like God peeling back your skull to rub a thumb across the molded surface of your brain like it's soft clay. Almost tender, that caress, but it leaves behind a mark. We took her because she would forget to eat. Sometimes she would go out to get the mail and forget to put clothes on first. You can imagine this naked, saggy, wrinkled old bag swaying in the breeze at the road's edge, peering into the box. Mama said it was either us or a home.

"I don't want her here," I told Mama. "I don't like old people. They're creepy."

Mama frowned at the crown of my head, the plain brown hair that she used to scrub with shampoo and spray with No More Tears and tease out with the comb every day, until at the late age of eleven, I decided I would do it myself. Since then, she's kept a few inches away from me on any side like there's an electric fence.

"You'll be old yourself one day," she answered, without the usual pointed "young lady" tacked to the end. Like she was giving me bad news gently.

So the old woman came, and I have to watch her close. Mostly it's my job, since Sidra is busy with horses, and Mama works, afternoons and weekends. The old woman has a walker and a plastic tube that goes up her nose and a can of oxygen that she carries with her as she wanders from closet to drawer, looking for my father's stash of cigarettes. She pitches junk out of drawers and mumbles "Goddamn, got a home, go home got damn." Not like she can't speak a perfect sentence when she pleases—any time the doorbell rings I have to get there before her and block the way, or she'll be on the UPS guy saying, "Might I trouble you for a cigarette?" Ten minutes later she'll be back on her rounds, sniffing through the same drawers she emptied an hour before.

It's almost funny until you look in her eyes. They protrude like wet black stones from a face of melting wax. Under the slide of her flesh, you can almost see how she was beautiful once, years ago. But if you look too close after what's vanished, her eyes become holes. They go all the way through her and past her, pull me in and down until I start to panic. Neither one of us can breathe.

I call to Sidra as she's on her way out the back door, yellow braid swinging. "It's your turn to sit with Grandma Ballard," I try. She bites into an apple. My voice never sounds big enough to touch Sidra's life.

She chews, considering. "Okay, then it's your turn to muck the stalls and clean my saddle." I make a face, and she continues elaborately. "Take Simon's bridle apart, scrub and oil every little bit, and then actually put it back together again the right way. Can you do that?"

Every weekend, Sidra has a horse show. If I keep pushing, she'll be ready to convince me that *this* show is the most important of all the shows, that it means everything and if I can't understand that then I just don't understand anything.

A couple of years ago, it was Jesus. If I mention it now, she'll pretend memory loss, but I remember it all, vividly—how, when she was my age, she was born again into eternal life. I was eleven at the time, and she sat me down on her bed, told me in perfect seriousness how Jesus came into her heart, how he changed everything with his holy love and he could do the same for me, if I would only ask him to. She pointed to paragraphs in her Good News Bible, gave me a handful of tiny comics to read. I was intrigued but suspicious, having experience with her hand-me-downs. I knew that nothing ever fit, ever looked the same on me as it did on Sidra. She'd never give away anything worth having, and sure enough, a few months and Jesus was cast aside like her treasured gold belt from sixth grade, long after it could mean anything to me.

Sidra doesn't have to wait for a reply. She knows she's won, goes waltzing down to the barn, the gold rope of her hair swinging carelessly behind.

~

Jennifer and I cut an hour of class most days to hook up with Donny and smoke. I call her Geronimo, so now Donny does too. She wants to name me, but she can't make anything stick. She's tried Tonto and George.

At first, Donny was impressive to have around just because of his age. He's nineteen, which is older than anyone Sidra knows, tall and gaunt with mossy black hair, delicate skin, a very red mouth. Cute, we decide. Cute enough. And an older man. But once he starts talking, nineteen doesn't seem so old anymore. You get the idea he hangs out with us because he doesn't have any friends his own age. If you ask him why he's a janitor and not in college, he'll tell you he's really a poet. A student of life, one who spends his paycheck on weed, comics, and video games.

Once, while we were sitting on the floor in the physical plant passing a joint, I kissed him. Which I did only because Geronimo did it first, and so he said, "That's not very original." Original being his favorite word.

"Is that a fact, Walt Whitman?" I said. "Why don't you recite me some poetry."

He tried to compose something on the spot about my eyes—*Your eyes are like . . .* and then he was stuck, staring and staring, while I offered suggestions. "Limpid pools? Blue flames?" Geronimo was amused. She joined in: "Sapphires. Diamonds. Transistor radios." I said, "Clock towers. Pigeon shit. Windows of the soul." Geronimo and I shrieked with giggles, fell in a heap.

Donny only blinked, stunned-looking, said, "Have mercy on me now. There ain't no word."

But Donny has a car.

⁓

Geronimo calls me on Saturday in a snit. Her mother is forcing her to go to a wedding for some horrible business associate. "I won't know anybody," she squeals. "And this dress she's making me wear—it's a joke. I could die."

I take the call in the kitchen, where I'm feeding the old woman her lunch. Sandwich, chips, and pickle—she pushes it around with her fingers. "You're a rotten one," she mutters at me. "An evil strain of blood musta got into you. Your mama, she don't even know about it."

"Don't talk to me, you old bat," I hiss at her, hand over the mouthpiece while Geronimo jabbers on.

"I know your secrets. I know who you are. Torturing an old woman. Who sent you? Answer!"

This is what she says to me, her own flesh granddaughter. I tell Geronimo to come over. I want to see what the old woman will say about her. She reminds me she has to go to this wedding, like she *just* said, and besides, she doesn't have a ride.

"Make Donny bring you."

I hang up. The old woman gives me a resentful look. "Lemme have a cigarette."

"Choke on that sandwich first. Then I'll think about it."

"How'm I supposed to eat with this . . . this—" She jerks at the tube that trails from her face. "You can't make me breathe this poison forever. I know about my own good, little miss. I'm seventy-two and I'll perfectly well kill myself if I like." Her voice is a wheezy quaver but she squinches down one eye and fixes me with the other, bulging and black with a star in the center, the only still point in a shaking body. Her hair is wild metallic floss, caught up in the faint corona that seems always to hum around her.

I shove the plate aside and lean across the table into her face. "Wanna see who can hold their breath the longest?" I puff my cheeks for a challenge.

"Get out of my face, hussy."

I stand back and study her—she's hunched and pitiful like some big, bony dog trying to sit in a kitchen chair. "You gotta be more creative. Any child will tell you holding your breath doesn't work."

"Wha's that?" she shrieks, cupping an ear. She goes deaf as it suits her, the way she plays when anyone else is home. I know it's an act.

It's almost an hour before the car pulls up the long, unpaved driveway. Geronimo comes to the door; I can see Donny, shadowy, waiting behind the wheel. The girl's all grin and shine, her breath coming fast. "Catch *this*, baby, I just walked out. My hand to God. See ya, Mom! So let's get out of here. Let's go!"

"Where to?"

"Who cares? Anywhere. *Any*where." Her grin drops a notch, awestruck with possibility, the limitless scope of a Saturday afternoon. She's the inverse of the old woman. Her gleaming eyes go careening like electrons from one side of my face to the other, like Judy Garland's eyes. Her next line will appear somewhere on the teleprompter of the face before her.

I lead her inside, to where the old woman sits on the living room sofa. The room is darkened in preparation for her nap, the zigzag afghan already over her knees. But she sits up yet and gazes across at the brass clock on the mantel—farther than anyone else would suspect she could see—while one hand probes like a separate little animal under the cushion behind her.

"Someone for you to meet, Grandma." I propel our visitor into position between the old woman and the clock.

"Who's 'at?"

"Judy Garland."

"Oh." The old woman gives a twitchy nod, and her eyes go narrow. "You smoke, honey?"

Judy sniffs and sticks out her chin, in case she's been offered a dare. "Sometimes, I guess."

"Ya too young for that. Hand 'em over."

"No, Grandma," I shout sweetly, like she has trouble hearing. "No cigarettes. Time for your nap now. Lie down like a good girl."

She aims her eye at Judy. "You must be a singer. This one, you know—" she waves toward me vaguely with one twisted paw—"she sings like an angel. Never tell a difference."

Judy smirks. "I don't actually sing. Just do impressions." She rolls her eyes at me and says with unsubtle emphasis, "I'll be in the car."

She lets the screen door bang. The old woman looks up to tether me, remind me that her blood runs in my veins, hotter and faster but still the same, still hers. As if we go forward or back together and no accounting for what I choose, what I will do. But she's feeble; with one blink she goes hazy-soft, forgets it all again.

"Lie back now," I tell her. "Go to sleep." I wait by her until her eyes close, thinking she'll sleep until Mama comes home and if she doesn't, she'll have a tough time killing herself in one afternoon. Her only methods are the slow ones. I'll be in trouble for leaving, but it seems inevitable now.

I kiss the spotted, pliable skin of her forehead before I go. It's so soft it reminds me of wild mushrooms, leaf mold, that wormy-rich black soil under disintegrated wood. How all things go soft in death.

∽

Here's where we go: Atlanta. Here's what we do: whatever we want.

∽

Once a year, Mama and Sidra and I go into the city, because Athens has no mall. We go shopping at Lennox and sometimes window-shopping at Phipps, and then we have dinner at Dante's Down the Hatch. The city has always been this one day a year to me: countless bags, fondue, and alligators.

Sometimes it takes two trips into the mall to get all the necessary packages to the car. Sidra's the one who drags us back for seconds, sure she's missed the perfect piece of clothing, the ideal shoe, and sometimes Mama says her feet are tired and she waits for us in the car. Sidra has to promise we'll stick together in the mall. But I know

I have to keep track of myself, because anyone who sees these two girls together sees the one with the long blond hair like flax and, beside her, the other one.

Dante's, where we go after, is a restaurant with a real ship inside, right at the center, that looks like Noah's ark. There's a gangway slanting up to the ship above; below on all sides, a moat of black water. Sidra and I trail the railing all along the moat, peering down to find the shapes of gators. They're alive down there, but so still you'd never know for sure. We split up to cover all the recesses, all the hiding places, rising several times during our meal of bread and fruit and silky cheese sauce because we have to look again. Signs everywhere warn us they're not to be fed.

My sister's hair is a gold beacon far along the rail, beyond the candlelit tables, her face turned down to the moat. I'm at the gangway that rises to the ship. Up above, I distinguish nothing but a faint blue light and the fainter voice of a woman, a blues singer. It almost hurts to hear that sound, half-imagined, the notes climbing each other so far out of range. Mama tells how there are tables set up on the deck of the ship so you can eat up there and listen to the music—live blues and jazz nightly. But there's always a velvet rope across the entrance. It costs extra to get on the ship.

"You can see the gators just fine from down here," Mama says.

When I come home on Sunday at sunset, the gold light still hangs in the oak that rubs its limbs over all the slanted roofs of the upstairs rooms. But the house looks a different shade of blue, as if years have passed since I've been up the front steps, reached for the screen door.

It turns out the old woman lived through her abandonment. Mama, though sick with worry, has not yet called the police. My father and

Sidra are out looking for me in Athens. The two of them are looking now, maybe from the window of a cafe where they're eating drippy warm gyros and coney fries, while he calls her Star and asks about her love life.

Mama is not quite yelling. "Where did you go? Where have you been? Don't you have a lick of sense? Answer, young lady!"

I don't tell her where I've been. I can't explain how, from Donny's car, the city is both more and less than I imagined. How we drove the Perimeter and looped down Ponce de Leon and into Little Five Points, to the places Donny knew. How I told him and Judy every-thing about Dante's and how we planned together to go there for dinner, to get a table onboard the ship—so high above and walled that I'd never even glimpsed the deck, could only imagine the way the tables would sit, where the singer would be. And we three would be ushered like royalty up the gangway, right into a waiting place onboard, like no place on earth. How it was supposed to happen.

Because it never happened. We drove into Buckhead, but I couldn't remember exactly where to go, and Judy spotted a poster that she *had* to have hanging in the window of a store, so we tried to find a parking space, and then we could no longer find the store. We were tired of walking and hungry and Donny wanted to drop in on a cousin up in Alpharetta, who had his own place and would buy us liquor and let us stay the night. Judy wanted peach Schnapps. We ate at a deserted Pizza Inn on the way to Alpharetta, and then found the cousin, who was less than excited to see Donny and gazed at us, his two compan-ions, with a distant, offended air. He bought us the peach Schnapps and then told us to leave.

I don't tell how later Judy was puking into the toilet and calling me her best friend, or how quick you could hate someone all because it's her fault you never got past a velvet rope onto a ship to hear the real blues.

Running away to the city, you expect to do more than get a room in a Motel 6 and drink peach Schnapps, your driver complaining the whole time that you girls are sucking his wallet dry. You don't imagine that the highlight after all will be a midnight run for Philly cheesesteak, in which, because the place is closed, you drive in circles in the parking lot and try to flatten a styrofoam cup that someone left standing lonely in the open like the center of something. I don't tell Mama how I asked to drive, how Donny got out finally to stomp the persistent cup, and when I pretended to leave him behind in the parking lot, he ran after the car as if his life were in danger and hurled his body onto the moving trunk with a thud, tumbled off the other side. He flashed through the mirror and was gone, lost in our wake as if the asphalt were water to draw him down. When he rose again and got into the back seat, he was trying to laugh with us, but he was shaking and white. In the mirror I could see blood beaded on his nose and chin, darkening the crevices between his teeth.

I could explain to Mama that nineteen is this young after all. No need to worry on Donny's account, not like you think. And if I crawled into his bed in the middle of the night, it was only the courage of Schnapps to make something, finally, happen—he never would have touched me otherwise. He didn't even want to wake up at first, waved me away and groaned, "Mom!" so that I sighed at the ceiling, wondered what I was doing. He rolled onto me, still heavy with sleep, began to fumble under my clothes, push against me, waking only when he felt that little pop, which made him gasp, as if surprised by this evidence that I wasn't truly older and more worldly than he. But then all of a sudden, I was. Not that a little thing like sex could change me, but that I found out it was nothing—neither a prison wall nor a parole, the way they always tell you.

What I tell Mama is that I'm fine and I'm home, that no one needs to worry because I know how to take care of myself. I don't want to talk about it. The old woman glares from her walker at the bottom of the staircase, and Mama stops short of following me into my room, of crossing the closed door. "I'm just glad you're safe," she calls, a bodiless, uncertain voice from the other side. The oak rubs its giant thumb against the roof overhead.

This is what I learned and don't tell: how life outside makes everything smaller than it is, than you think it is, than it ought to be. There's nothing can kill you after all. The more you face what scares you, the more immortal you become.

⌐

I can't remember why I started calling her Binky. When she sees me in the hall now, she screams, "*Mercy*, Miss Marcy," which she borrowed from Donny, his way of beckoning to me over long distances. In either mouth it sounds halfway like a real plea. We talk about "exciting weekend getaways." She wants to do Florida next. I say, fine, as long as it's a city. She says, okay, a city on the beach.

I look at school, my classes and teachers, the routine of hourly movements. I weigh it against my other life, the one in the open. The other one is getting bigger. This one shrinks. Pretty soon it will be no more than a dry speck to flick away.

"Donny's gonna bitch about the money thing." Binky rats her hair savagely in the mirror of the Girls'. Her every other word now is Donny, as though she's trying to maintain her priority over what I've slept with and she hasn't. We were still in his bed in the morning, at the Motel 6. Grinning and naked, Donny told her it was a drunk thing—we'd both been drunk, it was nothing. I just smiled and shrugged. "I'll do you next time," he offered sweetly, and she mustered so much instant disgust that for a second she turned into a Jennifer again. "In your dreams, Donny!"

"We don't need him," I tell her.

"He's got the car, remember?"

"Well, he's holding us back. I can't stand begging favors. Let's not even tell him we're going this time. We'll hitch."

"Are you insane?" She asks this like a reasonable question. We face each other, a little staring contest, and I notice her eyes have three colors like amber, but there's nothing caught beneath her glossy surfaces, only a gloppy black bit of mascara in one corner.

"I've got news for you, Bink. I'll go without you too."

She tilts her head, interested. "Why? Why hitch? Why go at all?"

"Experience." I smile like this is the answer to life, and once I've said it, I think it might be. "Because we can. What more do you want?"

She considers, and her coral lips pull back from her teeth until her smile fairly matches mine. She hooks her hands around my neck and I do the same to her and we press our foreheads together, grinning. We start to laugh, louder and louder. Our voices echo through the empty stalls and down from the ceiling pipes, and we spin a circle with our heads locked like two bighorn sheep flinging each other dizzy at the edge of a mountain.

⤳

She has a bikini in the bag over her shoulder. In Florida, she thinks, it's always sunny summertime, tanning weather, that we'll cross a border somewhere and this whipping rain will lift like a spell. We'll walk into a postcard, and before Monday we'll just mail ourselves home, three shades darker, to the envy of all the kids at school who spent the weekend roaming the new mall.

But it's Monday now; we're still slogging southward. I'm feeling shriveled inside my skin from the wet, like the old woman's softness is creeping closer the farther I get. Maybe I'll never get far enough.

Weather itself is a trap. The rain lightens enough that I can ease out from the shelter of the overpass, where no one ever sees us until they're already past, already vanished in the road mist. Binky unties the knot of her hair and finger-combs it. Twenty steps behind me in her water-heavy clothes, she wades through the sopping grass of the shoulder, no longer looking toward the road as if there is something to find. A semi sucks the air past her, whips the hair across her pale mouth.

"*Jennifer!*" she wails, as if calling someone back to her, forlorn, a last, desperate appeal. "My name is Jennifer, Jennifer!" But it sounds more ridiculous every time she says it, the syllables breaking, sliding apart, realigning. They've lost their connection to any sense, if there ever was a connection.

"You want some loser cheerleader name?" I have to shout back at her to clear the intermittent hum and rush of traffic, and my head echoes oddly with the words—I think it must have been hollowed by the pills a truck driver gave us last night. Maybe Binky hears the same way, as if we are alone in a tunnel shouting.

"Don't you call me a loser! I saved you from the fucking *chorale*!"

She turns her head away. Unseeing, she stares at the interstate, and for thirty blessed seconds not a car passes in either direction, so there's only the soft resonance of *chorale* to fill the space between us like an invisible choir. Whispered angel song rises into a hiss of insistence in the slushy passing of the next truck, and then it's just that gone. Red taillights in the distance.

"You know nothing about me." My response is softer in the next silence. She fishes through her shoulder bag; maybe she doesn't hear. "Now you know even less."

"Fuck!" she screams. "I can't believe you left my lipstick in that scuzzy bathroom."

I stand at the verge squinting for headlights, swallow against the sour aftertaste of coffee from three hours ago. Our next ride will have the heat going to blast us like a torch until our shriveled skins unpucker, smooth like ironed shirts. Out here, even in the mist, I can almost see the next thing coming.

"I can't believe I ever let you drag me out here in the first place. God, I'm soaked!"

"God, shut up already!"

A truck slows and pulls off onto the shoulder up ahead. It waits. I turn back to catch her eyes, but she barely seems to notice the truck. Her face is a twisted fury. "Why don't I just leave something of yours behind? Huh? What would you say about it then?"

She's close to tears, which would almost make me feel sorry for her except for the fact that she knows and I know she has already left something of mine behind us, long ago. I hardly recognize myself this way, voiceless, half-gone, as if singing had always been the most visible part of me. For some things, I'm finding out, there's no going back.

"Hurry it up, Binky."

She's sulking at a near standstill, and I start to imagine the truck will pull away without us, its hull cutting the road again like a ship from port to spray us with the wake of its massive leaving, before we have the chance even to touch it. We'll be left with nothing but what touches us—touching even now, that mucky water from under sixteen tires. I pick up a jog. I pass the mud flaps, two naked girls sitting arms back, legs out, facing each other.

"Are you coming or not?" My hand is almost at the door of the cab, which is so high above me I wonder if I'll be able to reach it. But it opens from the inside, and a guy with brownish teeth and a baseball cap low over his eyes grins down.

"Going to Florida?" I'm breathless. I'm a child asking her daddy to take her to Disney World.

"Take ya as far as Valdosta," he answers. "That's purty close."

"Sounds good to me."

The rain begins to spit again. I look back toward the girl who lingers behind the truck, wave for her to come along. Just in that moment she stands naked, skinned. The pleading in her eyes approaches the heat of blood, so that it's almost possible from this distance to hear the slushy sound it makes as her heart pushes it along the looping tracks of arteries and veins. For an instant I think I can see straight to her insides this way, where she's organs, systems, networks of impulse as schematic as some textbook on human biology. One foot pushes against the earth, begins to propel her body forward. She runs to catch me.

～

We never make it to Florida. Here's how we get home: a ride from the police.

～

Under house arrest, I'm allowed to take little field trips with my old pal Dad. He takes Sidra and me to see a movie in the crowded student union at the university. While Dad waits to buy our tickets, Sidra sits at one of the numerous little tables and pulls a book from her bag; she pretends to read, in hopes that someone will mistake her for a college student. I scan the notices posted around the wide columns of the lobby. The students are selling things, buying things, offering to tutor. They want to share rides to places like Raleigh-Durham, New Orleans, Memphis.

When I was six years old, my family lived for a while in an apartment in Memphis. We lived a lot of different places while I was young, and I remember almost nothing to distinguish one from another except for some avocado wallpaper with a worn velvet pattern in it—maybe that was Memphis—a girl named Dawn with long braids who was my friend. Dad was restless back then, Mama says. He would have moved us to a new town every six months till kingdom come if she hadn't put her foot down, settled her children into the old family house in Georgia and told Dad he could come if he liked. The rest of us were staying put, the end.

Sidra, who was eight, remembers more about Memphis than I do. She remembers the incident that I slept through, that moved us home to Georgia for good. Dad liked to drink in those days, and he liked to bet greyhounds. He'd go to the track over the river in West Memphis, and once, after he and Mama had a fight about it, he snuck Sidra out of bed in the middle of the night and took her to the track with him. She was good luck, he told her, had a sense about dogs. "Pick me a winner, Star," he'd say and put his money down wherever she liked one dog's name, another's color. Well, someone decided they looked suspicious, a grown man and a little girl so late at night, the man half soused. Maybe Mama had alerted the cops. Two uniformed officers came between them and one took Sidra aside, started asking her questions about Dad. By then, Dad had vanished with the other cop and didn't return until she was home again and it was three days later.

Sidra can't remember being afraid, troubled by Dad's vanishing. Instead there was only a change of scene: the excitement of the dogs spinning along the track, and then this sudden, handsome policeman who had charge of her. Nothing bad could happen. She felt charmed, miraculously independent. She can't remember the questions he asked or her answers, only her effort to make the right response. To make an impression. It was fun, she said, like choosing the right dog, this process of answering correctly. Maybe the brilliant-eyed man in the badge and the navy blue uniform would call her Star.

Even now, she can't imagine why Mama had to pitch such a fit over what turned out to be, what remains, the best night of Sidra's life.

Dad has our tickets now and his glasses wink uncertainly as he scans the crowd of students for my sister's blond head, so much easier to spot than mine. In front of me, a sign from Katie says she wants someone to share a ride to Memphis. I already have her phone number memorized.

≈

When I go outside, into the world, I tend to get caught up in other people's lives. I don't mean it to happen that way. People simply attach, full of their own strange, private needs. They pull you in their directions. But sometimes they can be useful. They share their lipstick, their drugs, give you a place to sleep when you don't yet know the lay of things.

In Memphis I meet Will, a sleepy-eyed boy who says he can show me how to break into houses. He calls it "checking in." There's a skill, he says, in picking the ones where people have gone out of town. The whole point is to move in for the weekend, eat what's in the refrigerator, and watch their TV from the velvet luxury of their furniture for a day or two, before stealing the set. He knows where to look for their drugs and guns. But he does it because he likes checking in to someone else's life as if it were a hotel, roaming around inside for a while, seeing himself in their mirrors. He doesn't understand when I try to explain that I just finished checking out. This is different, he insists. It's not like home again. No one goes back.

But I do—I go back. I open the front door of my house and walk inside, shoes squeaking on the hardwood. The house holds a reverent silence, dust motes trapped in the last sunlight at every window so I want to hold my breath or pray. In the kitchen, Mama is setting four places at the table, laying silver alongside the plates. She sees me when she turns, but she barely looks. First I think she is punishing me with invisibility. Then I see that if she doesn't look up, doesn't acknowledge, then I won't have left. All along I've been close by, playing outdoors or tucked in my room under the oak-rubbed eaves. I'm under her eye, the eye of the old woman, and together they keep this part of me like a lock of hair, the shadow of where I would be, would have been. Without speaking, she sets another place.

At school I find Jennifer, who is no longer allowed to associate with me, and vice versa. We are each other's bad influence. I've hardly seen her since the police dropped her off at home two weeks ago. "Where have you been?" she asks, aloof at the outskirts of her hallway pack, Jennifers and Kimberlys. I tell her Memphis. She says, "Is that so? Well, la di da."

Two hours later, she's wailing in the Girls'. "Why did you *leave* me? Just answer me! Why? You have to take me with you! You need me! At least ask me next time. Don't you care? Don't you care about anyone?" Her eyes are shiny with tears, desperation. But we are so separate now in our own lives that I have no answer.

"Promise," she pleads. "Promise you won't leave me again that way." I see how easy it is to take hold of her hands, give the promise she wants.

"You shouldn't go alone," Donny says later, wistful and vaguely wounded. "I'd go, you know. If you just asked. I'd drive. God, I hate this shitty town. Besides, you need me. Don't you?" He speaks this to Jennifer as well as me, as if she and I remain together and only he is alone, the forsaken one.

I have no way to tell them what Memphis was like, how it could have been any city at all. There's no way to explain the maps I follow now or what it means to me to be outside. Here, where the silly impotent bells of second period, third period, arrange their lives into hours and tick it away, how could they imagine a place with no clocks at all? Even Jennifer doesn't know. I'd open their eyes if I knew the right words. I'd offer them this.

I say, "I'm not on vacation anymore. Next time I might not come back."

But they assume I'm lying. There is only this one way to understand, I decide—know by doing, by living through it. I could have my own church now, invite them to come to the front and accept this doctrine. To say yes, which is its own power, the power to say yes to anything.

⤳

Will tells me I can make big money turning tricks. All the girls do it sooner or later. Young and fresh is what pays. He says he'll introduce me to a guy who runs things, sets up dates, if I decide I want to try it. When I mention it to Jennifer, she wrinkles her nose. "I got money out of my mom's *wallet*. Thanks anyway."

Donny says we could all stand to be more open-minded. "I'm open-minded," Jennifer protests, glaring at Donny, who's watching me sideways as he watches her, as she watches me. We balance this way at each other's edges, a game of Dare waiting to begin. We have come to Memphis. We are like the first explorers brought up short by the fact of the Mississippi, who paused on the riverbank to mark their maps, to gather their forces and see who would turn back, who would continue past the terrible water.

I'm conscious of the need to impress them. To hold sway. Donny wants to do Atlanta over again, liquor and a cheap hotel. Jennifer wants to go to Graceland. But I'm in charge this time, and I have a better idea. I call the beeper number that Will gave me. We stand at a pay phone outside a supermarket that offers a special on chicken necks, two for one. A savage cold wind lashes us toward any shelter, but we huddle in the open and wait. An old man sipping from a brown sack watches us without interest. We wonder if the phone will ever ring.

But it does, and we hook up with Will outside a diner that serves the best fried chicken in Dixie. He talks us into eating—into feeding him, as it turns out—while he tells stories we don't know whether to believe, his tumbling speech punctured with a high colt's whinny of a laugh. His hair is tied back with a twist-tie off a garbage bag. Under the diner lights he appears ridiculous, thinner, more flawed than I remember.

He takes us to a place he calls a "safe house." To Will, "safe" means safe from the police, which shows you how fast things get inverted out here. There are some mattresses and blankets in one corner, and some other kids gathered around a central staircase that goes nowhere—about halfway up it's burned away, charred black as the space above where it once led. There's no reason for anyone to feel warm here, as if that old fire still burns cozy and quiet as a stove for us to gather around, but I feel warmth in my bones. I feel as if I've bought this house—I own it now. It hums with a sound like a single struck chord, like the sound of my life beginning.

So when Will draws a syringe full of what the others have shot into their arms, I think about how safety gets inverted when you're in your own house. The golden glow off the liquid in the syringe is as warm as what grows inside me, tiny fire like the candle flame under the spoon. I look at the strangers on the staircase who drift in and out of awareness, whose arms are covered with the old marks of their survival, whose faces are so young. I look at the two I came with, shivering together, staring and dumb like tourists in a bombed country. Two who will drive home to Georgia and settle into the routines of everyone else, no matter how they talk now. Who will go on believing they are brave to have come this far. Another weekend getaway like a tent revival, put a little spark of holiness into their daily lives. But they are unconverted. They will not live forever. Will offers the needle with a general sweep. He could mean any of the three of us, but I go forward. I kneel beside him and roll up my sleeve.

saving felicia

I had seen her several times before, of course, on my route. The neighborhood is out on the east side of Athens, one of those temporary kinds of places with little rectangular duplexes made of brick or that plastic siding that's supposed to look like wood. People grow flowers there some, but they also let the poison ivy come right up. It's the kind of neighborhood where people go out in their backyards, not the front, except for a few greasers messing with old cars in their driveways. Some of them let their dogs run loose. I carry a tire iron through there, for the dogs. Folks almost never get packages, but all the boxes are up at the doors. When I stuff a box, I can put my eye to the window, not obviously looking or anything, but you see a lot that way. You get to know some pretty interesting things about the people on your route. I could tell some stories, but not about Felicia.

That was how I'd seen her, though—through the window like that. Mail to that house came for Mimi Dupree, sometimes Mrs. Dupree from those places that don't know any better, but I knew there was no Mister. A while back, there was this guy Manny Rodriguez. He would sit on the couch watching the tube all day, and the couch faced the window so I learned not to look, or he would catch me, his eyes the empty black you'd see looking down the muzzle of a gun. But you

93

can tell when a person's not around anymore. Every so often he still got mail, but he was long gone and didn't leave a forward. So his mail piled up there or she burned it, one or the other. Once I put it in the box, I have no control over how people treat it.

But I figured Manny R. was Felicia's daddy. She was the sort to listen for the mail to drop into the box, and then she'd come to the window and stare back at me, very serious. Her eyes were that same kind of black in a round face, the same look of "What the hell do you think you're doing?" That's what I thought at the time, at least. It's different now. Back then, I guess I didn't pay her much notice, but I must have thought it was an odd expression for a baby. Like maybe she knew more than she ought to be able to. She couldn't have been two yet. Now I can say, "Felicia is eighteen months old." But at the time I didn't know her name was Felicia or even for sure that she was a girl. She toddled around in nothing but a diaper or maybe one of those unisex T-shirts. And of course she didn't get mail.

The mother I had seen before and thought, *Fat cow*. Not that she was that fat, really. It was more the cow thing—and if you ever notice, people say "fat cow" all the time, and cows aren't really that fat. A cow can be plain skinny. It's just they have that look in their eyes that makes you think fat, like that animal is made to consume whatever's at hand. Mimi could have been one of those overgrown pregnant cheerleaders—all hard eyes and popping gum and bangs sprayed up in a big puff. She got welfare checks. She was always home when I came by there, eleven-thirty or so, usually yakking on the phone so loud you could hear her at the next house.

All this I had in my mind with the stuff I knew about the other people on my route—Julie Bruce, who ironed in her underwear; Mr. Carrouthers, who had every Star Trek on tape and got all these packages from sci-fi places; sweet old Mr. and Mrs. Deal, who, you wouldn't believe it, got mail from white supremacist groups—I mean, the Mrs. made me cookies at Christmas, for God's sake! You don't expect to find Betty Crocker on the other side of mail like that. I'd deliver a package C.O.D., some big box from "New World Order" that was probably a do-it-yourself bomb kit, and she'd say to me, "You seem like a very nice young man."

I'd say, "Yes'm, I try to be."

And she'd say, "It seems to me people aren't friendly with their mail carriers like they used to be."

And I'd say, "That's the truth." But I grew up right on the other side of town, not that long ago, I guess, but still, I don't recall a thing about my mailman. We weren't ever what you'd call on friendly terms. It seemed like a thing that happened only on those old TV shows from the fifties—that magical land where I imagined the Deals came from. And not that I wanted cookies from every screwball on the block, but sometimes I did think it would be nice if people waved, or knew my name. After all, I knew all of them.

But, like I say, I knew only certain things, and none of it took much of my attention. I didn't single Felicia out of the neighborhood or think about her much at all, until the day she became important. It was a usual day, a July Saturday, and nice weather—which in Georgia means not heatstroke hot. The ones without central air had their windows open, and when I came up on the Duprees', last house on the west side of Burnett, I heard Mimi squawking on the phone, even over Mr. Ostrander's everlasting weed whacker. But I didn't take time to look in the window because of this fight I just had with my sister, Cassandra. Cass has a duplex just like all the ones on my route, only on another route. I had to move in with her this summer because I got evicted from my apartment downtown, which was not my fault but mainly on account of one of my roommates, who decided he needed a pot-bellied pig. Anyway, it works out for me and Cass because I pay rent. She can't say she doesn't need the money. Instead, she finds other ways to dig at me.

Like she'll say, "Lyle, when are you going to grow up and get a real job?" Cass has this way of standing with her spine in an S-shape, her head all sideways, which tells you how frustrating she finds it to have to arrange your life for you. She's also got big, thick glasses that make her look like she must see everything about you, or at least like she's smart enough to know what she's talking about.

"I *have* a real job," is what I tell her. "You don't get more real than the mail."

Cass works for a little branch of a national company that does standardized test preparation. So she's all into potential—measurable quantities of it. She'll quote my own test scores to me and rave about how I'm wasting my life. She's also into *levels*. A job is worth nothing if there are no levels to climb, if you can't be the assistant boss and then the boss of the boss and then the king of fucking everything.

"UPS!" she raves at me daily. "You could get in with them, deliver mail for a while, and then you have a ladder to move up. You went to college, after all. And you realize, all the executives at UPS started out driving the trucks. It's true."

"I like my job. I do it, and it's over."

I learned a while back to stop telling Cass I was "really" a musician. The Postal Service gives me time to write songs, mess with my four-track recorder. I can go home early, or I can stay out late playing with my band, drag myself up at noon and deliver the mail hung over—who cares? It's only a paycheck to me, better than wearing a paper hat. When people ask me what I do, I can say, "I'm a musician"—you don't get to say that if you're some ladder-climber.

Now, if I were a *successful* musician, then maybe Cass couldn't get to me like she does. "What's wrong with the mail?" I ask her.

And she says, "It's embarrassing, that's what."

The problem—and this is what I was thinking about on my route that day—is not just that mail is embarrassing. It's that most of the time it's even *more* embarrassing to say, "I'm a musician." This is where, if you're dedicated to music, you have to fight yourself all the time. Because anyone who was ever great was small once, and they had to believe in the music. But at the same time you always secretly know you're a loser like a thousand others and your life is nothing on the slow train to nowhere.

So this is what I was thinking halfway around the block. *Loser. La-hoo-oo-zer. L is for Loser, it's good enough for me. L is for Loser, fell off the loser tree.* I started writing songs about my unfortunate condition, marching out a beat between the houses. Pretty soon I was singing that song from back of the drums in a packed football stadium—not that I actually sing a lick, you understand, but since it was my dream, what the hell. Somewhere in the audience, Cass was so twisted her head was nearly upside down, like one of those little dogs when it's really confused. But then I decided to forgive her for doubting me, and I put her backstage with the rest of the groupies, hands clasped under her chin like she couldn't believe she was so close to greatness.

By then I was past Duprees', down and up Highland Terrace and coming back around toward Burnett again, kind of an oblong circle. I'd just left the Deals' box when I hear screaming, porpoise-level, no words. At first I think someone hit one of those damn little yappy dogs and it's dying in the road, over on Burnett. Then I see Mimi Dupree running out of Burnett and across Highland Terrace, kind of waddling side to side. She's got the baby mashed against her chest. She's not looking at anything or going anywhere but in a more or less straight line across the street, screaming. Two steps into the Johnsons' yard, she crumples onto her knees. The screaming doesn't stop.

I look around, and there is *no one*, I mean no one, outdoors on the whole block. The weed whacker over on Burnett is silent. So I do the only thing I can do—take off running across the street to see what's the problem. She looks at me and her eyes sort of go past me. Now she's shrieking words, "Help me, help me!" and all I can see is the black hair at the back of the baby's head—its face is crushed against her chest, and she won't let go.

I think about slapping her, but now I'm kind of panicky too, saying, "What is it? What is it?" I grab hold of the baby's shoulders and shout, "Ma'am?" which sounds weird because Mimi Dupree is no older than me, but I can't just call her Mimi. "Ms. Dupree" seems too long for the crisis.

I pry the baby loose, and the first thing I look for is blood. But she just looks like she's asleep. Mimi gets articulate all of a sudden. "She's not breathing! Felicia! Felicia!" So that's how I found out it was a girl baby named Felicia.

My sister, Cass, who thinks she's so intellectual, is actually addicted to trashy TV shows like *Hard Copy* and *Rescue 911*. Since I've lived with her, I've sat down nearly every day to watch these old *Rescue 911*s in syndication, just because Cass had them on. So I'm kneeling there running over the different emergencies in my head, trying to think what you're supposed to do in this situation. Mouth-to-mouth! That's the first thing I think of, if you can believe it. I lay the baby on the ground and look at her. She's definitely not breathing. Her lips are kind of blue. I open her mouth and take a deep breath, and now Mimi's screaming "Save my baby!" That's when it occurs to me maybe we need some help. I grab her arm and yell in her face. "Go call an ambulance! 911!"

She stumbles off, and I feel better as soon as I'm alone with the baby. I fit my mouth over her mouth and nose and blow. But I can feel it going nowhere, into her mouth and nowhere else. I do it again, and again. No result. I remember chest compression so I push on her chest a little. She's wearing a spotty white T-shirt that's rolled up over her round belly, and her chest feels like the littlest, most delicate thing I've ever touched. But that gets me nothing as well. She's motionless—soft limbs, hard skull against my arm, so real and unreal. I go a little nuts because I'm out of things to do and she's got to be dead pretty soon. I roll her over on her face, lift her under the arms, and shake her, flop her, fold her over my forearm, smack her on the back, flop her to the other arm like a rag doll. When I lay her back down again, thinking I ought to try another breath, she's got color in her lips. She opens her eyes and looks at me.

"Oh, my God," I say, or something like that. "Hi, baby. Hi, Felicia." She starts coughing and kind of whimpering so I pick her up, and right away she goes quiet. She leans her head on my chest and starts sucking her thumb like the sweetest thing you ever saw. Like she knows I saved her life, and everything is just fine now.

⟋

By that time a few people were poking their heads out of doors, coming to stand on their stoops. Mimi ran back from the Deals' with the same shuffling girlie steps, kind of a high-speed waddle with her knuckles up around her face. But for all that, she seemed monstrous, her face twisted, mouth open, a huge force descending on the tiniest, most breakable thing. I had the idea the she might forget to stop and just plow straight over me and the baby too, like a runaway train. But she stopped after all, on her knees in front of me, moaning that her baby was alive.

"She's okay," I said. "She just started breathing again." Felicia seemed sleepy, pressed her head harder against my chest and took no notice of her mother. Under her skull I could feel my heart racing, so that beat must have been all she heard. I adjusted my arms around her. "I think she's just tired and scared."

"The ambulance is coming." Mimi's hands came for Felicia, then hovered around my arms, over the baby's head, pulled back. She looked over her shoulder. "They're on their way."

"Good. Because they should check her out, I think. Make sure she's okay." I pictured myself handing Felicia half over to a paramedic. Maybe we could hold her between us while I explained what had happened. My story would be clear and accurate, just enough information, not too much, and all in the right order. I would be just the sort of guy they always hoped to find at the scene of an accident.

"What happened anyway?" I asked. "Ma'am?"

"I don't know." She mumbled it like she wasn't sure there was a real person there asking her questions. She was busy looking for the ambulance. Now that I saw her in the light, her skin was creamed–coffee-colored, with a few dark freckles on the cheekbones. I was staring at her right cheek when she turned to face me like I had just shown up. "I mean . . . who knows really? She was, I don't know, just *lying* there." She held her palms open, fingertips thrust toward the ground in front of her as if that gesture alone would throw light on everything. "I was in the next room, couldn't have been a minute I had my back turned. I don't even remember."

"I'm Lyle," I said. "Harris. Your mailman."

"Maybe it was she choked on a peanut." Mimi shook her head. "I'm just so glad she's alive, you don't know. My little baby."

I was getting antsy for the paramedics to arrive so I could start telling my story. Mimi was bent toward Felicia, just close enough to touch the naked baby foot that bounced along my thigh. A curly black ponytail dropped forward over one shoulder.

"I saved her," I said. Suddenly it was hard to talk. I couldn't get any volume and the words sounded strange. "I think I saved her."

"You did." Mimi giggled, kind of experimentally, and started bouncing on her heels like a hyperactive child. "You really saved her. You're like a hero."

"I am. I think I kind of am." I smiled then, and Mimi smiled back. Felicia, still leaning against me, started humming a few notes around her thumb. Mimi moved over beside me so that she could hold the baby's foot in her hand while we waited.

⌐

Cass handed me a steaming bowl of mac 'n' cheese just as *Entertainment Tonight* came on. "What's this for?" I asked.

She sat at the other end of the couch, stirring through her own bowl. "You're a hero. I thought I'd cook for you."

"Deluxe, even. Thanks." I took a bite, set it aside. "Oh, man, that one moment. When she was breathing? It was like—"

"Like you were alive?"

"Yeah. I guess."

But that was wrong. It was what I had said an hour before, which was two hours after I'd started telling Cass the story. I still couldn't get to the center of the thing. "Not just alive. Like it was *me* breathing. It's like you make a connection with somebody, some other person. And maybe you're giving them life, but they're giving it back. Like that's where life *is*, and all of a sudden you're inside it, like you never were before."

Cass nodded encouragement with a mouthful of macaroni. But still what I was saying felt wrong—the words or the order, something.

"You should have done the Heimlich maneuver," Cass said. Her voice was quiet, almost wistful.

"I know. It was choking." One of the paramedics had actually found the peanut in the grass, so we knew.

"First thing is A for Airway. You can't do mouth to mouth without an airway."

"I know, I know. I could have done it better."

"But it's still a great story," she added, brighter. "I bet *Rescue 911* would want to use it. They should at least put you on the six o'clock news."

Since it came out that I had tried to perform CPR on a choking victim, I was almost glad when the news cameras didn't show up. Somehow when I rag-dolled her around—this was the paramedics' theory—I must have accidentally knocked the peanut loose. Saving a baby's life is one thing, but you don't really want to be famous for doing something stupid. Maybe not exactly stupid, but half-assed.

"I just wish I could explain how amazing it was. And scary, and—" What I couldn't explain was that I needed to tell the story to keep it. Because after the ambulance had pulled away and the last of the curious neighbors had drifted back indoors, I had caught sight of my mailbag over on the Deals' lawn where I had dropped it, and *that* was the most depressing thing I had ever laid eyes on.

Cass nodded. Her owl-eye glasses flashed in the TV light as she glanced from me to *ET*, where Tom Cruise was talking about the problem with Hollywood. Cass was good at doing two things at once.

"Here's the thing," I went on. "It was only about ten minutes of my life. What if that's the only ten minutes I ever get?"

Cass swallowed and looked at me carefully. "You should be telling all this to your girlfriend."

"What girlfriend?"

"I thought that blond girl—Sidra?"

"Oh, my God, Cass, don't say that! I mean ever!" I shot a panicked look around the room as if it were possible that someone else was in the house with us. I lowered my voice. "Sidra is Curtis's girlfriend. They're practically engaged."

"You said she was the love of your life."

"She's not. I was kidding. Forget I ever said that, really."

She shrugged. "Okay, sorry. Whatever you say."

"God, why did I tell you that?"

"It's forgotten." Cass smiled at the TV. Suddenly I could see Sidra sitting there in Cass's place, exactly where she had curled before in the dark with her eyes glued to the late late movie. Sometimes Curtis was there beside her, but other times he was back in the bedroom smoking pot or passed out on my bed. I knew every shadow of her face by TV light, no makeup and not what you'd call beautiful. Maybe I wanted her only because she belonged to Curtis. Sidra was another one of those things I couldn't explain, like maybe she was sitting so close to the secret of life that words wouldn't get there. One thing I knew—she would have understood about Felicia. All of a sudden it seemed urgent that I find her, tell her. Maybe I wanted to impress her, but it was more than that. Sometimes I had this thought that she deserved better than Curtis—not me necessarily, but just someone or something better. She deserved a little of what I felt that afternoon with Felicia. Maybe if I figured out how to tell the story right, she could feel it too.

"She would understand," I said. "Sidra. She's easy to talk to."

"Mmm," said Cass.

"She's *so*, you know . . . God. Curtis's girlfriend."

"You should tell her."

One time it had been the two of us alone on this couch, the volume down low on the set. We kept our voices low too. We each sat in a corner of the couch that seemed twelve feet long and all I wanted

to do was touch her, just touch her anywhere—her face, her hand,
her foot would have been enough. With Curtis dead to the world in
the back room, anything might have happened between us. But I
never got close enough to touch, and kissing was really past hope.

But now even fantasies of Sidra wouldn't stay in my head. Felicia
was closer, deeper, her little feather lashes, the blue sliding over to
pink in her lips. The weight of her was printed on my skin, the cer-
tainty that I had touched her, I had been touched.

"But when you tell it," Cass added, "say you did the Heimlich."

For a minute I watched the TV light playing over my sister's glasses
and the pale flesh of her face that drooped just a bit along the jaw. I
thought about how she spent most nights in this dinky little house
reading novels or doing crosswords. She was nice about letting my
friends come over, even though she was older; I knew she thought
most of them were stupid and immature. But the truth was, if it
weren't for us, she'd almost always be alone.

I picked up the bowl of macaroni, stirred some steam back to the
surface. "I can't believe you cooked for me. Man, Cass, I wish you
woulda been there."

"Me?"

"You woulda known right what to do."

⤷

By the next day, Cass was telling me I should become a paramedic.

"Why?" I asked. "A paramedic is just a paramedic forever. No lad-
ders to climb."

"Don't be obnoxious."

"You don't work for years and then one day you're . . . head
paramedic!"

She considered that, her head laid sideways against the door frame, then took off her glasses and rubbed them on her shirt. "Maybe you could just be happy."

But happy is never enough for Cass to hold on to for long. Happy is relative, Mom always told us. She'd say to Cass, "You can be as happy with a rich man as with a poor man," and now it looks like Cass might never have a date, let alone a husband.

"Medical school!" Cass decided later. "Why not? You could be one of those ER doctors."

On Monday I went back out on my route as usual, since nothing had really changed after all. I half expected some reception waiting for me on Felicia's street, like the neighborhood might turn out to welcome me and slap me on the back or something. But of course they didn't. I fell into the usual rhythm of bag-to-box, collecting the outgoing mail when it was there, glancing into windows and over fences, into the yards, until I forgot anything else was possible. I had played with the paramedic idea. I had even thought for three seconds about medical school. But who was I kidding? My life had a beat already driving it, the beat of the mail—six days a week it didn't stop or change by much, and there were no breaks. No putting it off while you dream up other lives.

My band had held practice the night before, but I couldn't get into it. I couldn't think of a song I felt like playing or a person I felt like talking to. I'd been hoping that at least Sidra would show up with Curtis, but then when she didn't show, I was relieved. I sat on my stool with my head tipped back against the wall, drumsticks crossed over my forehead, while Curtis, who played bass, and Kent, the lead singer, argued about whether "Pale Blue Eyes" was an overdone cover. I had no opinion at all. It occurred to me, as it usually didn't, that I was nearly twenty-eight, which was three years older than the rest of the band. What was I doing with these boys? What could they possibly understand about anything? But after a while I didn't hear their bitching anymore, just a voice in my head saying maybe I'd lost music and now what?

At Felicia's I dropped the mail in the box. There was nothing waiting to go out. Eye grazing the window, I caught a dim view of the deserted, familiar insides—couch and macramé wall hangings and baby toys strewn over the rug in the white light of the glass patio door. I stepped off the stoop toward the Reillys' next door. Then I went back and rang the bell.

Mimi opened the door in a cloud of perfume. Her lips and cheeks were painted matching pink, and all I could think of was this stuffed cow my mother keeps on her mantel that sits up like a person, dolled up in a lacy dress and big curling eyelashes.

"My hero," she said. "I thought you might stop today."

Distantly, like in some house three doors down, all my alarms were going off. But I said, "I wanted to see how Felicia was doing."

"Just fine." From behind the door, she lifted Felicia to her hip and there she was, blinking in the light. "Just perfect. Mommy's angel."

The sight of her was like one of those smacks to the nose that brings tears and stars even before you know what hit you. And believe it or not, she stretched out both hands, leaned out into space over the threshold. I took her without thinking. She was warm and smelled like cornflakes and fit so perfectly into my arms that I kissed her forehead without planning to or aiming for it. It was just there to be kissed. All of a sudden I had a wild, desperate thought: *Mine*. Next, *I am not giving this baby back*. It was like the voice of God. Or a voice that was more me than I was, telling me how it was going to be.

Mimi smiled out of her baby-poisoning vapor and said, "She knows you. She's only eighteen months, but I think she understands what you did." So that's how I found out she was eighteen months old.

Felicia patted my cheeks between her hands, squealed when I put my nose up to hers. "Da," she said. I caught my breath and held it like a bird in my chest. Half-Assed Hero Turns Baby Snatcher, news at eleven. Behind me was just another sunny summer day, the mockingbirds going, the empty street, my truck parked back around the corner out of sight. It was a street I had looked at nearly every day, in all weather, for longer than I cared to think. I knew every house and yard and all the side roads in and out, but it seemed like now there was nowhere to run.

"That's some parcel you got there. Why don't you come in for a bit?"

It took me a minute to hear the question. Felicia in my arms, I mumbled something about I really had to go. The mail.

"Don't go yet. I have a letter to send." She was gone, and the door stood empty and open.

"Ma'am?" I called out after a while. She didn't answer. Felicia and I looked at each other. Under my hand, her tiny bones were sprung across her back. We were rib to rib, my heart pounding out a crazy beat that must have echoed through that little chamber of hers, but she didn't seem afraid. Like she was ready for whatever would come.

"Ma'am?" I tried again. "You all right?" No answer, and from where I stood it sounded like there was no one breathing in the whole house. We stepped inside the door, picked a slow path through toys that littered the rusty carpet, the sunlight that fell beside the TV.

"Just a sec!" Mimi called. I let out a gasp of relief, didn't know I'd been holding my breath until then. Felicia sucked her thumb. We turned to face the front window, where a breeze ruffled gauzy curtains along the screen, and together we watched through the gap, alert, as if she had something to show me, as if any minute now I might pass by to rattle the box, familiar and fleeting and gone.

boys' club

For a year, I've been trying to tell Curtis that his band needs a girl singer. "*Everybody*'s got one these days," I argue. "People expect it. Get with the times."

Curtis gives me that patient, reproving look that makes me want to bite him. He sits on the edge of my bed, picking out chords on his old acoustic. I kneel behind him and trail my fingernails over the back of his shirt. "And here I am, the perfect candidate. Isn't that convenient?"

"We've got a singer, Sid."

"Kent. Oh, yeah. He's *okay* and all. But he's shy. He's got no spark."

"Spark?"

"Yeah, you know. Zing, flash. Skin." I kiss his bent neck, touch it with my tongue—he goes on strumming, unmoved. I slip my hands around to his chest and breathe in his ear. "You got talent, right? Now all you need is something to make people take notice. Think about it—sultry little chick in a red dress, husky voice, howling, smearing lipstick on the mike like she's gonna swallow it—"

"Sidra," he warns. But the guitar falls silent, speculative. Together we consider the sounds of the house, whether my mother is within listening distance, the way I used to when I was a teenager.

He shrugs loose. "Listen to this chord progression."

Curtis is a bassist. If the guys in the band were within a mile ra-
dius, you wouldn't catch him thinking about a guitar. I'm about the
only one who ever gets to hear him struggling through these melodic
attempts with the acoustic, each new chord hesitant, feathery soft.

"Wait, I fucked that up. Let me start over."

"Sweetie, baby, let me sing. Just once. I'm your *girlfriend*." I don't
say "fiancée," which I technically am. But I can put a point on just
about any word—pizza, lawn chair, fire escape—so that he hears that
other one beneath it, that and the diamond he still hasn't given me.
"I can't believe you won't let me have this *one* little thing."

"Sidra. You know it's not mine to give. Can we just change the
subject?"

"Why? Because you have no answer? Go on, Curtis, say it. Right
to my face. *You can't sing.*"

"Sidra—"

"You're thinking it right now, aren't you? *Sidra, you can't sing.*"

This is how I know my chance at stardom has been in his hands
alone, all along—because he once answered me in just those words.
Imagine it. *You can't sing*, like the verdict was his to make and might
as well be tattooed on my forehead.

It's more than that, of course. The band is his sacred fraternity. I
know if I push him on the topic, he's bound to fight. "Sid, it's *band
business*," he'll tell me. "It's got not thing one to do with you." I'm
barely allowed to comment, even little stuff—like telling him at
sound-check that the mix is wrong, I can't hear the singer for shit,
whatever. "Turn it up," I'll say, gesture with my thumbs and point at
Kent. Curtis thumps the bass and looks straight through me like I'm
not in the room.

But then, during the show, Curtis looks straight through everyone. He's a zombie on stage. Meanwhile, Jeff, the only one of the four
who doesn't look like he wears a tie to his day job, lets his hair shag

over his face and studies his Stratocaster like watching it is the only way to get music out. Lyle, a lanky scarecrow with a jutting Adam's apple, spins his drumsticks and shouts "yeah" every few minutes, grinning. That goofy energy is eye-catching, I suppose—though not necessarily in a good way. Kent, same as Curtis, looks like your mom's idea of a prom date: athletic, possibly young Republican, no visible tattoos. At ten paces you're sure he pays taxes and slows for yellow lights. It's because of those two, Kent and Curtis, as much as the music, that the local paper sneeringly calls them "frat-boy rock."

Kent's the dark one to Curtis's blond, denser in build, hairier, not the kind of face you'd mistake for gorgeous, except when he sings. The band's small, loyal crowd shows up for him: his intimate voice, his bedroom eyes that can make anyone in the audience feel alone in the room with him. But as soon as the song stops, that spell is broken. He's as dull as the others—mumbling, self-conscious, not quite sure what he's doing on a stage. I swear, a stage is the one thing I would know what to do with, but no one in the band, least of all Curtis, will listen.

"Boys' club," I'd mutter to Kim Fisher, this groupie chick who used to run their lights. But since Kim got married to the last drummer and moved to Lawrenceville, I have no one to bitch to.

⌐

It's not just to punish Curtis that I started hanging around with Paul, his kid stepbrother—a term to which Curtis would prefer any number of alternates that avoid the "brother" issue altogether, most of them involving "faggot." I try to point out that they don't share a drop of blood, but Curtis says, "*Still*," and shudders head to toe. As you might guess, Curtis has decreed the topic of Paul, like the band, closed to my input. He'll barely tolerate being in the same room; you can see the violence rising in him like sickness. It's pitiful too, to watch Paul squirm, try to figure out how to act so Curtis will like him. I figure I need to go out of my way to be nice, big-sistery and all, just to compensate for Curtis's nastiness.

Besides, Paul needs handling. He reminds me of an Arabian colt, hot-blooded and skittish and a little too smart for the barn. I think his folks are nervous around him, truthfully, pretend he's an interesting pet and let him go in the field because they don't quite know what else to do with such an exotic breed of boy. Not a *gay* boy, of course—they don't have one of those. I doubt they'd admit to knowing the word.

I figure all this is my business, at least a little bit, since Paul is maybe my future stepbrother-in-law, though I wonder sometimes if Curtis is too mean to marry. I've talked it over with his mother, Muriel, who seems to believe both her wayward boys are fixable. "Oh, honey," she tells me, "you marry Curtis, and he'll sweeten right up, mark my words. He's so much better with Paul anyway, since you been around."

Her mouth, under pink lipstick, is Curtis's mouth—the upper lip strong and flat, the lower rolled out rounder and softer, just the hint of a pout. I try not to stare, but the likeness is fascinating. When she smiles, the skin beside her eyes folds accordion-style. She holds my hand with her tanned, ringed fingers and strokes it lightly to make the words sink in, this mission she hopes I'll take. "I do think *you* could be the one, Sidra, to finally bring this family together, the way I always pictured it."

Then she chuckles with a little snort and adds, "Lord, I wish I had two of you. I'd marry one of you to Paul!"

I tend to have hopes for fixing Curtis myself. Paul, I'm not so sure. Muriel likes to call it a phase—"it" being, of course, nothing so specific as a desire for men, but only whatever quirk or social maladjustment keeps him from noticing girls. If I report her verdict to Paul, he smiles fondly and says, "Tell me about it," like I'm the only soul in the world who understands him. He talks to me as if his life is a book I've read; I watch his mouth form the words, and I can't help wondering where that mouth has been. It's hard to picture, and hard not to.

⌒

I've been giving Paul riding lessons. I saddle one of my mother's old mares and string her out on the lunge line so she trots a circle around me. Paul figured out posting right away, so we've moved on to the sitting trot. "You're doing great," I tell him. "You're a natural." His knees creep up to clamp the saddle, but he pushes them back down without being told. Relax, relax. The effort to relax without falling spreads blood under his cheekbones. The mare pounds on, tireless, stretches her reinless head down to cough dust and blow. The saddle leather creaks rhythmically.

"Am I a redneck yet?" he asks. This is what I said when I first called him, out in Greene County, two counties over. If you're gonna be in my family, it's time you learned to ride like a real redneck. He went out and bought a pair of alligator boots for the occasion.

"Any day now," I answer. The overheated flush of his face is indeed spreading along his neck in a red streak. It's way too hot to be wearing chaps, but Paul insisted. You'd think the happiest day of his life was when I zipped him into my black suede schooling chaps and they clung to his slender legs like they were custom-made, only the long ends lapping the tops of his boots.

"We'll have to get you in a Western saddle before long. Wish I had one."

His hands rest on his suede-covered thighs, like I've told him. Each bounce is an effort to keep the tiny patch of exposed denim on his butt glued to the saddle. "Those other kind of saddles," he asks with a grin, bounce bounce bounce, "they got more padding?"

"You don't need padding. You just need to learn the motion, push forward from your lower back." Feeling mischievous, I add a helpful hint from my old dressage instructor, one meant to make teenage girls pay attention: "It's like sex."

Paul loses his balance laughing and grabs the pommel to right himself, while I wonder, *Now how stupid did that sound?* I mean, I don't know how guys do it! I'm a little afraid he's about to tell me how wrong I am, which I don't know that I want to hear about, let alone from Paul, who's just a kid and probably shouldn't know technique yet anyway. Though, probably, he does.

But he says, "I'll have to tell Curtis you said that!"

"Oh, pish. Curtis's heard it before. I taught him to ride too, you know."

He groans a laugh. "Gawd, Sidra. I don't want to hear all your nasty bedroom secrets. You're gonna make me fall off." His face is glossy, his grin so acute now it looks painful. More flushes are spreading down his fair skin, piebald, oddly attractive: a ruby wedge on his chest, rising from the scooped neck of his shirt.

"Just trying to help you relax," I say innocently and cluck to the mare.

The farm—my mother's place, now mine again—gets a nice breeze through the fields even in summer, but it's too hot to keep this up much longer. Come fall, I think, we can have longer lessons. I wonder if Paul really wants to learn, or if he's doing this only for a chance to escape Greene County for the day. The way he speaks of the place—not with hatred but with a kind of disconnection, or in the past tense—makes me wonder if he might run away from home, with only a year of high school left. Maybe by fall he'll already be gone.

I halt the mare, begin to coil the line. "You're a good student," I tell him.

"Thanks." Dropping the stirrups to stretch his legs, he balances on his crotch, pushes the sweat back through his butter-blond hair with both hands. His chest heaves softly. "Yeah, people can say that at least. I make A's in everything."

⌐

Xeroxed blue signs around town announce that Clok, which is what Curtis's band is calling itself this week, is going to be playing tonight at Slocum's. I never call them anything but The Band, since the name constantly changes. For a while it was Neon Clock, changed from Fried Baloney, when they thought this guy Chet was going to sit in and play sax, and they figured out that the first letters of their names would spell CLOCK if they made Jeff Ostrander go by his last name. But Chet never worked out, apparently, so they had to drop a C. No one told me why they dropped the "Neon."

I bitch to Paul while we're unsaddling the horse. "Tell me, how exactly are they ever going to make it big when they can't even settle on a name?"

Paul smirks. "Let me try. How 'bout the Intolerant Shitheads? The White Trash Wannabes?" I laugh, but he dims and shakes his head, unsatisfied. "You try it."

"Oh, Lord, have I tried. They don't listen to the first word I say, and my ideas are inspired compared to theirs. Don't get me started on the playlist either. Same tired covers they were doing in college when they were called the Keggers—gawd! If I hear 'Stepping Stone' one more time—"

"What's that?" Paul asks, bright-eyed.

"You know, 'Stepping Stone.' The Monkees, frat house torture. *Ah-ah-ah-ah-ah'm not yer steppin' stone.*"

"Sounds awful," he agrees. But his voice has a wistful note, and—stupid me—I remember that Paul didn't go to college with us. He's probably never seen the inside of a frat house.

Then it hits me. "Paul, you've never seen the band, have you?" But of course he hasn't, his own brother's band.

"It's not like I even want to," he says. He lays his cheek to the plate of bone between the mare's sleepy eyes and looks at me. The gaze is simple, innocent as the surface of water. But underneath, something moves, deep and shifting, adjusting focus, until I get the idea he's no longer seeing me at all.

I've seen that look before. Once when he drew me aside, out to the back steps of his house in Greene County, to explain the fading bruise under one eye, the only real mark I'd ever noticed on him. "He wasn't always this way, you know," Paul said then, with that soft, slipped-away look—I could hardly believe it at the time, that he was apologizing to me for Curtis. "When I first knew him, when I was young and nothing was, well, decided, I guess, he would act like my big brother. You know, take me places, tell me things about his life. It was just little things. But I always thought they were these holy secrets. He was nice to me."

I've tried to tell him that it's hardly his fault if Curtis is an asshole now. But I know how those eyes turn to look back over the evidence, thin as it is, and he decides to blame himself or forgive Curtis, provisionally, all the while clinging with one hand to that raggedy old dream of possibility, before it was all decided.

Last week, I told Paul how horses communicate by blowing into each other's noses. Now he holds the dozing mare's muzzle propped in one hand and blows softly through the tunnel of each nostril, murmurs baby talk. "See wants a carrot, doesn't see? See wants a widdle snack." I raise her damp coat in circles with the rubber curry.

As if bored with her suddenly, he drops the mare's head. He slides over one loose shoulder of his tank top and studies himself, presses a finger to the skin. "I think I'm burned. Feel."

He offers the back of a shoulder. One hand caught through the curry on the mare's back, I reach toward him with the other, lay four fingertips to the skin. It's hot and soft, his androgynous shoulder. No extra muscle, no striking thinness, just a pure shape like something original that's never been altered or touched. He's watching for the verdict, head turned back and tipped, mouth parted. On his skin, the marks under my fingers show white before they darken and blend again, trackless.

"Scorched," I say, then amend it. "No, it's not bad." It hurts me somehow, to think that he would peel.

⌒

Paul's in the shower down the hall. We're going out. Dancing, I said, though I'm not sure I can get him in the door anywhere. He barely looks as old as he is. Athens gets pretty near dead in summer, but I figure any night in this town has got to beat Greene County's best effort. I want to make him happy here. I don't know how the world must look from his eyes, but I want to show him he doesn't have to leave altogether. Sometimes he acts as if he barely believes there are gay men as close to home as this college town, doing the same things they must do in New York City bars and bedrooms—though I have to suspect he knows better. For some reason it's maddening to wonder what he knows.

For a long time after the shower cuts off, Paul's still in the bathroom. Curtis will do that on a lazy day, clear steam from the mirror and spend twenty minutes shaving over the sink, inspecting every inch of jaw and lip and throat for lingering roughness. I love the smell of his shaving lotion, the way he draws the razor over his skin. "Let me," I beg. I'm mad to shave him. He laughs, says he can't think of anything scarier than me with a razor in my hand, coming at his face. But then, sometimes, he lets me anyway.

Surely Paul's not shaving, though. Nothing but down on those cheeks, smooth as my own. Not that I've touched his face to know for sure. Maybe he shaves, just so meticulously that stubble is never allowed to emerge. His chest is hairless; but then, so is Curtis's. I try to picture Paul stretching his upper lip before the mirror, the blade in his fingertips scraping delicately. But even under his own touch, surely that fine skin would shred and bleed, fall apart like tissue paper. As if nothing has ever really touched him or ever safely could.

He emerges finally and traipses into the bedroom, flops onto the bed beside me. He's wearing my peach silk robe, smells of my apple blossom shampoo. Silly, he sprawls propped on one elbow and asks where we're going.

"You're adorable," I tell him. "The robe is you."

"Oh, pish. Are we going to see that horrible band of your boyfriend's?"

"I guess we could." I scowl. "I don't think they deserve us though. I don't even want to speak to Curtis right now. Honestly, you tell me." I pop up onto my knees, the old mattress springs creaking between us, to display the hollows at my hipbones, the long stretch of my body; I fluff my hair and stick out my A-cup chest. "Don't I look like I could sing?"

"Absolutely," Paul agrees with a little nod. He's utterly sincere.

"I know I could sing. I've always known that." I lie down and stare up at the ceiling of this room I grew up in. I've been back home for only a few months, since I ran out of money and needed a place to keep my horses. It's a temporary arrangement. But this room works strange tricks on me, makes me feel twelve years old again, back when I used to lip-sync along with 45s and dream nothing but spotlights, the mass adoration of rock stardom. "Do you ever have feelings like that, that you just know in your gut how a thing belongs to you?"

Paul is flat on his back beside me. "You mean singing."

"Yeah. That mike, you know, that spot. On stage. I'd know what to do with it. I swear I'll never forgive Curtis for this. Tell me, how can I marry someone who won't even give me this one chance, when it would cost him nothing?"

"You have to marry him," Paul says reasonably. "If you didn't, then you and me wouldn't be related."

I grin, roll up on one elbow, and lean in close enough to touch his damp hair with my nose—a quick breath of apple blossom. He's so clean and pink I want to lick him. Then I feel about to burst because I want so badly for Curtis to see me do it. I wonder if Paul has ever been this close to a girl.

"Maybe I'm too skinny," I chatter. "Maybe if I were fat, I could sing better. You think there's a reason opera singers are fat?"

"There's a lot of skinny singers," Paul counters. "Curtis doesn't like fat girls."

"How do you know?"

"Oh, I know." He wrinkles his nose. "You wouldn't want to be fat. Look at you." Palm up, his hand offers my body as exhibit in a little spokesmodel sweep. "You're so totally perfect. You know how he feels about you—like you hung the moon. Like there wasn't a girl alive until you came along."

"*Hung the moon?*" I press my face into the pillow, lift it again. We grin at each other, giddy and conspiratorial as a pair of middle-school girls. The bedroom must be working its spell on him too.

"Curtis loves me!" I shriek.

"Shh!" He puts an arm around my neck, mouth brushing my fore-head as we stifle our giggles in the pillow. "You'll wake up your gramma."

"Okay, shh, you're right." We calm down; our grins fade a little. The air between us is humid with apple blossom. He looks a little embarrassed and turns back to the ceiling.

"Me and Curtis are always messing around in here," I whisper. "We say we're not gonna start and then we do anyway, and we have to struggle to keep our voices down so Mama won't hear. Gramma Ballard doesn't hear a thing. It's Mama's got the ears."

"You have sex in here?" he asks, frank, pointed. I'm surprised that he would be interested. He gazes upward, the peach silk fallen open in a V at his chest. The overheated flush of his skin is still faintly visible in a pink diamond in the center of his breastbone. I try to imagine a man's mouth kissing him there, touching with the tip of a tongue.

"Hardly ever," I say. "But sometimes. Sometimes it's like we can't help ourselves. Maybe it's exciting in some twisted way, to be overheard."

"Oh, pish. You just can't keep your hands off each other."

I smile, picturing Curtis on the stage at Slocum's, the way he'll look tonight, glowering over the amps or adjusting his monitor with the shove of a foot. His intensity during a show is sexy and endear-ing at once. If I go around to the darkened sidestage, before they start, between sets, Curtis will soften a little when he glances my way. I might even climb up to plant my mouth on his mouth, turn and be gone again before he can find the first word of "not now."

But what would I do with Paul? Slocum's cards anyway, so I'd be lucky to get him in the door, let alone past Curtis's forbidding eye. The divide between them is so deep, so treacherous, and somehow I'm the one who's supposed to bridge it. It seems impossible.

"What's it like?" Paul whispers.

"What's what like?"

"You know, you and Curtis," he rambles, shy now, his eyes dipping. "How he can't keep his hands off you." I feel a weird shudder from his words as if something is happening between us. It can't be. But then, maybe he's curious. We're so close, after all, and he's still male, half-naked, maybe vulnerable in some way to the same hair-trigger urges. Here we lie, somewhere close, I think, in the realm of possibility, before anything was decided.

"I'm being nosy," he says. "But just tell me one little thing. Anything." His eyes promise me he can handle it, this foray into the dark unknown of hetero sex.

"Well, okay. He touches me—" My hand steals up to my throat, trails back down along the neck of my shirt, and I watch Paul closely. He watches back with a wary interest. "I just melt, that's all. I wish you could know. He's different with me. I swear he's a lamb underneath. But, God, he has this incredible power over me too, this force. He touches me, like this, just the pads of his fingertips. They're all callused and rough from the bass—"

As I speak, his eyes shade darker, slip out of focus, and I sense that I'm not in control of this. I stumble on what I'm saying, can't remember what I just told him.

"Show me," he whispers.

He turns onto his back, closes his eyes. I set my fingertips on the pulse at his throat. My hand casts a shadow on his skin, traces his collarbone, wishbone, moves slow along the soft, hairless chest. It darkens the diamond between his nipples, trails along the silk edge of the robe. But my hand is still Curtis's touching me, my body prone on the bed in peach robe and apple blossom shampoo, as if I see through my lover's eyes what it is to be him in one stolen moment. I've almost forgotten where I am, who I am, three of us in these two

bodies, when Paul says, "Stop." But we've barely started. This is nothing, not enough. He catches my wrist hard, and his face is locked tight,
anguished, as if I've burned him. In the few seconds too long that his
fingers squeeze my wrist, I realize that I've been Curtis for him too.

He lets go. I draw my hand away, stunned. We are only ourselves
again, sharply drawn in daylight from the window. His chest rises and
falls soft as wings, the arc of his rib cage marking and unmarking his
skin. All that's left of desire is an urge to comfort him, but I'm afraid
now of the smallest touch. I want to cover him up, close the robe,
protect what's exposed.

"Sorry," he says after a minute. "I shouldn't have asked."

"That's all right."

I need to say something else, but I don't know what. I sit up, lean
against the headboard, and look around my room: posters of horses
and rock stars from the eighties, these familiar pictures unchanged
since childhood, returned to me again like dreams. When are you
going to grow up anyway? I ask myself, hearing my mother somewhere
in that, the voices of the guys in the band: *Jesus, Sidra, grow up!* But
never Curtis—he likes me this way. Even now I can see his mouth
curving into a smile, as if he knows he has been with us just now,
and he lingers in the room, amused. Paul's eyes are shut, but that third
presence is close enough to heat the nearby air—he feels it as well as
I do. In the doorway, Curtis stands, arms crossed, immovable as a
bouncer, with a bouncer's slitted, mocking eyes. The world is his.

"Well," Paul says after a minute, blinking up at me. "That was an
adventure. I, uh, oh, God. I've never done that." He giggles. "I'm
going to hell."

Hesitant, I touch his hair while he chokes on breathy, fitful laughter, finally presses the back of his wrist to his mouth. He gives me a
concerned glance. "You probably shouldn't listen to me. I just blather
sometimes."

There's something I want to ask him—whether or not he hates me. Even in my own version of an outcast state, I step through the door at Slocum's, crawl into Curtis's bed when I please, no permission required. But he stares fixedly at the ceiling, and I can feel him encasing himself in a shell of his own careful breathing. I don't want to risk cracking it again.

I try for a light tone. "Let's not go to Slocum's, okay? God, I'm so bored with the damn band anyway. The same stupid songs, over and over."

His breathing is quiet now, and he gazes upward as if there's no ceiling at all, nothing between him and the open sky. "We can go," he says, "if you want."

rest stop

Greene County was talking about Muriel Foster's stepson. People had always talked, always kept one eye on the Foster house like they were waiting for a bad seed to bear what they knew it would. So far Dan's boy, Paul, had been quiet, good in school, but it was like he was *too* good—they couldn't quite put a finger on it, but it wasn't natural. It marked him that he was smaller than the other boys, with a fragile look, that by high school his inquisitive eyes hadn't gone dead like a normal teenager's but instead sharpened with the sidelong cunning of hidden designs that made other boys want to shove him against lockers for walking by.

"Just a boy," the county said now, as if shocked.

"Seventeen—that ain't *just a boy* no more."

The police were involved, so no use in keeping quiet about it, not even for Muriel's sake. Poor Muriel, they said. She made another bad match, her second marriage. The first one, you know, was bad enough to put her in the hospital from stress. Now this. You heard about it, of course, the Foster boy. Got picked up at some rest area over in Rockdale County, one where that sort of thing goes on, apparently. Well, *yes.* I suppose there's all kinds. Don't get me started on the sickness of this world, Lord have mercy. At least it didn't happen here.

Muriel knew they were talking, knew there was nothing she could say to make them stop. In the beginning, she'd wanted to scream in rage, scream the shock right out of their eyes, these gossips who presumed to know it all. They didn't know a thing. But she closed her lips and kept to her house. Inside, her family was safe from words, the silence clouded here like a settled weather that gathered about the boy as he ghosted from room to room and back behind his own door. Almost peaceful, as if she and Dan and the boy had agreed on a preference for softer tones, agreed to speak only what was purely necessary.

"You keeping those biscuits for yourself, Paul?" she'd ask gently at the supper table. With the briefest glance from under his lashes, he'd pass the basket, whispering "Sorry." "Sorry," he'd offer to the house in general, as he bumped a chair where no one sat. "That's all right," she'd answer, and if he came close enough, she would take hold of his arm, almost fiercely, as if to assure him of the fact. Later he would come to say good night and linger another minute in the doorway of their bedroom, saying nothing. His dim blue eyes wandered over the two of them in their bed, then over the items on Muriel's dressing table and Dan's nightstand without ever finding a place to land.

"It's late, Paul," Dan would murmur. "You need something?" For a minute she and Dan would listen to the boy's careful breath, his silence, and before he could manage another apology, Muriel would suggest that he get some sleep.

After Paul had gone to his own room, Dan might meet her eyes with a glance so quick it looked like guilt, just the way his son looked at anyone those days, before leaning away to set his reading glasses on the nightstand and switch off the lamp. In the dark they would lie barely touching, unspeaking most nights, as if it had all been said so many times.

"He didn't do it—those things they say," she had tried to insist one night, for Dan's sake. This was back in the beginning, before the silence began to feel like a comfort.

Beside her, she could sense Dan staring at the ceiling, turning the problem over for himself in his detached way, a purely intellectual puzzle. "How do you know that?"

"This is Paul we're talking about. He was only hitchhiking. He wouldn't lie. He wouldn't . . . *do* that, what they say."

"So, because you can't conceive it, it didn't happen?" He might as well have been musing over something he had read in the paper, something that happened to other people. Again Muriel had to remind herself that Paul was not her child.

But he was. Or he was like her child. When the awful call had first come from Rockdale County—Paul's scared voice, tuned to a wispy tenor—she felt his instant relief in hearing it was her on the line, his trust that she would be the one to understand as always. "I got arrested," he said. "They won't set bail till morning."

He tried to explain what had happened, but she couldn't get a picture, couldn't think of anything beyond the cell where he would have to spend the night. Surely the place was dirty and cold, maybe dangerous, no place for a lamb who would never hurt anyone. She was certain he'd be injured by the experience in some deep and permanent way, so that the change in him would be visible by the time they arrived to post bail.

But the boy who emerged was the same one who had left her house the day before: seventeen-going-on-fifteen in a white T-shirt, cutoff shorts, high-top sneakers, and a faded baseball cap. Dan hugged him first, without eye contact, the gesture both tender and automatic on both sides. She went forward more hesitantly, peering close at his face to find the change. As if the boy would escape, she held him around the small of the back—he was inches taller than she was now—and lifted off the baseball cap. Underneath he was still Paul, unmistakable, his delicate features and bruisable skin, the same short, winter-grass hair and the faint blue vein etched along his temple. She was used to other eyes, though, narrowed and foxy with humor, irony—that look was gone. Her fingers reached toward the vein above his eyebrow, but he pulled away. "I'm okay," he mouthed to her clearly, soundlessly, glanced once at his father, took back the hat.

Their lawyer had arrived then, a woman, and from the start she hadn't set right with Muriel. She was too young, too pretty; to Muriel, she didn't seem to know what she was about. A competent defense lawyer ought come in already raving about malicious prosecution and police corruption and such. Instead, this one calmly stated the charge against Paul, solicitation, cited the cop's statement, all as if it were fact. She might as well have been one of the enemy. Serious and cool as a mortician, she set her clasped hands before her on the conference room table to address Paul. "I'm going to ask you to tell me what happened. Do you want your folks in the room for this?"

Muriel had gone cold at that, so cold she couldn't turn to Dan for guidance. It was that lawyer's fault, twisting things this way. The baseball cap was turned backward now on Paul's head, giving him the slick-eared expression of a dog that had just messed the house. He looked at Muriel and then at his father, and she saw in his eyes that he wouldn't say no. That he was willing if they were, that they would not be sent away. Instinctively, she reached for Dan's limp hand, lifted and squeezed it hard and said, "Maybe we'd best wait outside."

An hour later Paul had emerged, face rubbed blank, erased. She took hold of his thin, bare arm above the elbow and stroked with her other hand in small circles, as if his arm were a separate creature, a fussy infant she meant to soothe—she had no clear sense of what she was doing. Dan made arrangements with the lawyer for the hearing, which was set for two weeks off. The three of them got in the car. Paul sat alone in the back seat, and all the way home no one spoke a word.

By day, in those long days before the hearing, she caught herself hovering, listening, outside his bedroom door. He was in there, moving around, the door cracked an inch as if anyone were free to peek in. On the outside was the Yield sign he'd taken off the road—an innocent crime, she'd always thought. Boy stuff. Instead of looking in the door, Muriel stared at the sign's glaring yellow and black, the rust that collected in the battered edges. Paul liked to issue such theatrical commands when they were alone together, joking in the kitchen while she fixed supper and he set the table: "That's enough out of you," he'd bark, straight-faced, aim an index finger, so abrupt that she burst into giggles. Play-acting suited him.

But when she tried now to hear that "Yield" in his royal tone, it sounded only dark, threatening; she could hardly recall what had ever been funny. How long had it been since he'd spoken in his real voice? Or was this the boy's real voice after all, this chaff of sound lighter than air? When his rustling inside stopped, she caught her breath as well, motionless. She thought they were listening for each other now, with only the door between them.

She pressed his one suit for the hearing. Dan took the day off from work and the three of them drove together back to Rockdale County to meet their lawyer at the courthouse. In the marble hall, the lawyer spoke briefly to Paul, and then without fanfare they were all four in the courtroom before the high-throned judge and the district attorney and the bailiff and the stenographer and other people who sat scattered in the wooden pews like this was some kind of a show. She looked in each face to make sure there was no one she knew. Things happened more quickly than she expected: the D. A. and the judge exchanged words like a secret code, and Paul's lawyer stepped forward to enter a plea that was neither guilty nor innocent and sounded to her like Spanish. "What was that?" Muriel gripped Dan's arm, frantic. "What'd she just say?" Paul stood beside the lawyer, his back military straight, hands locked before him. She wanted him to turn and look at her, to let her know he was in need of rescue. Maybe that lawyer really didn't know what she was doing, for even the judge looked disgusted as she entered the plea.

The judge called Paul forward and began what sounded like a lecture. Muriel could see the man's nostrils flaring. "Are you aware, son, of the laws against sodomy in the state of Georgia and before God?"

"Yes, sir," Paul answered. His voice was gruff, surprisingly audible, nearly echoing in the high-ceilinged room.

"You claim you were hitching a ride *this* time, is that it? A ride from Officer Kendrick, whom you propositioned?"

Again, "Yes, sir," his eyes on the judge and not even shifting for the lawyer, who was five steps behind him and not moving to intervene.

The judge shuffled papers. "You have some reason to be in Atlanta, I assume?"

"To see a friend."

"What kind of a *friend?*"

Paul hesitated but kept his eyes raised to the bench. "A good friend."

The judge massaged the bridge of his nose wearily. "Son, are you going to stand there and act like you don't know what *solicitation of sodomy* is? I do get sick of having to look in the face of a pervert every day in this court and—you know what I would like? I would *like* it if y'all would *stop*. Stop defiling this state and my courtroom."

While the judge spoke, Paul remained silent, though at each rhetorical punctuation his dropped shoulders spread farther back, like wings. And suddenly he was answering yes, calmly, to a barrage of questions that Muriel thought would never stop. *Yes, I have taken money for sex. Yes, I have traded blow jobs for rides. Yes.* Until Muriel was standing, unthinking, screaming at the judge, "Stop it! He's a boy! Stop bullying him. You're confusing him!" Dan's hand was on her arm, and the judge growled, "Counselor, shall I ask your clients to step outside?"

It wasn't Dan who sat her back in the pew, mouth shut, but a cool, leaden density that seemed to have gathered inside her like a weight she could no longer resist. She sat, heavily. *Not your son,* a voice reminded her. Not Curtis, surely. Curtis had a college degree, a job up in Athens, and a girl he could up and marry any day now. That boy had been fatherless from the age of ten, later sent to live with his grandmother so that Muriel could take what they called "a little rest." And after all that, the boy had turned out fine. This one, on the other hand, was Dan's. She was fond of Paul, naturally, wanted him to grow up well, to turn out fine. But this sharp pang of responsibility, like a cord was twisted somewhere inside—it didn't belong to her.

In the end, when the judge delivered the sentence, she felt extraordinarily lucky. After such vicious words, she'd expected that he would take Paul in chains back to the cell and close him in for good. But the sentence turned out to be no more than time served plus a little probation and community service. It was nothing. It was over now, she told herself in giddy astonishment, as they drove back to Greene County. They could put it all behind them. She wanted to chatter about the scenery, to smile with relief, smile especially at Paul, who sat slumped and bloodless in the back with his tie pulled loose, his collar undone. But she found she couldn't meet his eyes, and she wasn't sure why. She sat back in her seat, facing forward as Paul and Dan both faced forward. They all remained silent during the drive.

As the car pulled into the driveway at home, they saw where their journey had led them. An angry black scrawl crossed the front door and onto the white clapboard of the house, trailing huge under all the windows like an evil vine that had sprung up in their absence. *Burn in hell faggot*, it read, unmistakably.

They sat unmoving in the car. Paul was the first to open a door. Dan and Muriel remained seated while he walked across the lawn, cracked the seal on the screen door, which broke across the U in BURN and then settled back into a legible word again, after Paul had already vanished inside. Together, Dan and Muriel followed. They approached the house with slower steps, Muriel with a sort of hesitant horror as if the message would bite, Dan in a thoughtful study. He surveyed each letter while Muriel waited, wanting him to offer something that would fix it instantly. He drew and released a deep breath, then chewed the corner of his lower lip the way he would if he had discovered mole tunnels or termite damage. "I'll go by the hardware store and get some paint," he said.

He returned to the car and drove away. Muriel felt sick, afraid to face that message alone, so she went inside as Paul had. Inside was still safe. It was her own house, the familiar dim ticking, cool with air conditioning, the smell of potpourri and floor wax. Inside had nothing to do with outside.

She went to the kitchen to wash their breakfast dishes. Without checking, she knew that Paul was back in his room again, closed behind the Yield sign. Even in the kitchen she felt, rather than heard, his restless moving at the opposite end of the house. Each minute made her more certain that he needed her, needed for someone to speak and it would have to be her, what with Dan gone. At the least, she must bring him out of his solitude, get his help with the dishes so he would know there was still such a thing as regular life. That no hate could break through, nobody's words could change them inside these walls.

She shut off the faucet and turned with a dish towel pressed in her hands to fetch him. But there he stood before her in the door frame, in the afternoon light of the kitchen window. He had changed clothes: cutoffs rolled up tight around his upper thighs and an ancient shirt of Dan's, sea-green button-up with the sleeves pulled off, worn to translucence. His hair swept back from his forehead in a little wave. In his ear shone the gold hoop—the one he never wore in the house, wore so rarely, in fact, that Muriel wondered how often he had to repierce the hole himself. His school backpack, which normally carried books, hung on one shoulder.

"Muriel," he said, "I'm sorry. I don't know what else to say. That's all, I guess. Tell Dad I'm sorry, and not to worry. I'll miss him, and you. You were a good mom." He turned and went out the back door.

She followed him out onto the porch. "Hold on now. Just what the devil's going on? This is no time for—" She waved her hand, in search of a word.

He was down the steps, out into the sunburnt yard. "I think it's exactly the time." As he glanced back, she noticed the way pieces of him glinted in the sun, a boy dusted in gold.

"Your father's gone for whitewash," she called from the porch, twisting the towel in her hands. "He'll be back directly." She heard the desperate rise in her voice, threat and promise. She meant somehow to say that whitewash would fix it, that Dan would know what to do. That Paul had no business running off on her, choosing the precise moment when his father was not around. But it seemed he was doing just that.

Called her *a good mom*. How odd that sounded from him—more like something Curtis would say when he was a boy, urgent to raise her out of the sadness she couldn't shake in those years. Eventually Curtis had learned to hide behind a tougher shell, but there for a time he'd been as sweet, as pretty blond as this boy. This one never said *mom*, called her Muriel, *darlin'*, treated her more like a sister. Teased, scolded her. But past that, underneath, they'd always had a kind of understanding, how she was not to acknowledge the hunger in his eyes but merely feed him, quietly. That was being a mother, she supposed. It was all she really understood to do.

She started after him across the grass, in shorter steps than she meant to take because she still wore the cream-colored suit and hose and wedge-heeled pumps she had worn to the hearing. "Paul, stop."

"What?" He spun to face her, his breath quickened, chin tipped up. She knew that look, though she had never seen it on Paul's face, and her upper body tightened, shoulder to fist, like a single muscle.

"Get back in that house," she ordered. "Right now."

He raised his eyebrows. "What, I'm grounded?"

"Hell, yes you are." She jutted her chin up toward his. "Now do what I tell you."

He began to smile like this was one last joke between them, and she saw instantly how he would defeat her. He would laugh. Laugh and turn and go, her too-late efforts nothing to him. But the smile quivered to a smirk, ended there. "You can't stop me," he said, and the blade edge that pressed hard across the tremor in his voice wasn't sharp enough to cut it. How much he wanted to defy her in some typical teenage way—she felt it like pain. This boy who didn't own a hard look was trying to put one together from scratch. She almost cried to see it—not because it changed him, but because he failed to change at all. The hardness wouldn't take, the way it did on other boys.

She shook her head at it. "Don't you try to sell me a load. I know you."

He tipped his head with a softer look, curious, almost pitying. "Do you?" he murmured, and as he turned away, his backward glance along one shoulder seared her with a smoky eroticism that made her breath catch.

She flared with anger. "I've known you from the age of ten!" she shouted. "*Ten*, Paul. And you are still a boy."

With backward steps, his eyes leveled on hers, he flicked open the bottom buttons of the shirt, gathered the tails into a rough knot above his navel, and jerked it tight. But she could only think that between that and the earring, he looked like a pirate prince, dressed for some make-believe game with the neighborhood kids. The most they wanted back then was to stay out past dark, to keep playing their game. Always it was "five more minutes, ten more minutes, *please*, Mom?"

But that was Curtis, not Paul, their old neighborhood in town— why couldn't she keep them straight? This was not her son. This was Dan's son, who was turning again with his shirt tied up and his pack hitched on his shoulder, walking away. Still no sign of Dan. Paul lobbed the bag over the barbed wire fence of the Hendersons' cow pasture and ducked through the middle strands. So effortless—how many times had she watched him go that way, come home by the same route? She'd always admired the economy of motion in the way he caught the wire back one-handed above the graceful contortion of his body that slipped through clean, without a snag.

She trailed him to the fence. "Paul." He ignored her, and she snatched his wrist over the wire, propelled by a sudden rage that would not be restrained. "You'd do this for sex?" she hissed. The wire prongs bit at the breast of her suit. "Those . . . things, whatever you do with them? It means that much to you, to ruin your family, ruin your life like this?"

"Yes." His answer was instant. The unadorned word made her eyes drop, made her afraid to look at him as he leaned close to her face, said it again. "*Yes*."

She released him like a breath. He turned, went away from her. He was like an air that whistled through her, gusted across the hot, still humidity of July and over the tops of the withered field grasses, the distant, fly-twitching backs of milk cows, and lofted easy toward the loblolly stand that darkly etched the horizon, before she knew there was anything left to say. By then he was past calling back—small with distance, harmless again. She focused on his familiar blue pack, urgent to read its shape before he vanished for good. Did he have any food, any money, enough clothes? A knife, perhaps—something to protect himself with? Too quick to trust, that boy. She had loved him just that fast, from the beginning, because he trusted her without proof. It was the very thing that terrified her now: his unmasked hunger that nothing sated, that left him vulnerable to anyone's version of love.

The fence held her; in her narrow skirt, she couldn't duck through. Paul was cresting the next rise, almost to the pines' edge, and not looking back. So many days that summer she had watched him leave that direction. Gone out to see his friends, he said. Of course he had friends, though she'd heard the county talk as if he were some kind of outcast, too peculiar for the company of other boys. He would be home again by supper, almost never late. Out again after supper, he'd make the midnight curfew and act sweet about it, never a minute's trouble. His teachers talked of how he had a chance at being valedictorian next year. A boy like that, to go so wrong—it didn't make any sense to her.

She watched the angle of his shoulders and his stride, as he vanished without a pause into the pine and blackberry at the other end of the field—as if he knew his destination. Then she knew it too: Highway 12 and the Lake Oconee Bridge. Unmistakable.

She stumbled back down the lawn, back inside the house. Her bulky leather purse sat in a kitchen chair and she grabbed it up, feeling more prepared now that she had her hands on it. She fished out her car keys, looked at the phone on the wall. Surely there was someone to call. The police, maybe, or she could try to call the hardware

store. A minute withered and died while she tried to calculate the
difference between calling Dan and leaving a note. But there wasn't
time for this. Just go, she told herself. You don't need anyone's help.
She pictured the face of the doctor she still saw once a week over
at the county hospital, hardly more than a pleasure visit these days.
You can handle this, he would assure her. *You are capable.* I am capable, she responded, and he nodded with her. Their heads bobbed
in rhythm.

She went out to the carport and ducked into her little Honda
Civic, backed out. Accidentally, her eyes swept over the front of the
house, and the defacement twisted inside her like a new assault, seared
her throat. Her own home. Who? Those highschool boys who loi-
tered around the Phillips 66—they would do this. But then, she
thought, so might their fathers.

She pulled out onto Highway 12, which curved in front of the
house, and followed it the familiar mile down toward Lake Oconee.
Below, beyond the concrete barrier along the bridge, sun glared on
the water. Paul was halfway across, shedding the same light from his
hair so she had to squint to be sure it was him. She slowed the car to
a crawl behind him. He turned once to look at her without stopping,
his expression unreadable in the light.

She rolled down the window and shouted his name. Behind her, a
sleek black pickup loaded with teenaged boys blared its horn, then
shrieked across the dividing line. Passing, they leveled malice at her
from their identical eyes, for the crime of driving too slowly, like the
weapons of a trained militia. Boys she'd known in past years would
drink and whoop and holler, raise harmless hell up and down the
county roads. Not these. They gave her the creeps, boys today—so
contained, self-righteous, humorless, gazing out at the world like it
gave them matching cases of indigestion. Her own Curtis had turned
out a little that way, she thought.

Another car approached from behind, and she pulled to the right as far as she could against the concrete wall, rolling, the tires crunching over stones and glass. The boy walked steadily, maddeningly, away from her. In the middle of the bridge, she hit the brake and threw the car into park, left it. On foot, she marched after him along the white line. Swallows twittered and chased each other past their heads.

"Stop, Paul, I mean it." One pump slipped off the slick nylon at her heel, and she paused to jam her foot back inside. New shoes—the leather was stiff below each ankle, rubbed and pinched at every step, and her stride became the mincing gimp required to hold the shoes on her feet. "Slow down, honey, *please*."

Nearly to the west end of the bridge, he stopped and turned to face her, arms crossed tight over the knotted shirt, head tipped toward one shoulder. She caught up slowly. "These darn shoes." She chuckled. "I can't believe I never changed out of my good clothes all this time. Ain't that stupid?"

Unsmiling, he flourished with one hand back toward the bridge. She turned to see the Honda parked half in the road at the center, the driver's side door hanging open. "Oh. Oh, Lord." She looked at Paul helplessly, back at the car.

"There's no stopping on the bridge," he said.

"You wait," she ordered. She leaned close to his face but not touching him—his posture was forbidding—and jammed an index finger under his nose. "Just wait right here."

She trudged back to the car, shuffling a few running steps whenever she could stand it. Already she could feel a blister coming up on one toe, and both heels were raw. Not until she reached the car did she turn to look after Paul, and he was already gone from sight.

She drove across the bridge, and he was standing in the paved loop of the pull-off. A few cars were parked there for fishing along the water side. At the other, near Paul, a lone sedan spotted with rust idled

close to the exit. The car looked familiar, one Muriel had seen before around town.

As she pulled in, Paul was at the sedan's passenger window. At
that distance, in those clothes, he looked like someone else's boy:
older maybe, hands in his front pockets, a lazy curve in his spine. She
strained for a look at the driver, the dim back of a man's head she
thought she could almost place. Paul leaned in at the window now,
ignoring her. Wild with fury, she drove up right onto the tail of the
sedan, bleated the horn. The sedan rolled forward a few feet and Paul
followed, speaking fast words into the window. Muriel slammed her
car into park and got out, fists balled. Whoever was in that sedan,
she was going to drag him out with her own two hands and smack
him senseless.

But the instant she was on her feet, visible in the daylight, the
sedan leapt forward like a spooked horse and laid rubber out onto the
road heading west. She gasped at the sudden exit, before a low, steady
thrill came over her. She had this on her side at least—a mother's
power to put the fear of God back in a man.

Paul stared after the car, closed his eyes for a moment. Open again,
they looked as scrubbed as sea glass, the same blankness of the first
day in Rockdale after he had emerged from the room with the lawyer. He turned without looking at her and went to sit on the low wall
along the woods, facing the road. She regarded him as she reached
in to switch off her car's engine, closed the door.

"Who was that?" she asked conversationally. He sat pulling the high
weeds that grew nearby, peeling down strips of the long, bladed leaves
in his fingers. She approached the wall. "Did you know that person?"

He shrugged. "Yeah, I guess so. Sort of. What's the difference?"

"Well, it matters. It surely does." She crossed her arms tightly,
hoping to conceal her confusion. "If you know him. If you think he
. . . means something to you. I don't know, Paul. You tell me."

He gave her a pained look, and his eyes went back to the road. "He doesn't mean anything."

"You were about to get in his car."

"I have to get away from here," he said. "That's all he is. He's a ride."

Weariness had slipped into his shoulders, his eyes—her Paul again, not that stranger she had glimpsed by the sedan. "Guess that's over for today, ain't it?" she said. "Nobody's stopping for you so long as I'm standing here. And I ain't moving."

He sighed. "You stand there all day, it won't change anything."

"All I'm looking for is your rear end back at home."

"I can't go back there. Don't you get it?" He looked away and swallowed, hugging his rib cage. "I just don't want to cause any more trouble."

So young, that face—it was like looking at a memory, something already lost. "Sugar Pie," she murmured, brushed a hand over his knee. He flinched at the touch. "I should wish for so little trouble—" But at the same time, she could hear the echo of Dan's words from the night before, after they had turned out the bedside light: "We haven't begun to see the trouble this will cause." Maybe even now, they had only begun to see it.

He got down from the wall, hoisted the backpack again with a glance at the sun. "Go home. Help Dad paint the house." He began walking away, toward the road.

"Paul, now—" She started after him instantly, but already losing ground to her narrow skirt, the rub and slide of her shoes. "Paul!" At the road's edge, he cocked a thumb for a car coming over the bridge. She held her breath until it was safely past, then ran up the embankment after him, fairly losing a shoe in the process. Headed west, his strides were long and easy, his pale head passing from sun to shadow between the edge of the woods and the road. She knew she'd never keep up, that she couldn't trail him in the car either—not along the twisting pike of Highway 12, where people always drove so fast you'd think Greene County was no more than a road between two other places.

But she gimped anyway along the roadside grass, as much a spectacle herself, she figured, as this strange stepson who pursed his lips and gazed so intently at every passing car. She stopped to knock a stone out of her shoe. When she looked up, the same black pickup full of boys was rounding the curve toward them, engine gunned. As it passed, a can shot from the back, full, winging in a straight line close enough to Paul's head that he threw an arm up in defense. It smacked the grassy edge beyond him, hissing with foam. Another, crushed and empty, clattered on the asphalt near Muriel's feet. Over the engine's roar, hoots and howls of laughter seemed nearly unconnected to human mouths. The truck crossed the bridge and was gone.

"Jeez Louise," she gasped, hand to her chest. Paul gazed after the truck, mouth open, the defensive fist sinking by degrees back to his side.

"That was that Baker boy driving, wasn't it?" she said, not sure if she was talking to Paul or herself. "And that one in the back—I know him too."

Paul, flushed and breathing hard, came back to the place where she stood and gripped her upper arms with surprising force. She stared at his face, mouth dropped open and dumb. "Go home, now," he said. "You leave me alone, and I'll have a ride in two minutes, I'll be *fine*. You keep this up, and we'll both get hurt. Go home."

He set her back a step, as if she were the child. Bewildered, she stood where he had placed her, while he turned and went on walking. Was it possible he was right? Maybe he understood his situation better than she possibly could. Uncertain, she looked back at her car, the direction of her house—the same direction the truck full of boys had gone. She tried to picture those hard, young faces, attach their names. They would be back soon, she felt sure, and Paul might still be walking the shoulder, hoping for anyone to stop. Any car at all that might pass along this wooded stretch of the county, where she no longer knew people.

With a moan, she started after him. He had nearly gone out of range, beyond the next curve, and she shouted his name so loud her voice broke. But he didn't look back.

She took a few running steps to keep him in her line of vision. That was all, she thought, just to keep that close. As long as she could see him, he'd be safe. Whole caravans of Greene County boys might throw whatever garbage was handy, but no one would lay a hand on him. No car would stop. But she saw, too, how a man who knew what he wanted might snatch Paul up so fast she'd never make the license plate at that distance, let alone the face. Desperate, she quickened her pace, running five strides, walking five, trying to separate herself from the pain in her feet. Finally she took off the shoes and carried them, picking her way along the shoulder in her stockings. Her eyes flicked between Paul's distant head and the stones and broken glass that littered her path.

Whenever a westward car came along, Paul stopped and put out his thumb. Muriel gritted her teeth and ran in choppy strides, hoping only that by the time she looked up from the treacherous ground, Paul would not have disappeared. Once she had walked through the feet of her stockings, she tried putting the shoes back on and found they stuck better to bare skin, slipped less and allowed her to hold a steadier pace. They walked a mile this way, the gap slowly closing. Paul seemed to slacken and match her stride, head down. In the second mile he paid less notice to each passing car, his thumb out in a halfhearted effort, but still he refused to look back at her. She stopped calling for him. They walked.

Before she noticed it happening, the sun sat along the tops of the trees and she and Paul were nearly abreast, trudging along almost companionably, as if they had agreed on a single destination. Paul raised his eyes for the next passing car, but that was all.

Just past the next curve, she calculated, was the Ellis brothers' filling station. After all that walking, they were still so close to home. "Boy, I could use a co' cola," she said. "You think we might rest a bit up here at Ellis's?"

He shrugged. The knot in his shirt had fallen loose, and the open edges flapped back from his pale, adolescent belly in the gust of a passing car. "You're doing this for Dad," he said, "because you think he wants it. But he would've let me go."

"You're wrong." It was hard, she found, to speak without panting for air. "You're twice wrong there. Your dad—I don't know what you want from him, but you're the one, Paul. You pulled away from him. I watched it happen, from years ago."

He didn't answer, though his jaw flinched at the words. Maybe after all these weeks he'd run dry on apologies. Softening, she added, "I wouldn't be out here on his account anyway. You're my son now too."

He smiled miserably, eyes on the grass. "I sure ain't Curtis, am I?"

"No," she said. "No, sir. You don't need to be. Curtis ain't no angel—you know that as well as anyone. He hasn't been since he was a little boy."

Their pace dragged as they approached the curve, and Muriel felt a strange urgency to get the filling station in sight. As if the presence of buildings and other people, the business of daily lives, would somehow save them.

"I tried, you know," Paul said, addressing the trees. "To be good. To be like I'm supposed to. And then I tried to be good in Greene County and bad everywhere else, like I could keep those two people separate. But it all comes home sooner or later. It doesn't matter what you do."

"Paul, now, I don't know that I—"

He stopped, facing her. "This is what it comes down to. What you don't want to know. What I do with them."

"Just—" She squeezed her eyes shut, palms flashing out. "Please. It's not that I don't—" Defeated suddenly, she searched his face, tried to light on the words she needed. "I know how you are. I do. But do we got to talk about it? It's just that you're still so young, is all. There's still so much time—"

She heard the pleading in her voice, the sound of a child begging a favor like a magic trick—something beyond reason. What *did* she want? It wasn't that she hoped he would suddenly wake from this curse, to be like other boys. It was not to be asked of him. She simply wanted him to find his way back somehow, agree to take his place at home as the child. Return to innocence, become a virgin, begin again. Go more slowly. Allow her to keep up.

He drew a breath as if to explain, but then stepped out away from her, gave her the back of his head. The filling station was in sight now, so she felt easy that he would only beat her to that resting place. But in the soft gold hair at the nape of his neck, she glimpsed how close he had come to vanishing before her eyes in a sparkle of dust, this trick he had mastered without her notice. The Great Escape— it was how Dan spoke sometimes of his first wife's leaving, pain masked in irony, as if he saw something to be envied in that brand of magic. He insisted, too frequently, that Paul was born the image of his mother. But Muriel hadn't known the woman, saw only in a hundred lights how Paul would study out a problem with his father's face, his father's gestures.

No customers were parked on the filling station's gravel lot, and for that small favor Muriel felt immense gratitude. She approached the store on the last steps she thought her feet would take, eyes locked on the Coke machine back in the shadows of the wooden porch. Paul sat out in front at the porch's edge, eyes closed, head tipped back against a post of peeling whitewash stained along the base with years of tobacco spit.

"Lord, my purse is in the car," she muttered. "Honey, you got a dollar? I need a flat one."

He reached for his pack, pulled his wallet from the zipper compartment. From a sheaf of crisp-looking bills, he drew a twenty. "You'll have to get change," he said as he handed it to her, not meeting her eyes.

She stood blinking for a moment, words floating just beyond her immediate grasp, then went into the store with the bill. Harvey Jr. stood behind the cash register, a huge boy a year or two older than Curtis, his small, dewy eyes peering from beneath a Skoal cap. She went past him to the refrigerator case and selected a pair of plastic-bottle Cokes. At the register, she offered a brief smile and the twenty. It occurred to her that her legs were striped with open runs, that her suit was ruined, that she was coated all over in sweat and gritty dust.

"How you today, Miz Foster?" the boy said in his high-pitched drawl. She listened for any shift in tone from his usual greeting.

"I'm all right, Harvey." She smiled again once he'd counted the change back to her, his usual grin pasted on his face. His expression remained dull, benign, locked in place as she rang the bell of the front door going out.

"Here, honey." She tapped Paul's bare shoulder with one of the cold-sweating bottles. He looked up and took it, and she held the wadded change of the twenty out after it. "You're gonna have to tell me about that money. The money I don't—" The words choked her. She clenched her jaw and looked away. Setting him aside for the moment, she sunk to the porch steps and slipped off her shoes, felt the sweet, aching wash of blood returning to throb in her toes.

"It's not what you think," he said.

She cracked the seal on the Coke and took several long swallows before speaking. "Paul, if you're gonna lie, you mighta started with that judge."

"It's not." Head still tipped back against the post, his shut eyes squeezed harder as if to block the tears his voice betrayed. He took a breath and went on more calmly. "I don't do it for money. It just happens that way. This is all from one guy. He just gives it to me, I can't stop him."

She sipped the Coke and watched him. "Paul, honestly. You think this man cares about you? Loves you?"

"It's not that, exactly."

"Well, if it's not, darlin', you are tossing away your life for a pittance. I don't think you got the first idea what you're doing."

"Don't tell me that." He shot her a red-eyed look, opened his bottle with a vicious twist. "When you were my age, tell me you didn't know what you wanted. Tell me you hadn't figured out what a man was for."

She flinched against his comparison, but found herself answering steadily, without a pause. "You think you know it all, I guess. About me and sex and everything else. I'll tell you what. I don't care what you done—you don't know squat about this world yet, the danger you're facing. I hope you never find out. And I'll tell you another thing. You don't know how a mother feels about a child, and I doubt you ever will."

A car carrying three black teenagers, two boys and a girl, had pulled up beside one of the pumps. She could feel their eyes, hear their half-muffled hoots and laughter. So everyone knew. Paul sat motionless, exposed at the porch's edge, head still tipped back as if he would bare his throat to any attack, as if he expected nothing else. This choice had lost him every protection in the world; that was what she couldn't bear. She touched his shoulder, was surprised to see tears spring instantly along the seal of his lashes.

"I don't know what you want from me," he whispered. He covered his face and started laughing softly, at the edge of hysteria.

She slipped an arm around his neck, and his forehead dropped to her shoulder. "Come home," she said, stroking his hair. "Have mercy on me, Paul. All I know is I don't think I can walk any farther with you."

Against her shoulder, she felt him nod, a tiny motion. She tightened her hold reflexively, flooded with the same relief that had washed through her feet when she took off the shoes. To be home—what a dream, what paradise.

"I won't be able to stay, you know," he said. He separated himself, easing back against the post to gaze toward the snickering kids at the pumps. One of the boys squalled with laughter and shoved the other forward when he saw they had Paul's eyes. "This is our life from now on, anytime we step outside in Greene County." He nodded toward the pumps. "This here is the good part."

"It don't matter," she promised. "We can just stay inside."

He laughed a little, as if she had made a joke. But why not? They could simply keep to themselves, away from county boys in trucks and men in rust-spotted cars. Home is yours to make, her doctor told her—these words he said were his own good mother's. Home can be the whole world if you choose it.

"I'm going to call your dad to come get us," she said softly, earnestly, close to Paul's ear. The carful of kids had torn off, and he gazed at the dust that hovered now at the verge of the road.

Inside, she borrowed Harvey's phone. Through the receiver, her own phone rang at home—soon they'd be there too. But for how long? Maybe it would be only a week, a month, before Paul left in the night, not risking good-bye the next time. From where the cord tethered her, she couldn't see the spot where he sat, and in her exhaustion—Dan picking up the line—she felt a moment of transport to some near future in which Paul was not the subject of her call, no longer this sweet trouble to be balanced awkwardly between them. "Dan? I'm down here at Ellis's," she said, the other words she needed for the moment beyond her reach. The window's limited view held only the dust that persisted, shot through with the last sharp rays of daylight, out over the road.

rapture

be careful what you wish for

At the end of summer, Florie Ballard acquired a house guest. She wasn't sure how she had happened to say yes, when her daughter proposed that they keep this boy, board him for a year. "He's practically related," Sidra had argued—this based on her notion that at any hour she might run off and marry the boy's stepbrother. Florie had yet to see a ring. Back in the spring, this grown daughter had hauled her college degree along with eight garbage bags full of laundry up the staircase, stowed four scruffy horses in Florie's barn, and hadn't budged since.

Now another boarder. Paul needed their help, Sidra said, after getting into some trouble at home, needed a new high school for his senior year. Florie could have guessed what sort of trouble. One look at him told the story, though Sidra supplied the lurid details: an arrest for prostitution, of all things, and his parents' house covered in graffiti in the aftermath.

"He's harmless," Sidra said. "The arrest was bogus. But still, he can't stay in Greene County. He can't go back to school there—those rednecks would kill him."

"I don't know about that," Florie tried halfheartedly. "People are usually more tolerant than you think."

All that summer, Sidra had been bringing the boy to the house for little visits, nudging him toward Florie to say his hellos. So she'd guessed, even then, that something was up. The boy had a habit of cupping the side of his neck with one hand, the arm curled tight to his chest, and she found herself noticing how the bones protruded at his wrist, how fragile he looked. *He's one of those boys*, she'd thought with a start—remembering the young men she had tried to forget, the ones who always surrounded them whenever she'd taken Marcy to the hospital, eighth floor, Infectious Diseases. She'd wheeled Marcy's chair clear of them, as if they were somehow different in their contagion from her daughter. She commandeered a private corner, half-concealed by a potted palm, and refused to look. It seemed an accident that her daughter had fallen into their midst. A mistake. Somebody would need to correct it before long.

Now, back to haunt me, she thought, looking at Paul. And perhaps those thin boys she had shunned had once been very much like this one—who was healthy, young, and electric with nervous bravado, balancing at the edge of the world. It had been wrong to blame them, she knew, when Marcy bolted for the edge of her own free will. She was a girl who went as far as she could and laughed at the hands that reached for her, and the bitter echo still found its way into Florie's dreams some nights. Paul's laugh was not Marcy's. Even his squinty, pale eyes couldn't touch hers—those striking spheres, rounder than round, violet blue.

Look, look, a blue-eyed child in danger, Sidra seemed to say with every nudge. As if it were that simple. As if any little resemblance could remind her of a dead daughter who was never out of mind to begin with. But Sidra said, "If we don't take him, he's going to run away." And Florie discovered, to her dismay, that she couldn't let him go.

So she agreed, almost against her will, and Paul Foster moved in.
A relation, Florie told herself to smooth it over, though she found
she didn't know how to feel related to this boy, who looked like a
boy in every way but what counted. He dressed like a boy, cut his
hair like one. But there was a girl somewhere inside that body, she
was certain. She had seen about such things on TV. Once taken in,
he seemed to relax and expand; she glimpsed him, when he thought
he was alone with Sidra, strutting with the haughty air of a runway
model, or posed in *femme fatale* curves against doorframes, perfectly
lounging on the furniture. Even when boyish, as he behaved in Florie's
presence, he had that shy little smile, the kind of innocence only a
girl would know how to fake. And those eyes—not his eyes, exactly,
but *behind* his eyes, a girl peering out through gold lashes as if from a
curtained window, trapped.

He made himself useful around the house, more than she could
say for Sidra. He would rush to carry groceries in from the car and sit
her down in a kitchen chair while he put them away, chattering a
blue streak about school. Not about the friends he made (she wondered if there were any) or sports or class schedules, but the teachers
and books, the stuff he was reading.

"You've read *Candide*," he would say, as if everyone had. Ignoring
her blank stare, he would rattle off the story as if to remind her, then
go on to other books for comparison, books similar to *Candide*, about
Candide. . . . This depth, she was certain, they couldn't be teaching
in high school. It seemed suspicious, somehow—but suspicious of
what? That he was ditching school to crash a college course? To hide
out at the university library, sneaking books? She wasn't sure how to
be responsible for this restless creature not her own, or where her
authority should end.

She found herself listening for his return from school, or wandering her rangy farmhouse in the afternoons to see where he was holed

up. Often she'd find him out in the driveway in the old Dodge, which his parents had bought so that he could get back to Greene County on the weekends. It was an ugly, boxy thing, the color they called "flesh" in the old Crayola boxes, but he had transformed the interior. The upholstery was hidden under mismatched swaths of fabric: orange silk, a leopard-skin print, squares of suede. Green tassels edged the back window. Tacked over the whole ceiling, zebra stripes. The result seemed to satisfy him, so much that he would park the car under the oak shade, and for hours he would sit in the back seat. The floor was forever strewn with clothbound library books, red and blue and green. He'd leave the doors open and sit curled with his bare feet propped on the front seat, reading.

Sometimes he and the car were gone. He never offered to tell where he was going, only that he would be home by dinner, home by ten. Must be the library, she told herself, suspecting otherwise. But maybe it was best not to look too close.

She and Sidra discussed him quietly when he was gone. "He needs to be treated like a young horse, I think," Sidra reasoned, her blond head bobbing thoughtfully—that gesture a new one to Florie. "Give him some rein, you know? A little freedom. So he learns how to use it, he doesn't bolt." Florie marveled quietly at her firstborn, with whom she so rarely managed a civil, adult conversation about anything.

From the living room window one afternoon, Florie watched Paul's bare foot, just visible through the Dodge's open door, flexing and pointing like a dancer's. *Lord*, she thought, *when did I ask for another daughter?* But she caught herself instantly—she *had* asked. Could one little prayer be that powerful, to warp the natural sex of someone else's child and then drop it on her own doorstep like a foundling? *The Lord must be having Himself a good laugh over this one*, she thought.

Another afternoon, when he was gone, she wandered into the room where he slept. The bed was made, clothes hung in the closet, a pair of jeans folded over the desk chair, books stacked on the night table. She thought she must be looking for evidence, something in plain view, though she didn't know what would qualify. Evidence of what? She lifted a paperback book from the bed—*Candide*. On the cover was a painting of a man who pushed a wheelbarrow while gazing wistfully at another man, who sat reading. She opened to the first page and read from a chapter called "How Candide was brought up in a beautiful castle, and how he was driven from it": *In the castle of Baron Thunder-ten-tronckh in Westphalia, there once lived a youth endowed by nature with the gentlest of characters. His soul was revealed in his face.*

what touches you

Curtis was late to band practice, came into the old trainyard warehouse they rented wearing the flushed, sullen face that meant he was fresh from a fight with Sidra. Resigned after a glance, Kent unplugged his electric guitar and set it in the case—no use rushing Curtis in such a state. He picked up his acoustic and settled down cross-legged on a crate in the corner, began working out the bridge to a new country song he was writing, one of many the band would never play, since they didn't play country.

Lyle left the drums to stand beside Jeff. Off among packing crates, Curtis sat and began to meticulously tune his bass as if he had walked into an otherwise empty room.

"Drama of the week," Lyle said.

Jeff muttered, "This is bullshit."

"Y'all." Kent didn't look up from the guitar. "Don't fuck with Curtis. We'll be here till midnight. And we got business. Our lease is about up, and it looks to me like we're getting kicked out."

"Great." Jeff tapped out a cigarette and lit it. "Well, you know, Curtis ain't the only one around here with places to be. How about you, Lyle?"

They strolled over to Curtis. "Rough day?" Jeff said.

Curtis cranked strings in a silent fume. "You don't get it. I'd ignore this shit if I could, right? But it's like it's touching me. I can't get it off, 'cause of what he did. He did it to my *mom*, you know, her house. Painted on her fucking *house*. She don't deserve that. Now it's like I can't even go visit my own mother."

One foot propped on the crate where Curtis sat, Jeff cocked his head, squinting through his smoke. Lyle hopped onto a box across the aisle and rolled out a soft patter against the wood with his drumsticks.

"It's like he's contaminated everything," Curtis went on, dropping the pretense of tuning. "I don't want to be in his family. I don't want him in my family. And now, Sidra, Jesus! He's in her house. He's living there! I mean, what's next, for fuck's sake?"

"Yeah, I know what you mean." Jeff shook his head in commiseration, exchanged an amused look with Lyle. "I mean, who knows? Maybe next he'll be in her bed! Then your bed. From there, well, hell—anything could happen."

Curtis glared. "It's no joke. Sidra's mom, she don't know all that faggot's up to under her roof, out sucking cop dick and God knows what all else. She oughtta know. I mean, she has a *right* to know."

"Damn straight." Jeff's grin strained against his best effort at a serious face. "I say you should follow him around a little. See for yourself exactly what he's doing, with who and which orifice, and then you can make a report to Mrs. Ballard. Official and all. Get your details straight."

Curtis looked off at the far wall, refusing to be amused. "Oh, yeah," Jeff said to Lyle, a stage whisper. "He probably don't want details. That could make him sick."

"You know, Sidra's doing this just to piss me off. Man, does she know how to jerk my chain. Why do I waste my time on this woman?"

Lyle jumped off his crate. "Just dump her already. Let's practice."

the extended family

Sidra was sick to death of Curtis—sick, sick, sick. The degree of her nausea was such that she sought her mother's ear one evening, a first in the two years she had been seeing Curtis. Florie made cocoa for the occasion, finding that she had to read the directions on the Swiss Miss box before she boiled the water. When it whistled, she filled the two mugs, set them on the oilclothed kitchen table with a plate of Lorna Doones. The wind chimes outside the kitchen window rang softly in the dark.

"So Curtis hates Paul. I didn't realize."

"He's been this way all along," Sidra admitted. She stirred her mug, poking at the tiny ready-puff marshmallows that trailed a creamy scum after her spoon. "He's hopeless. What am I supposed to do with him, huh? Am I supposed to fix him somehow?"

"I don't know, honey. Men aren't always fixable." Florie sat in the next chair, her own steaming mug before her. She was dissatisfied with the cocoa, this scene she wanted to create. The props of mother-daughter bonding had always somehow eluded her.

"But you try, right? You don't just give up. Abandon them." Sidra's voice was soft, measured, carefully nonaccusatory, because she and Florie so often fought their skirmishes against the backdrop of divorce. For years Sidra had been camped on her father's side, implicitly blaming Florie for breaking up the marriage over nothing, and she maintained a reserve of spite on this account to call to her defense at any time, whatever the topic. But now she didn't want to approach that battleground at all, if she could help it. She wanted to talk about Curtis.

"Depends on the problem, I guess." Florie sipped the watery cocoa, its syrup-sweet coat at the top. "This is about Paul, not you. Any man with a family comes with a whole set of problems already in place. I guess you inherit them too, in a way, but you're still an outsider. It's not your place to step in and solve it all like magic. Now if Curtis were hitting you, that'd be one thing. If it were anything to do with you—"

"Doesn't Paul have something to do with me? I mean, I know he's not *my* family. But he's important to me. He feels like family. More than Curtis sometimes."

"I'm fond of Curtis," Florie ventured. "And I see how you feel about him too. I know you. You're not gonna give up on him that easy."

Sidra met her mother's eyes, surprised by that easy claim—*I know you.* She looked back into her mug. They had called a truce, it seemed, over Paul, offered each other a provisional forgiveness. Now something was accumulating, thickening between them, like a sheet of ice over a pond. Fragile still. Neither was quite sure how to walk here yet.

"Funny those two wouldn't get along," Florie said, musing. "They're so much alike. I could mistake them for real brothers."

Sidra's jaw dropped. "Curtis and Paul? You're kidding, right?"

"You don't see it? They look similar enough, for one, same coloring. They've both got a sort of intensity in how they approach things. That enthusiasm for little projects that don't make much sense to other folks."

Sidra smiled in amazement. "Paul is going to die when I tell him that."

"Where's he at tonight?"

Sidra turned her gaze back through the doorway, knowing he was not in the house and the flesh-toned car was gone as well. "Out, I guess."

"Out." Florie smiled and Sidra caught her humor, a quick flash of light between them. Then it was gone. Florie's nail picked at a chipped spot in the rim of her mug. "The boy makes me nervous."

"Yeah, me too. A little."

"You have any idea who he's with?"

Sidra shook her head. "I get the idea it's no one steady." She pictured him as he had presented himself at her bedroom door the night before, five past ten, breathless, the flush of recent sex on his skin. So visible he only closed his eyes, bit his lower lip against the grin. Happy, at least. She couldn't mistake that, and she had intended, after all, to make him happy.

In Paul, Sidra had thought to offer her mother a kind of gift. The strain between them, a certain chill of formality, Sidra dated from the divorce—specifically from the night Florie had thrown Jimmy Ballard out of the house for the crime of surprising Sidra with a new horse. Sidra had nursed her grudge all these years, through the intervening drama of her younger sister's delinquency, which had actually started before the breakup—Marcy running away, again and again until she finally stayed gone for a good while. It was Marcy, they all secretly knew, who had strained the Ballards to the breaking point, shredded them so weak and raw that it was easier to blame anything else: one night, one horse, her father's innocent, thoughtless, definable act. Easier for Sidra too. Draw clear lines—choose a side.

Sidra had been in college the year Marcy, at nineteen, had come home to die. Her involvement in Marcy's care had been slim for several reasons, reasons that Sidra still listed for herself when she thought about Marcy, which she was doing more and more as the years passed. She'd been busy with school, living in the dorms, involved in one project, then another. Marcy, no denying, was difficult. Sidra had never understood her anyway, never felt close to her the way sisters ought to feel, and Marcy, once home again, went through spells where she didn't recognize people.

Then there was the nature of the illness itself, which, even after all these years, no one liked to say the name of if they could help it. Even now, if Florie spoke of Marcy's last year, she talked about pneumonia or lung conditions or stomach complaints, and shied away from dangerous words, like tuberculosis. There had been necessary social precautions, reasons to limit the number of people with access to the medical details, and Sidra had volunteered her absence. It seemed logical, and all her good reasons spared her having to admit, even to herself, that she was terrified to enter the house where AIDS lived. That she waited until it was gone.

That had been four years ago, and now Sidra was home again, feeling the void of her mother's house, vaguely accusatory, echoing around her. Father gone, sister gone—Sidra wanted to call it even, but she knew it was not. The imbalance ached, and she felt the need to offer something to her mother, or perhaps to the void. To make amends. But not knowing for what, or precisely to whom, until Paul came along. A surrogate.

She knew it would take both of them to save this one, though she had not counted on it being quite so hard. Paul didn't come braced with Marcy's stubborn sense of invulnerability. He was sweeter, more tractable. But there was a deafness in his pliancy, something she sensed hidden in plain view, his doors seemingly so open.

"I asked him if he was being careful," Sidra told her mother wryly. She twisted a lock of hair to one eye, examining the ends for splits. "Safe, I think is what I said."

"Did you, now?" Florie leaned closer with interest. "And what did he say?"

Sidra wrinkled her nose. Florie still waited for an answer, eyes soft with concern. So Sidra smirked—Paul's cheesy, theatrical grin—and imitated him. "Oh, *always*, darlin'."

"Being honest?"

Sidra shrugged. "Honest enough, maybe. Who knows what safe is? I don't know. He doesn't know. I mean, kissing's not safe, if you want to get nitpicky about it. There are so many degrees. And he just hates to be serious for two seconds at a stretch."

"And here he is now," Florie said, not bothering to lower her voice. Sidra turned to see the boy smiling behind her in the doorway. Alert tonight, not that sex-permeated haze of the night before.

"Speak of the devil and demons appear. That's how my stepmom says it." He took a seat, picked a cookie off the plate, and examined it. "Did I miss all the juicy stuff?"

Sidra laid her hand over his and offered a smile not really apologetic, but radiant with affection. Florie wasn't sure this boy deserved so much of her daughter's love, which was more than she had witnessed for anyone outside of Sidra's father. Not even Curtis rated looks like that. It puzzled her, the way Sidra threw her heart at a reckless child, who was charming in his way but who so clearly didn't know what to do with a girl's heart—or, as far as Florie could tell, anyone else's either. But then, she guessed how Sidra had made arrangements in her own mind for their three salvations, and it was easy to excuse her.

Florie frowned at her watch. Across the table, Paul matched her, checking his own watch, then glancing to Florie's wrist with elfish calculation. He turned his wrist, watch face out, in case she wanted a comparison—five minutes under the wire.

"Stop," Sidra whispered.

He tucked the watch under the table, glanced at Sidra with those fake innocent eyes. "What?"

Florie's first thought was to send her daughter out of the room, talk to Paul alone. But this was Sidra's project—no reason why Florie should have to play parent alone. Might as well give Sidra a look at what she was up against.

"You out with someone tonight?" she asked him, incisive, without delicacy.

Surprised, his eyes went round and blank for a second. Then he exhaled, ate half of the cookie in a bite. "Not really." He chewed, popped the other half into his mouth. "I met someone," he admitted. "I was with someone for a little while."

That was honesty, Florie thought with a shiver. Her next question came out flatter than she intended. "Is it someone new every night?"

Paul lifted another cookie, looking uncomfortable. "*Every* night? I'm not a rock star or anything."

"But these are strangers we're talking about. The one tonight—was that a stranger?"

"Yeah, I guess." He smiled privately. "*Was.*"

Florie sighed. This was a boy, she'd gathered, who outside of a court hearing didn't talk about sex, who simply was not asked about it, because nobody knew how to approach him. She certainly didn't know her way any better than his parents, but she had come this far. She asked, "You think what you're doing qualifies as promiscuity?"

He set his mouth against a propped knuckle and regarded her in thoughtful silence. "You're asking me?"

"I'm asking, Paul, what you think about this, what you think you're doing. Have you thought of maybe waiting? I hate to say *abstinence*, but all this activity . . . it could wait until you're a little older, maybe you could handle it better?"

He gave a soft laugh, courteous and a little lost, as if she had made a joke in some foreign language he only partly understood. Finishing his second cookie, he scooped a third from the plate and stood. "Well, I'm beat." He smiled at Florie's concern, checked his watch again. "Past my bedtime."

"Paul," Sidra said.

He turned to meet her intense, questioning gaze, and his own eyes softened a shade. He leaned to kiss her cheek. "Goodnight, beautiful." From the doorway he smiled back over his shoulder. "You girls be good now."

the perfect bite

It was early October, warmth persisting through the days, the nights crisp. Sidra decided to have a bonfire, because she was craving s'mores: marshmallows and chocolate oozing together, squeezing out of a graham cracker sandwich—some childhood image of paradise that wouldn't let go. And she wanted a party.

It began as a small, close gathering, circled around the fire above the Ballard pastures—just the guys in the band, some sorority girls Jeff Ostrander had asked to bring along, Florie, and Sidra. She and Curtis squabbled like kids over the proper way to build a fire, rearranging each other's wood stacks until together, almost by accident, they produced a competent blaze. The others were talking, and Sidra noticed how at ease everyone seemed under Florie's resonant voice, her laughter, how they let her turn the conversation around her questions like small children, that eager to please. No one else would have thought to bring a mother to such an event, but no one else would have fit quite so well as Florie Ballard.

Lyle labored over a pair of marshmallows until they were toasted to an unburned caramel color on every surface, and offered them to Sidra. As she stacked her first s'more, David from work tapped her shoulder. "You came!" she said. She and David had sniggered together in corners often enough, while waiting tables at East-West Bistro, for Sidra to size him up: dishy college boy, slightly goofy, definitely gay. She looked around for Paul but saw no sign, though he had promised he wouldn't miss it. David told her he couldn't stay long. She offered him her s'more.

He laughed. "Oh, Sidra. That's obviously yours—look at it, it's artwork. I'll make my own. There's always s'more, right?"

"No, that's not how it goes," she chided. "It's that you always want s'more."

"Oh, god, one's my limit. But if I know you, you'll make yourself sick." David liked to tease her about sneaking desserts behind the server line, even, on occasion, the untouched corners of leftovers from her customers' plates. "Somebody might have licked that!" he would point out, just to be perverse.

"I'll eat a dozen and go to the hospital a happy girl." She bit into the s'more, and the melted marshmallow goo fell over her lip, onto her chin. The perfect bite—but it was not exactly what she'd imagined it would be.

David sat with the sorority girls. Curtis was beside Florie, engrossed. Though Sidra was sometimes pleased, even proud, to have a mother she could bring to parties, it irked her too—especially that Florie and Curtis got on so fabulously. Well, let them have each other.

Kent McKutcheon, the band's singer, who had trouble talking without a guitar in his hands, was already taking requests from the girls. "Brown-Eyed Girl," "American Pie," his singing voice warm and velvety over the strummed chords. He ignored Jeff's "Freebird!" Sidra took the spot beside Lyle, who produced a vapor-cold beer for her before she thought to ask, and Curtis moved over to sit beside her. A long swallow of beer, a satisfied sigh for the fire—a success, she decided. Except Paul. She hoped it wasn't Curtis keeping him away. It occurred to her that maybe those two were the real reason for the bonfire—she needed to see their faces together, had somehow pictured them brought together in the glow of firelight. They wouldn't need to speak to each other, just be there.

She leaned across Lyle, got Jeff's attention. "Better watch out. Your brown-eyed girl over there is getting swoony over Kent."

"Another one bites the dust," Lyle added, cutting eyes at Sidra, who had once gone down that path, or so the band liked to believe—seduced effortlessly by their only real musician.

Jeff squinted across the smoke to where the girl he favored sat clustered with the others, their enraptured gazes on the singer with his goatee and downcast eyes and dark hair curling over his forehead. They had all seen it before, and firelight only enhanced the effect. "Now I ask you, is that shit fair?" Jeff spat into the coals. "Show-off."

"Hey, that's not about some girl," Curtis said, his elbow hooked around Sidra's knee. "That's just Kent. He's an artist, you know? Got a head full of music. He don't mess around with it."

Jeff conceded the point with a snort. "Well, I don't know why not. Someone ought to be getting some around here. Besides you, that is." The last was for Curtis, though he aimed his smarmy grin at Sidra. She turned to Curtis for an unspoken reckoning of how many days it had been since their last spat. Three. They smiled, sealing a truce for tonight.

But he clung to the anger of his principles, and when Paul arrived, Sidra knew it first by Curtis's silent bristling, like static on his skin. Paul stood off in the darkness, talking with David, the half-moon over the trees behind them. David had just said his good-byes, must have run into Paul on his way out. Maybe he would decide to stay now, Sidra hoped. But another few minutes and David was gone, Paul hanging back from the firelight, watching.

She kissed Curtis's temple and rose, walked over to where Paul stood. "What are you doing, sweetie?" He looked chilly in his thin shirt, and she took hold of his arm.

He stared past her, wary and transfixed, at the back of Curtis's head. "I told you I'd come." His voice was low, a dark, unfamiliar pitch. He extracted himself from her hands, and she wandered with him to the cooler, set back from the fire, where he fished a beer from the ice. "Your mom won't let me have this, will she?"

Sidra slid it from his hands and opened it. "There's Coke and Sprite."

"But I need it." The plea was half comic, though his eyes shifted back to Curtis.

She slipped an arm around his back, kissed his shoulder. "You cold?"

"No."

She touched the icy bottle to the crook of his arm and he jumped, smiled at her, caught out of his trance. "Finish it here," she whispered, "and get a Coke."

She got another beer for herself, went back to Curtis. But the tenor of the party was already changing, friends of Curtis arriving, more beer. The s'mores were forgotten. People stood in groups, milling about farther from the fire. Sidra played hostess with Curtis tagging along, holding her tightly from behind in the circle of his arms whenever he could, chin hooked over her shoulder. Silly, but at least he seemed willing to ignore his stepbrother. It was the most she could hope for, especially with a guess at how much he'd been drinking. She drank a few herself.

Paul was circulating well, though Sidra felt him often hovering close by, his voice louder than necessary—that slightly fey invitation to overhear that Curtis's presence compelled from him. He was a small boy testing his own courage at a tiger cage, sticking an arm through the bars, pulling it back. The next time, a little longer. Maybe the tiger's sleeping, maybe he's not. She laughed, knowing Curtis was a pretty tame tiger as long as she was nearby.

Later they were back beside the embers, everyone gone but the core group, Sidra's familiars. Florie was on her way to bed, but Curtis waylaid her again to talk in a rambling way about her family land, these eighty acres of horse pasture held back from the developers, now half-surrounded by suburbs. How their bonfire had five acres at least on every side—how they were free to stretch in this place, the last wilderness. Sidra tuned him out, sat with Lyle again. Paul had taken a seat by Kent, whose guitar hadn't fallen silent for ten minutes all night.

Lyle and Jeff were arguing music, rating the new bands. Sidra yawned. Curtis was distracted enough that she thought she might safely join Paul now, listen to Kent for a while. He was on "Girl of My Dreams," an original, the soft drawl of his country songs stretching through his voice, and she remembered when she had been the Girl of the song, back when she'd first met Curtis, and Kent for a time had seemed to pursue her as well, visiting her with near-nightly serenades. Stupid to take it personally, she knew now. She was only one of many girls over the years who had melted into moony puddles while Kent simply went on playing, as if their adoration were all for the music.

Behind her now, Jeff and Lyle seemed to be discussing the very topic in her head. "Beth, huh?" Jeff said. "What about Beth? He was with that girl, like, a year. She was a babe. He was nuts about her."

"That was two years ago," Lyle said.

"So?"

"I'm just saying. It's not beyond possibility, is it?"

"Look, I'm not even having this conversation. I know him. I went to high school with him, okay? And he's as straight as your daddy, I promise you."

"Knowing him however long just makes you less observant, sorry to say." Lyle grabbed Sidra's shoulder and waggled it, grinning. "Sid'll back me up, won't you." His eyes jerked toward the scene beyond her.

Nearly out of the reach of firelight, Paul sat with his arms on his open knees, leaning close to Kent, saying something—she couldn't read his lips, but it was earnest, intent. Kent's head was down as he strummed tentatively into the next song. She looked away, looked back, just as Kent laughed at something Paul said, their eyes connecting sharply for a moment. She caught her breath, looked away. Paul was speaking again when she glanced back, and she knew what he was saying now, knew it as surely as if she could hear it: "You're really great, your music, it's gorgeous, I could listen to you all night. No, really, I mean it." Paul, who hated country music, considered it a personal affront. Or maybe her bright, feline boy would be wise enough to say something different, something Kent hadn't heard already from a hundred girls.

She glanced around. Florie was gone, Curtis dipping into the cooler for his last beer of the night. "Y'all shush!" she hissed at Jeff and Lyle, but their eyes were roving, leery, and she found herself grinning too, at the edge of giggles.

This was nothing, surely. Still, she beckoned to Curtis as he approached, sat him down in front of her with his back to the serenade. "We were just renaming the band," she announced on impulse, and Curtis was launched on his favorite track, already arguing over her shoulder to Jeff and Lyle.

Kent would begin a song and cut it short after a few lines, laughing, shaking his head, Paul answering with a grin and his eyes spading for Kent's, fingertips brushing his flannel sleeve lighter than breath—*go on*. Curtis kept blocking her view, and the band discussion canceled all other sound in waves. None of her business anyway.

She settled for the conversation around her, and tonight they let her join in on "band business" because only Curtis pursued it seriously; Jeff and Lyle, intent on a game of innuendo, slipped among reasonable-sounding names, needed her attendance. "The Receivers," Lyle suggested. "The Backtrackers," Jeff tried. "Manhole." Lyle stifled a laugh, and Sidra wanted to smack them both lopsided. But she didn't dare, with Curtis so far oblivious.

But here they were, her two boys, Curtis and Paul. It was something. She held both at once in sight, touched with the same faint glow, though Curtis was brighter and closer and had not yet acknowledged Paul's presence. Then Paul rose, leaned to speak close to Kent's ear. Three syllables—she could almost read them by firelight. They felt like part of the fire. But she must have closed her eyes the next second, because Paul was gone, vanished, Kent still gazing at the place where he had been.

A minute passed, and Kent laid the guitar flat in its case, as if at some signal that the party was over—and it was by now, should have been, the moon gone, the still-glowing coals no longer cutting the chill of the night air. Sidra was cold, sleepy. Kent walked out into the dark. Her eyes blinked open. How long had they been closed? Maybe she had dreamed Kent's leaving, without a glance at them, out toward the barn or maybe the back pasture. The guitar lay in its case, unattended.

"Bedtime, children," she announced sharply. "Douse those coals."

No one rose, and she was almost relieved, glad for the excuse to get to her feet. She went to the cooler. Only soft drink cans remained—she fished them out and set them out on the ground, then dipped her hands back into the thick ice water, slapped them against her face, over her eyes. Clouds moved gray against black over the trees, and out in the fields she could make out the shadow of the fence line, hear the brittle hiss of wind in the long grass.

She carried the cooler back to the fire, where the boys seemed dulled, oblivious—maybe they hadn't seen anything. Or were simply keeping quiet. The coals glowed with latent heat, with the very words she had witnessed on Paul's lips before he vanished, and as if the words might be visible for anyone's eyes, she hurled the ice and water over the coals. The sudden collision of elements made a sound at once soft and startling—like God saying *hush*. A steam cloud rose against the night.

territory

While they were looking for a new place to store their equipment and hold practice, the band moved temporarily into the Ballards' garage. The building was at a distance from the house and beginning to collapse, the once-folding doors more or less rusted in place. With slots for two cars, plus a shed tacked onto the back, it was home— now seemingly permanent—to Jimmy Ballard's '72 Chevy ("almost a classic," according to Sidra), as well as to various ancient pieces of farm machinery, bikes, old straw bales, cracked and dusty pieces of harness, and stacks of crumbling horse magazines. They cleared most of the junk from the second car slot and stacked it against the walls or back in the shed, then set up the drums beside one of the rusted bay doors. They brought in milk crates for chairs, and Sidra cleaned an old bench from the shed for audience seating.

Curtis had arranged their new studio without consulting any of them, even Sidra. It turned out he had spent much of the party pleading their case with Florie, and the others couldn't fail to sense his motives for laying this particular claim. But they needed a place, so now, one or two nights a week, sometimes Saturday afternoons, their cars pulled in to the Ballard driveway, and Kent, as he parked, glanced automatically toward the windows of the house. He watched the porch swing, where Paul sometimes sat with a book, and noticed with relief when the flesh-colored car was away. When it was there, Kent went straight to the curtained side door of the garage without lingering, without turning his eyes.

One afternoon he strolled alone down to the barn, looking for something that was nagging, indistinct. He knew that none of the others would have questioned his reasons. Kent was like that, they would have said, thoughtful, distracted—had a tendency to wander off by himself. It was a sunny afternoon, Paul's car gone, the horses out in the field. The barn stood empty, except for a thin, smoky tabby that appeared with throaty mews to rub against his leg. Overhead, the loft was just visible, a high platform burning with sunshine and dust. It seared him—all that light—made some deep, muddled emotion well up in his chest. He couldn't stand more than a glance in that direction. He turned his eyes down instead to the supplicant cat, which he figured for half grown, at least half wild—thought better of touching. It probably had ringworm, or something worse. Sweet as it looked, it might lash around and bite.

During practices, he was distant from every other concern, and sometimes he looked up to see that Paul was there in the garage, having slipped in without his notice. He'd pause to whisper to Sidra on her bench, stealing glances at the band, then move away as if it were unnatural for him to remain in one place for too long. Often he ducked back into the shed, all that shadowy space behind the slatted wall, until Kent started to become distracted with a constant sense that the boy was lurking back there, spying. Though they hadn't exchanged a word or look since the night of the fire, he felt certain that Paul's presence now, demanding in its silence, had to do with him.

I'll say something to run him off, Kent thought. But he hung back, until the night that Paul lingered too long in the open, once practice had finished.

"That last one you did, that Lurleen song," Paul said. "You wrote that, didn't you? I remember it, something like it."

Kent blinked up, surprised to hear him speak so casually, in front of Curtis. But Paul's eyes weren't on him, and besides, "Lurleen" was Curtis's song. It took Kent a minute to put the two things together. Curtis stood glowering at near-military attention, making and un-making fists against his thighs while Paul wandered through the garage, touching this and that—the edge of Jeff's guitar case, a drum-stick propped on the snare—like a lovestruck girl. He seemed hardly aware that Kent was in the room.

Jeff and Lyle had gone. Kent was stalling, strumming a few whis-pery bars on his unplugged Fender, and seeing now that the situation was something other than he'd imagined. Not pursued after all, he could safely look at Paul, who wore faded jeans and a green-and-blue checked shirt that looked like a Salvation Army find, the top few buttons open. Around his neck was a hemp choker woven with ivory beads and an-other, slightly longer, with tiny alternating blocks of amethyst and silver. Had he been wearing those by the fire? Kent tried to remember, but he'd successfully buried the whole night and left no marker.

"I've heard you play it before, at least. At home. Like, through the door, you know?" The corners of Paul's mouth quirked in brief, pri-vate, almost-blushing smiles at every one of Curtis's scowls, which were the extent of his responses. He trailed a forefinger lightly, in passing, over the first three knobs of Curtis's amp. "I always thought you were too shy—"

Curtis reacted before Kent could see it, lunged at Paul and shoved, his shout incoherent. *"You fuckin' touch—!"* Paul hurtled backward, tripping over the mike stand to the smooth concrete floor, gaining enough velocity to bump and skitter back a little way on his butt. He caught himself with his hands, so that he was almost sitting on the floor with his legs open and bent before him, and smiling—actually smiling! not broadly, but with a little curl in his lip, a smirk of anticipation—as Curtis surged in toward him with undirected aggression, as if he might stomp on him or kick him or land on top of him and hadn't yet decided which.

That lack of clear intention was the reason he stopped so easily, with no more than Kent's hand on his chest. Face flushed, breathing steam, Curtis looked as if rage had replaced words, turned to Kent and seemed a little scared, to find himself so suddenly at a loss.

"That's enough," Kent said. "Go cool off."

Curtis's eyes shifted back to Paul on the floor and anger flared again; every muscle flexed. He hocked and spit over Kent's arm, onto the concrete beside Paul's leg. Paul looked down at the sizzling wad and back at Curtis, who was already turning to walk out, muttering *goddamn faggot*.

"You okay?" Kent asked, once the door had smacked behind Curtis. He spoke as if addressing a stranger who had earned his casual disapproval. He held out a hand, hooked stiffly.

Paul heaved a sigh, took hold of Kent's hand, and rocked to his feet. Checking his elbows and palms for wounds, brushing dust from his backside, he seemed to avoid Kent's eyes. When he finally looked up, the ironic awareness in his steady gaze was more than a match for Kent's, reaching as it did beyond the present machinations to the night of the fire. One look, and everything that had passed between them lay open for view.

"You don't have to do that," Paul said dryly. "Protect me, or whatever."

Kent looked down at Paul's sneaker, the glob of spit that bubbled just beside it. "You sure about that?"

"You don't owe me anything, if that's what you think. He's my brother—"

"Stepbrother."

Paul glared. "We have issues, is all. It's private." He lifted his eyebrows, offered a crooked smile. "But thanks for caring."

Kent bristled at the boy's cocky contempt, which seemed, at the very least, unfair. But he kept his words businesslike, reasonable. "You'd be smart not to push him, you know?"

"Push?" Paul blinked. His fingertips tapped against his mouth. "I don't think I touched him. I think I would have remembered that."

Kent sensed he had begun a pointless project. He considered walking out with something offhanded. *Whatever. Your funeral.* But Paul didn't need to get away with pushing him too; and whatever else Kent might have felt, he had no fear of this kid.

"You know what I'm talking about."

"No, I don't," Paul fired back, but just as calm. Hands in the front pockets of his jeans, he stepped closer, his words spring-loaded. "Maybe you could explain it to me."

"For starters, there's the way you look at him."

"Really?" Paul tipped his head in mock fascination. "And how's that, love?"

The light from above the door caught the pale centers of Paul's irises, and Kent sucked a breath, stopped himself from flaring back. *You know exactly how!* He was in danger of sounding like a jealous boyfriend—best to keep quiet. Meanwhile he was struck by what seemed to be Paul's unfaltering poise—it was impressive, really—and also, almost at the same moment, with his sudden likeness to a particular actress, some perfectly boyish, petite little pixie-dyke of a movie star with upthrust pointed chin, whose name he couldn't recall.

He was staring, he realized too late, and Paul's keen expression faded in surprise. "Like that, you mean?"

Flustered, Kent started to shake his head, explain what he didn't mean. "All I'm saying is, you should be more careful. You could get hurt."

Paul didn't seem to be listening, though he watched Kent steadily, eyes softening. "You're actually really beautiful," he said, fading back at the same moment on reflexive steps, as if such words might trigger a fist from anywhere, swinging. "In a way."

He slipped along the edges of the room, his gait that continuous, familiar wandering, in and out of shadows, that seemed to keep him safe. But he looked at Kent now as he made the rounds, never moved his eyes. *Great*, Kent thought grimly. *Perfect*. Well, he had managed to get the boy's attention again—the last thing he'd thought he wanted.

what you see

Teeth clenched, breath hissing out in short bursts, he pounded himself into the girl. Each thrust was strong, definite, no mistaking his power or his presence. He was sweating, she was sweating—his left knee slipped back along the sheet, found purchase again.

Sidra was below, gasping, clawing at the pillow, then pulling it to her mouth, to keep quiet, but he didn't really see her—saw instead a red, murky haze, a dangerous nothing. He needed to see her, the straw-yellow hair spilling over her shoulders, across her chest. He pushed his hands up under her slick thighs, lifted them, her knees up to her chin. Her eyes were slits, jaw tight, mouth pressed closed. *See me*, he thought. *Look. Look hard.* "Ow," she said.

"Shove my head into the board, why don't you," she complained, when he was finished. "Christ, you don't think my mother can hear that?"

"I was quiet."

"Yeah, *sort* of, but the springs were going like crazy." She grinned. They had never been so rowdy under her mother's nose, and no matter how Sidra bitched, he knew the abandon of it pleased her. He dropped beside her on his back, smiled at her contentedly.

"Who's the man?" he asked.

"You are." She flipped over and crawled onto his chest, snuggled up under his chin. "And who turns you on?"

He pulled her long body up tight against his, stroked the curve where her lower back dipped and rose into her beautiful ass. "That would be you." With his other hand he lifted sections of her hair and draped them, arranged them, over his arm. Her hair felt amazingly good against his skin.

"Are you through being mad at me yet?"

He had to rouse himself from a sudden drowsiness. "Mad about what?"

"About Paul moving in here."

The name brought an instant scowl. "Goddamn—that little wanker! I don't want him in the garage when we're not around, Sid. I mean it. You *know* he goes in there and messes with our shit." He shook his head, made himself shut up—he knew what she would say.

"What would he do that for?"

"You don't know him, okay? You think you do, but . . . he's a first-class shit-ass weasel, is what he is. You know how he messes with me." He was getting angry all over again, angry especially that there seemed to be no words to explain to Sidra the truth of what he felt so strongly.

"Just now," he tried, already sensing the futility of the effort, "he's out there trying to talk to me! His usual namby-pamby faggoty-ass bullshit, and he's got his fucking hands on everything in the room! Do you know, I mean, do you have any *idea*, how expensive that equipment is?"

"Just talk back to him, hon," Sidra said. "It won't hurt you."

He was silent a moment. "I can't." He looked down at her, folded a strand of hair back from her hopeful face. "I know, you're right. Sure—in theory. But when it comes right down to it. I mean, honestly, the only reason I didn't cream his ass just now is Kent was right there."

"Kent?" Her eyes went round, as if it Kent's presence were somehow noteworthy.

"Yeah, you know, right after practice. Stopped me from—" He gritted his teeth, shook his head. "Whatever. But right in front of me, okay, the pansy's turning knobs on my amp! You fucking believe that?"

Sidra sighed, burrowed against his chest. "If you'd just talk to him like a person, he'd back off."

"No. He wouldn't. He'd just worm up closer. He'd be on his knees in two seconds asking pretty please for my dick." He met her eyes again, cracked a smile—he even laughed a little at his own thought. There, now let her call him a homophobe.

She swatted his chest. "You're awful."

A floorboard creaked out in the hall. Curtis tensed, his grip tightened on Sidra's back. "That's him," he whispered. "That prick's listening."

"That could be my mother," she said, scowling when he tried to shush her, "come to see what all the noise is! Or Paul's just walking by. Or the dogs, for Christ's sake."

They kept still, listening, silent for several minutes. "He's asking for it," Curtis whispered. "You deny he's asking me to kill him?"

"That's not funny, honey."

"You hear me laughing?"

worse ways to go

The boys' cars were lined up in the driveway when Sidra got off work, though she heard no sounds from the garage. It was ten-thirty. They'd be in there practicing another half-hour, maybe an hour, then she'd lure Curtis out for a drink—a big margarita, she was thinking. Lots of salt. Maybe a pitcherful. She bolted straight upstairs for a quick shower.

Paul's door was open, and she glanced in to find him sprawled upside down on the bed, his head at the mattress edge. A skinny book was poised over his face. "Hi, honey, I'm home," she called, breezing in. She bent to plant a smacker kiss on his mouth. "You taste like grape soda."

"I know, isn't it gross? But I get these cravings." He rolled onto his side languorously, an arm stretched out under his head, the book closed on his finger. "Can I be you when I grow up?"

She giggled. "Why do you say that?"

"Because you're gorgeous."

"Oh, pish. Really, you know, I'm *raw*ther plain." She flipped the long hair back theatrically from her shoulder. "And at the moment I smell like food." Sitting beside him, she peered at the title of his book. "*Winesburg, Ohio.* Why, may I ask?"

Outside, below Paul's window, the drum started up, sputtered and stalled. "It's not that bad," he said. "It's about apples—how sometimes the twisted little apples are the sweet ones."

"You'd know about that, wouldn't you?" She went to the window and looked down onto the garage, yellow lights emanating from the small square windows on the two visible sides. A shadow shifted within. Three sharp drum cracks, and they rolled into a muffled song—an R. E. M. cover.

"How can you read with all the noise?"

"I like it," he said, with a softness that made her turn to meet his eyes. He looked sad, pensive—that expression, open for her to see, made her own chest tighten. She had never been able to ask him what had happened with Kent, or what he had wanted to happen. She had not heard another suggestive peep from Jeff or Lyle, as if their collective speculations at the party had, after all, come to nothing. "Did I tell you how happy I am," he said, "to be here?"

She didn't disbelieve him, though he didn't smile. She nodded, waiting.

"Do you think—" he dropped his eyes, picked at invisible threads in the comforter, Marcy's comforter, Marcy's old bed—"that Curtis is getting, I don't know, used to me being around?"

Oh Lord, she thought. "Sweetie—" He frowned, pressed his forehead against his arm on the bed, as if to discourage her too-tender approach or whatever she was about to say next. "Paul. Don't hope for so much, okay? Please. You know, if he'll just ignore you, that might be the best you can get out of him."

He nodded, opened the book, and creased the page carefully along the spine. She looked at the cover again. "I think I actually read that once." He looked up with guarded curiosity, and she went on. "Someone made me read it in college. You know what I remember? That guy, Sherwood Anderson? Died by choking on a toothpick!"

"Really?" He smiled, laid his cheek on the bed.

She laughed. "Can you believe that? And that's the one thing I can remember about that book. Isn't that a shitty death for a famous writer guy? Or, hell, for anyone, I guess."

"I could think of worse ways to go." Paul raised the book again, his face still resting flat on the comforter. She wondered if the tough floss of the stitching would leave a pattern on his cheek. She went to take a shower, touching his hair on her way past.

When she got out of the bathroom, in a robe with a towel twisting up her wet hair, Paul's light was out, the door still gaping open. But he wasn't inside. She walked in, over to the window. Below she could hear the voices of the boys, Kent's and Jeff's, outside the garage—practice breaking up early. Yellow light from the garage still lit the yard and part of the driveway where they stood talking, Jeff calling back as he walked up the drive. Kent moved along the tall hedgerow toward his car—Sidra could see the keys in his hand—when he stopped abruptly at the point where the hedge ended. Another shadowy figure stood before him, blond in the trace light, might have been Curtis if he weren't standing so suddenly close.

Sidra caught her breath, ducked back, and peered past the curtains, though they couldn't have seen her up in the darkened room. What were they doing? Talking, it seemed. Kent, the dark head, perfectly still; Paul in motion around him—sidling up close, rocking away. She could see his folded elbows held in his hands, as if the game allowed no touching, but there was an intimate tilt to his head, especially as he leaned close to speak. She recalled the three fire-wrought syllables she had seen in his mouth that night—was it nearly three weeks ago?—before she flung ice to the coals.

Sidra was so absorbed in fear and hope and suspense, hardly knowing what she wanted to see, that she forgot to watch for Curtis. The garage lights flicked off and he came striding out the side door, toward the hedge. Kent and Paul were in the shadows just ahead, and she didn't have time to check to see whether they had reacted to sound or the lights going out. Her hand smacked against the window. She rapped hard with her fist, until Curtis stopped to look up, and she tugged at the sash, forcibly hauled the sticky window open to the cool night air.

"Hey," she called down, bright as bells. She didn't dare shift her eyes from Curtis's upturned face, his smile at the sight of her. "I'm here! I'm clean! I want a margarita!"

who you are

Walk with me, Paul had said. That was all. Fingers stilled on the guitar strings, Kent had looked up—the mutter of voices, Curtis, Sidra, Jeff, Lyle, audible nearby—to see the boy's face haloed in a blurry heat, or maybe it was wood smoke from the dying fire. One look, passed along his shoulder as he went away, not waiting for a response. And Kent, unthinking, had followed.

Walk with me? he said now, with the question mark added, waylaying Kent by the dark hedgerow after practice—why more tentative on a second approach? This time Kent refused, without hesitation. But he didn't move away. *Kiss me*, Paul said, like a challenge, upping the ante with his uptilted chin, and Kent couldn't help smiling and maybe hesitating a little before he answered with the same simple, inflexible *No*.

He found himself now, more and more, trying to bring back the forgotten night. What, for instance, had he been thinking, to say yes to those three words? He had only the three words to go on: an invitation for a walk. It might have meant no more than that; it might have meant anything. But it didn't matter. The command itself was magnetic, and Kent didn't think.

He left the fire behind and ducked through a fence, into the near pasture where the grass had grown long, ungrazed. He couldn't see the ground before him, could barely distinguish the dark shape of the barn at the end of the field. But he kept walking, and Paul was suddenly before him in the path, waiting, hands on his hips like Peter Pan. He had been running—the sound of his breath came that fast. But as Kent approached, it changed to breathy laughter, and before Kent reached him, Paul turned and ran again, laughing out loud once the dark had swallowed him.

Kent ran too, chased him. His own laughter joined Paul's in the night air, weird and alien. It felt like something tearing him as it ripped loose, a thing freakishly separate from him because nothing was funny. His chest ached with the effort to breathe, to keep quiet. But the sound of his laugh grew lighter until it was weightless, rising around them on bat wings.

Paul, just ahead—pervert, hustler, Antichrist—only a picked handful of Curtis's words for him. "You're *Paul*," Kent had said baldly, after a moment's confusion, when the boy had introduced himself at the fire. Though wise enough not to expect anything like accuracy from Curtis, he was nonetheless startled to be faced with a human being, one who looked so scrubbed, the hair glittering brightly where it swept back from his temples. Paul had laughed at his reaction. "Am I that famous?" Now it was the same spontaneous, boyish laughter that drew him, that was tangled with the breathing from just ahead.

Kent followed the sound into the barn where Paul vanished, where the darkness deepened, and he couldn't tell a shadow from a solid thing. He stopped, started forward again, hand trailing a rough wall. Close by, a horse blew, took muffled steps. He could smell the animal's flesh, the quick sweat of his own skin. He didn't know if he was chasing a shadow or becoming one, stilling his breath so he could melt into darkness; but he moved slowly forward until he felt himself enter a sort of balance with the dark, and his hands lashed out. Before his eyes ever adjusted, he had hold of the boy, both upper arms in his grip.

Paul let out a startled sound—a thin, girlish squeal. "Hold still," Kent said, though Paul didn't struggle. The only answer was a deepening of breath, and Kent thought he could feel it, warm and then cool against his throat. He let go, stepped back. Afraid the boy might bolt again, he left the fingers of one hand resting on the white shirt, which was gauzily visible, all he could see. Then he took the hand away too.

In letting go, the tight ache of his chest eased a little, and Paul relaxed as well. "What are we doing out here?" Kent asked, the echo of the laugh ringing his voice. Perhaps they were conspiring in some prank against the others.

"Why are you whispering?" Paul whispered.

"I don't know. The horses. Why do you keep laughing?"

"I can't help it."

"Tell me the joke."

"I'll tell you later. Maybe." Paul stepped closer, brushed slowly past. "I want to show you something."

He took Kent's hand as he passed, took hold of it firmly and easily and offered no alternative, as if this were the normal way for one man to guide another through a dark place. He led him to a ladder and began to climb. Above was a blackness the quality of velvet, and even the white shirt was consumed as it rose. How odd it felt to hold the boy's hand, odder still to be released so suddenly, to be climbing now higher than he thought the barn should go, as if they were no longer in the place where they'd started. But he never felt as if he were falling, even when the ladder ended and he was pulling himself up onto a platform that he couldn't see, into a loose bed of hay that he could only feel and smell under his hands. Where Paul waited.

In that absolute black silence, unruptured by anything other than touch, he could have been anywhere, with anyone. He might have been drunk or half-dreaming in his own bed, and Paul, when he reached him, found him, might have been a girl for all the skin his fingers found—taut rib cage, shallow gully of spine, flank in denim. By touch, inhabitants of a sightless world, they became something other—a meeting of bodies, of mouths, and then only Paul's mouth, on his throat, his chest and stomach. So slow and careful, even tender, as if they knew each other.

What happened in the loft was more than Kent wanted and more, he knew now, than where it ended—the somehow-canceling act of fellatio. He recalled the very quality of the boy's skin.

Weeks later, musing over these recovered details he had all-too-willingly banished, he repeated his own first words from the fire. *You're Paul.* But what had he really said, in the loft? It was only Paul he remembered speaking, once the spell was broken. Had it been those words, rather than the act itself, that canceled it all, reduced it to a perfunctory transaction? *Well, babe . . .* He'd lifted himself out of Kent's embrace, where he had been lying afterward, face notched in the hollow below Kent's bare shoulder. *That's one I think I'll remember—blowing a straight boy.* He laughed with the same soft lilt, almost a giggle, and not unkind, that Kent had been hearing all night. *How about you? Something to tell the grandkids?* By then, Kent's brain had been static, ooze. He'd barely registered the rustle of the boy finding his shirt in the hay, slipping it on to go.

But they had made love, in a way, no matter how either tried to deny it. And it was Paul's mouth that had met him in that place, Paul who laid him back in the hay so that he never had to decide what he would do or what he wanted. He hadn't needed to do anything at all, it turned out, not even say yes to this, only breathe and release himself fully to the shadow he was in.

advice

When Sidra answered the phone Sunday afternoon—Kent, asking for Paul—the request seemed to her almost expected, a normal thing, touched by her own secret thrill of a voyeur's proximity to high-school romance. *She said that he said that Tommy said that Fred likes you!*

"He went home"—Sidra's best phone voice, full of casual, chatty ebullience—"to his folks', but he'll be back tonight. You want me to tell him you called?"

"Um—" The line fell to silence, as if she had asked a difficult question, and maybe she had. "I don't know," he stammered. "No, I guess not. It's nothing." He paused. "I don't actually know why I'm calling, I just—"

She waited through his next silence, heard him breathe. "Sidra, let me ask you," he said, earnest now, dropping all pretense in a heap. "I shouldn't be doing this, should I? Shouldn't be calling. Shouldn't be . . . anything."

"Oh, I don't know about that."

"Okay, seventeen—that's awful young, isn't it? I mean, *too* young." He spoke as if already convinced, handing her a position clearly marked, so that she could talk him out of this. He was right, of course. They both knew the reasons it was a bad idea, reasons that didn't begin and end with age.

"Well, Paul's not at all your usual kid," she heard herself argue. "He's insanely smart, for starters. I forget all the time he's not as old as me."

"I had that idea, but . . . I don't know."

"Kent, honey?" she said finally, when it seemed he might have become permanently lost. "How 'bout I just tell him you called?"

And that was it, the call. When Paul returned, she reported every word.

"Well," he said, with nothing more revealing than a secretive smile. For a minute he was thoughtful, chewing the nail of his pinkie. "Guess I'll have to call him back," he said brightly.

Monday evening after dinner, Paul was on the phone in the kitchen. Sidra stood in the den behind the love seat, brushing her grandmother's hair, long strokes back from her forehead with a soft brush. At eighty-one, the woman had nearly a full head of hair, though it was so fine and white that the liver and purple and charcoal spots on her scalp were visible at each stroke. Calmed by the brushing, she sat quietly examining her nails in her lap, which her granddaughter had just trimmed and filed. Sidra didn't have to make much of an effort not to eavesdrop, since Paul's voice was audible only when he laughed.

"Well?" she shouted, once he had finally hung up. "Give me details."

He came into the room and dropped onto the overstuffed ottoman in front of the old woman, a smile flattened between his teeth. "He wants to cook me dinner. Is that hilarious?"

Sidra frowned. "No, I think it's sweet. Why shouldn't he cook you dinner?" She continued brushing, while her grandmother examined Paul's face with mild, vague eyes.

"It's just, gawd, I don't know." Nose wrinkled with displeasure, he nibbled the nail. "It's so—"

"Romantic?"

Paul pantomimed sticking a finger down his throat to gag. "More like stupid. Like he's trying to be all respectable, or something. I mean, I am not Molly Ringwald, okay? This ain't *Pretty in Pink*."

She laughed. "Don't tell me no one's ever cooked for you."

"Hell, no." He scowled. "Well, okay, there was this one guy. Loser. Always trying to get me to eat, and these fancy gourmet meals. I mean, please. I don't have the time."

"But you're going."

He shrugged, a small, guilty smile slipping past. Sidra singsonged, "Paul's got a boyfriend!"

"Shut up," he muttered. "Do not." He lifted a bottle of seashell pink nail polish from the end table, turned it over studiously. Elbows on his knees, he gazed up at Sidra. "What do you think? Of Kent?"

"Kent's great. He's a great musician—"

"Doesn't he just look like one of those J. Crew guys?" Paul said with sudden enthusiasm. "Not that fakey, plastic kind of gorgeous, but like he ought to be out camping in the woods or something. You know what I mean? Someone you can touch, get your hands on. Like, he's *real*."

"Real?"

Paul nodded gravely, silent for a minute. "But honestly, the whole thing is too weird. Don't you think so?" His voice took on the same false assurance she'd heard in Kent's—handing her the invitation to play devil's advocate.

"Well. I guess he's a little old for you."

Paul scoffed at that. "Twenty-six? Honey, that ain't close to old. I mean, when you look like this—" he swiveled a wrist in a casual, splay-handed sweep, body to face, rolled his eyes. "Sidra, you don't even want to know what I get. I'm midlife crisis bait. Guys with bald spots and kids and two mortgages and a Porsche!"

She paused in her brushing, tsked her tongue as if to speak, but nothing came. After such stark admissions, she never knew whether her job was to scold or offer a sermon or inquire further or keep her mouth shut.

"I mean because of Curtis," Paul clarified. "I was thinking. I mean, what's he going to do, if he finds out?"

She stopped brushing. Paul's solemn, staring eyes looked ready to be awed by revelation—what *would* Curtis do? "Like, Kent is his best friend, isn't he?" he went on. "I mean, really, out of all those guys, Kent's the one—"

"He won't find out," she said firmly, hammering both T's. "You'll be very, very careful, and he won't know anything about it. Until he's ready." Even at her last concession, Paul didn't blink. Sharply maternal all of a sudden, she added, "You hear what I'm saying?"

"Oh, I hear. He won't find out." Paul sighed. His eyes fell on the grandmother's fingers, and he gently lifted one hand from her lap, touched her nails. She smiled down at him, and he smiled back, searching her eyes. "You want me to paint them?"

She made no response, but went on smiling benevolently. Paul glanced at Sidra, shook the bottle of seashell pink so that the silver balls inside rattled. He began slowly stroking the pale color over the nail of her index finger, checking her face after each stroke for response. Sidra put the brush away and sat beside her grandmother.

"That guy Lyle, the drummer?" Paul said, the speckled and twisted hand balanced lightly across his palm as he worked.

"Lyle's a sweetie."

"No kidding. He's got a crush on you, darlin'."

"Please!"

"You ought to be with someone nicer than Curtis," he murmured, looking at the grandmother and not her. "That will be pretty, won't it?"

The woman watched her hand as if it were separate from her, a photograph of a kind face she remembered from long ago. She held it stretched and still but for a little trembling. "Yes," she said. "Very pretty."

"You do nice work," Sidra told him.

"Don't I though?" He cast her a playful glance. "I am going out tonight."

"You always took good care of me," the grandmother announced in a loud voice. Clearly she was addressing Paul.

Paul almost laughed but caught himself. "Is that right?"

"And your voice," she went on, each word carefully pronounced, though strained and out of tune. "What a voice for a child! You sang like an angel. Sing something for us, dear. What is that hymn I like so? About have thine own way, Lord—"

Paul halted the manicure and gave Sidra a pointed look, eyebrows raised.

"She thinks you're Marcy," Sidra whispered.

Paul's humor vanished. Open-mouthed, he continued to stare at Sidra, spooked, waiting for guidance or rescue. She shook her head with a slow shrug. Swallowing, he pressed his lips closed and went back to the manicure. The next stroke wobbled a little from cuticle to tip.

"Have thine own way, Lord—" The grandmother's brow folded in distress. "You remember, dear."

Without warning Paul began to sing, softly and on key. "*Have thine own way, Lord. Have thine own way.*" Sidra smiled and joined him. They sang a few lines together—"*Thou art the potter, I am the clay*"— but Sidra had forgotten most of the words she had learned so long ago, and Paul finished alone. "*Mold me and make me after thy will, while I am waiting, yielded and still.*"

The old woman's gaze remained fond and distant, registering neither the song nor its conclusion. A silence fell for several minutes after. Paul completed one hand, each nail smoothly coated and blemish-free except for a few wavy brushstrokes. He blew on the nails a little, then handed the task of drying to Sidra.

He was about to begin the second hand, when the old woman caught his eyes, leaned toward him with a confiding air. "I know I'm old, dear," she said with effort. "I know I'm a little foggy sometimes. Out of touch with how things are now. But you're too young to date."

Paul betrayed no amusement but leaned closer, nearly on his knees before the ottoman, as if to catch a glimpse in her face of whatever she saw. Wry now, almost humorous, she tipped her head toward Sidra. "Same goes for that one."

law of gravity

Wednesday evening, when he opened the door to let Paul in, Kent knew something was wrong. It sent a little quiver through his gut, made him want to steer the boy back out into the hall, to say it had all been a mistake. "Hi," he said instead, and Paul said "hi," ducking his head a little, tilting it to peer sideways past Kent and into the apartment. Kent stepped back and Paul moved in fluidly, hands in the front pockets of black jeans. He wore a soft-looking gold shirt, cuffs buttoned, tails loose, and a bright spot from the track lighting balanced in his hair as he wandered through the room. His eyes roved with interest over the stereo equipment, the plush cream-colored sofa, the hardwood floor, and twelve-foot ceiling with windows that stretched nearly the full height, looking out onto the shops and bars of Clayton Street, the center of downtown Athens.

"Wow," Paul said. "Nice. How do you afford all this?"

"It's a sublet. It's temporary."

"That figures." He picked up a blue pillow from the sofa, turned it over. "Doesn't look like you. You mind me saying so?"

Kent stiffened reflexively but shook his head. "No, I guess not."

Paul's tour took him to the end of the room and the abbreviated hall that led to the bedroom. "It's smaller than it looks," Kent added, as Paul took a peek around the corner, turned to grin at Kent, to meet his eyes for the first time—not lurid exactly, but something expect-ant there, waiting. Crossing his arms, he made a little gesture with his mouth that Kent couldn't read, didn't know if he was meant to—as if shifting a wad of gum from one side to the other. Maybe it was unconscious, meaningless.

"The guy who owns the building—it's his place," Kent said. "I'm just watching it for a while." He looked at his shoe. Paul strolled back to the stereo and began examining the long shelves of CDs. "It's a pretty good deal, for as long as it lasts."

Paul seemed engrossed in reading titles, one finger paging casu-ally through the cases. Kent, at ten paces, stared at the side of the boy's face, then allowed his eyes to drift down, to imagine the line of the slender body through the clothes while he tried to decide if he felt anything like desire under his numbing, unfocused fear. He wasn't entirely sure how he'd reached this decision, to bring Paul here.

Paul picked up a small framed photograph. "Whose sailboat?"

"Mine," Kent said. "Well, she will be, once I get the money. Kind of a junker, but—" He felt himself ready to launch into some emo-tional reverie about childhood sailing trips and stopped himself. "You, uh, want something to drink?"

Paul looked up from his examination of the boat and smiled, said sure. "Pick out some music," Kent said. But Paul followed him to the kitchen, where the makings of dinner were spread on the counters, and leaned in the doorway watching. Kent felt the boy's eyes as he gazed blindly into the refrigerator, thinking, *Just dinner. A casual thing. Nothing has to happen.*

"There's tea, Coke, beer." Could he offer Paul a beer? It seemed ridiculous now to think he was too young. But he was—too young. He went on gazing into the bright case as if he would eventually see something else to offer.

"What's that?" Paul nodded toward a bottle of red wine that Kent had set out on the counter, a corkscrew beside it. "How 'bout we open that baby up?"

"Oh. Yeah, good idea." He opened the bottle. Paul peered at the dishes, a long pan of lasagna, bread wrapped in tinfoil, a wooden bowl of dark green salad already tossed.

"You, uh, want to reach into that cabinet over your head? The wine glasses are up there."

"Looks pretty fancy, all this food." Paul retrieved two glasses.

"It's not, actually. Just easy stuff." He poured one glassful carefully, passed it to Paul, and they held the glass for an awkward second between them as if it were in danger of falling. Kent laughed, moved past so that they switched places in the narrow kitchen. "I'll turn on the oven. Dinner will be a little while, I guess."

Paul sipped his wine against the counter, watching Kent over the rim of his glass. Barely turning his eyes, he reached back one-handed for the bottle and poured the second glass, splashing a bit on the counter. "It's good. Try some." He held out the full glass, and Kent saw the irony in the boy's eyes going full bore, locking into him, saying, *You need this. Drink up.*

Kent sipped the wine. They watched each other with seriousness now, the polite veils of host and guest having fallen away in one direct look from Paul.

"You know, you didn't have to do all this," Paul said with a diffident tilt of his head. "Cook dinner. We could just—"

"What?"

"Fuck."

Kent's heart stuttered at the bluntness of the word, but he was determined not to react—he wasn't about to let a mere schoolboy shock him. "I thought maybe we could talk."

"*Talk?*" Now it seemed it was Paul's turn to be shocked, though he tried to pass it off as more irony. And Kent saw him completely in an instant, like revelation, Paul's eyes darkening as he sidestepped without apparent intention and wandered a few feet across the kitchen to brush the opposite counter.

"Talk," Kent repeated, smiling. "Have a conversation. Eat some dinner. You don't ever get hungry?"

Paul sighed elaborately, his sweet smile quickly composed. "Whatever you want, babe. I'm game." He sipped his wine. "So what do we talk about? Sports? Politics? Global deforestation? Alien abductions?" He seemed oddly to relax as he spoke, his smirkiness draining away until the topics he offered sounded sincere, almost hopeful. "My sex life? My arrest for prostitution? Any of that . . . interest you?"

"You interest me," Kent said.

Visibly stricken—terrified, almost—Paul had to close his eyes for two seconds and breathe. Kent felt a twinge of tenderness, the urge to go to him, touch him, or maybe just ask if that was so hard to believe. But he continued casually, with his back against the oven. "How do you like living at the Ballards?"

"It's all right." Paul brightened—grateful. "They're nice, really nice, to take me in. The curfew sucks, but I had that at home."

A few sentences, and Paul became animated. As if stepping under a spotlight, he performed a few bits he might have rehearsed: dinner conversations at the Ballard table; Florie's halting efforts to sound at ease discussing sex; the grandmother who thought he was Sidra's sister, back from the dead. His stories were funny and at the same time strangely sad, full of misunderstandings, failed connections. Kent watched, laughing now and then, drawn to the drama of the boy's face as he spoke. He was truly beautiful, in flashes; the next instant, no more than ordinary.

Paul wandered closer to stand beside him, pausing to reach for a bowl on the counter. "What's this?" He lifted a corner of foil.

"That"—Kent peeked with him—"was supposed to be salmon mousse. I gave up on it. Not that I know what I'm doing, but I don't think it turned out right."

"Never had salmon mousse." Paul dipped a finger, dragged it through the pinkish goo. "This is my first time." He took the finger into his mouth, pulled it slowly out, his eyes on Kent's. He moved closer, as if by gravity—Kent didn't know which of them had actually moved, only that he felt a little dizzy, a little panicked, as in a dream of falling, and Paul's mouth was the only ground.

Dinner cooking, and they were in the half-lit bedroom, caught between the door and the bed, clawing at buttons and zippers, tangled in sleeves, heels snagged on pants cuffs. There was no sound but quick breath, whispers that ended before making sense—"there" "don't" "here" "wait"—as if speed were crucial. It seemed to take forever to undress, threatened to become comical—Kent almost thought they would start laughing and fall in a heap on the floor. Then, of course, they would regain their senses, put a halt to this.

But no one laughed, nothing stopped, only moved swiftly to the bed, where he glimpsed Paul above him naked in silhouette, Paul glowing along the tapered line of his hip, his thigh, where the light of the hall caught in the fine down of his skin. Kent wanted to hold that image still, if only for a moment, to get his bearings, but there was no stillness possible, only the ferocious speed, building, a roller coaster, and if someone threw the switches it was Paul, Paul guiding them through a tangle of bedsheets and producing a condom, Paul who hissed "Yes," against Kent's half-uttered resistance and kissed him deeply and put the condom on him and there was no choice, it seemed now, and never had been but to give Paul his way. So there it was—difficult at first, awkward, but soon it was simply sex, mechanical and glorious and done.

Beneath him, the boy lay breathing, filmed in sweat, mouth open against the pillow. Something—the smell of him, the hard little body still turned toward the bed—or maybe it was something else entirely, but it struck Kent without warning, a revulsion so primordial, so physical, that it erased thought. Nothing had been spoken and Kent still didn't speak, only separated himself delicately. Naked, he went out to the hall, into the bathroom, closed the door and locked it. He held himself upright over the sink for a moment, eyes closed in concentration, before he folded before the toilet and vomited.

Later he heard Paul's voice at the door, softly. He didn't answer, though Paul called a second time.

Much later, he went to the kitchen and opened the oven, which was only warm, the baked lasagna cooling inside—Paul must have turned it off on his way out. He closed the oven, thought of cleaning up but left all the food where it lay. Though he moved gingerly, his stomach seemed to recover with amazing speed, to turn solid, even flicker with a feathery hint of hunger. In an hour, he might be well enough to eat.

Done. Over. Gone. So quickly. Of course, Paul had left—Kent could hardly blame him. He sat on the sofa and hugged himself, remembering the glow along the boy's skin, one image held against a miserable welter of self-loathing and confusion. It was the mousse. Had to be. He'd tried it earlier, thought it tasted funny, maybe the mayonnaise turned. Maybe Paul would be sick too, later, and then, then he would understand.

nude at the gates of hell

In the restless days that followed, Kent began walking rather than driving the two miles to the Science Library, where he managed the computer system. His walk took him from the downtown shops that surrounded his apartment, across Broad Street, and through the black iron arch to the campus. Past the green, deep magnolia and oak shade of the quad, he crossed more roads, passed the stadium. Students with backpacks were everywhere, quiet in the mornings in their light coats and hiking boots. In the afternoons, on his way back home, he passed them posed under trees with books or throwing frisbees across the quad. Downtown again, college kids moved among wandering home-less men and sedentary clusters of street kids—those suburban high-schoolers who panhandled and tried to look homeless—and Kent passed through them all with long, steady strides to his apartment.

It was more than a week before these walks, meant to clear his head, yielded a glimpse of Paul. He was just ahead by two storefronts, com-ing out of Rocky's Pizza, and laughing back over his shoulder—it was the lilt in the laugh that reached him first. A man followed just be-hind, a swarthy Hispanic who promptly leaned in with a mustached face to kiss Paul good-bye.

The scene halted Kent, made him gasp like a blow to the gut. It was no more than an affectionate peck, slightly off-center and returned—the way Kent's mother kissed her lady friends at luncheons. Part of him even stood back and admired it (two guys, in the middle of downtown, mid-afternoon—that was balls). The man departed, leaving Paul stalled a moment facing Kent, and by then it was too late to look away, for either of them to pretend they hadn't seen the other.

What now? There was nothing between him and this person, just a meaningless encounter or two—exactly as Paul had planned it, Kent was certain. There was nothing to justify jealousy or his painfully adolescent need to escape. He might have simply done that, walked away without a word, except for something in Paul's eyes—a mirrored wince in the recognition.

It was Kent who finally spoke, who said something about coffee, and then they were drifting together down the block to a café on College Square. Inside were smoky, high ceilings and exposed brick. An exhibit of charcoals hung on the walls, corpselike nudes with fiercely blackened eyes and mouths. Paul headed for the restroom. Kent took a table near the back, found himself staring at a long-limbed man, sprawled upside down and perhaps masturbating, his mouth the howl of a black, gaping abyss. Against the corded muscle and contours of the flesh, the skeleton shaded faintly.

Even if he had, on some level, been looking for Paul, he hadn't planned this meeting. Now he wanted to get up quickly and leave. What was there to say? He felt intensely that he should be home by now, closed up safely in his lofted rooms. But Paul had returned, still not speaking a word, his hand fallen in a hesitant caress along the back of the opposite chair.

"I'm sorry," Kent blurted, "really sorry, about the other night. I don't know why—"

Paul slipped into the chair. "It's all right."

Kent nodded, hands flat on the table. It was a weird relief to have the boy sitting across from him. Paul started to smile and Kent rose, the chair clattering back. "You want some coffee or something?"

"Mocha cappuccino."

"I'll get it. You wait here?"

Paul tucked his chin, made that sly, shifting motion with his mouth again, offered no other answer. Kent took a few hesitant steps toward the counter and looked back; the boy hadn't moved.

Once the machine had labored through their orders, Kent delivered two cappuccinos to the table. "Thanks," Paul said and put his hands on his cup. They faced each other without eye contact, but leaning in toward the lamp light at the table's center.

"I need to know something," Paul said after a time. "And, well, I'm just going to ask. Was it so awful? You know, that—"

"No," Kent said. "No. It wasn't awful."

"Okay. But you won't look at me."

Kent lifted his eyes, straight into Paul's intimate gaze, so close across the small table, and felt a little queasy. God, what was wrong with him? "You probably think I'm some kind of virgin," he said, glancing down at his cup. "I guess I am, really. I had this roommate in college once. We would mess around, you know, get drunk first for an excuse. Nothing serious. There was one other time. I met this guy, out somewhere. I was so drunk I don't remember what we did. I think that incident just scared the shit out of me, maybe."

"I know you date girls." Paul's fingertip traced the rim of his cup. "You like girls?"

"Sure, I guess. Not so much lately." The crowded coffeehouse dimmed and blurred around them, and Kent forgot to wonder who was there and eyeing them, perhaps eavesdropping, forgot to imagine what anyone thought. "How about you?"

Paul laughed in surprise. "Me?"

"I mean—" Kent stumbled. "That guy you were with. Is he, like, your boyfriend or something?"

"Raoul? God, no. I don't have a boyfriend. I don't really believe in the concept. He's just a guy, a friend, I guess. If that."

"You sleep with him?" Kent's voice had fallen to almost a whisper, but he forced himself to meet Paul's eyes.

Paul hesitated. "No. I mean not . . . yet, at least."

"It's not my business."

"No, no, it . . . you can ask me anything you want." Paul laid his knuckles to his lips, dropped the fingertips to brush over Kent's hand, which rested on the table—so light he could barely feel it. "I'll tell you anything."

Kent was silent. Paul's brow bunched. "You have to understand what it's like for me. Being here, this town, it's a new world. I feel like I can breathe. I feel normal."

"That's funny," Kent said bleakly. "I feel the opposite."

Paul leaned closer. "Look, I don't know if you want to hear this. But I want to tell you. I used to have sex in cars mostly, for money— I didn't know any other way to meet guys who wanted me. But here. It's easier here, you know? I've met, oh, so many men. Nice men. Beautiful. Some, sure, it's twenty minutes in a bathroom stall, but others I spend time with, get to know a little. I've been in love maybe three or four times in the past three months."

His nostalgic gaze had gone beyond the table somewhere, and Kent's stomach tensed as if he had actually left, perhaps risen to walk the gantlet he imagined now—rows and rows of men that waited between their table and the restroom. Stop, he wanted to say. But he couldn't speak, couldn't say that he wouldn't hear more, that this was all clearly a mistake.

"But I haven't met anyone like you," Paul said. "Not even close." He paused to register Kent's stunned expression, sipped his cooling drink. "Put it this way. I'm not giving up on you yet."

Kent drew a few short, gasping breaths, an unsuccessful effort to laugh. "What if I don't give you the choice?"

"You will."

Paul was all confidence now, certain enough for both of them, and Kent looked down at his own callused fingers on the table, felt them both bowing their heads this way over the closing space between them. There was nothing he could do. His skin flushed hot and cold, and he felt intensely that he needed to leave, that he was ill. "I don't know why I'm even here," he said. "I don't think I'm in control of this."

Paul smiled. "Good."

"You're too young."

"I have experience. It equals out."

"You're—" Did Paul need to hear the list of all he was? Kent searched the smoke haze along the ceiling for some kind of deliverance, but felt only the agonized gazes of the nudes, from every wall—"oh, God, in every way, the last person I should feel this way about. I feel like I'm losing my mind." He laughed under his breath. "This is ridiculous. Isn't it?"

Paul watched him with a heated, tender look that belonged in a bedroom. "Are you finished?"

"Yes."

"Then walk me to my car. I gotta be home for dinner."

neverland

When Sidra returned to her bedroom, having fetched a couple of beers from the kitchen, Curtis was on the phone. He sat on the edge of her neatly made bed with its sea-green ruffled skirt, where he looked for a moment like one of her high school boyfriends visiting her still-little-girl room.

She needed only a few minutes to dry her hair and get dressed, then they were going out. She nudged a beer toward Curtis, and he waved it away sharply—waved her away. His hand was clamped over the mouthpiece, and he was listening intently. His face was rigid with concentration. She stood dumbly holding the beers, her throat suddenly dry.

He was listening in on someone else's conversation. Someone else in her own house could only be Paul, and if Curtis was still on the line, then the other person was Kent. "Curtis," she said. By then he had hung up the phone, sat staring at the space just in front of him. She set the beers down on her dresser.

"You knew about this?" he said after a minute. His voice was small. "What's happening?" Neither was really a question, only an expression of his shock.

"Curtis," she whispered, shaking her head. "I knew you'd just get upset."

He looked dazed, hunched over his knees at the edge of the bed. "You know what's funny. What's actually fucking hilarious. I didn't know, until the last minute—until they just now said good-bye." He chuckled flatly. "I thought it was about the band. Why he'd be talking to—" his jaw tightened, relaxed again—"about the band, don't ask me that one. 'Curtis will be upset if he finds out'—something like that. And I thought, well, Kent is dumping us, hooking up with some other *band*."

Visibly pale, he stood without meeting her eyes, began to move aimlessly through the room. "They even said 'we.' And I thought, well, maybe the little shit's decided to get *musical* or something." His voice rose incrementally as he spoke. "Maybe they're forming their own band! How stupid is that? They're gonna have dinner to talk about their new band! That's how willing I am to believe anything else."

She wanted very much to laugh, though there was nothing to laugh about. He pressed his lips together, met her eyes for the first time, and she got a glimpse of how deep the wound went. "But then they said good-bye. Just the way they said it."

The door was already open, Curtis out in the hall. "Curtis!" she shouted, following. "Wait! What are you doing?"

But he was headed the opposite direction, away from Paul's door. When she realized he wasn't going after Paul, her voice fell away. From the top of the stairway, he leveled a cold look that seemed to combine everything before him and judge it as one, then cast it off like soiled clothing. "None of your business."

He was gone down the stairs, and she turned to find Paul standing in the hall behind her. "He heard? I . . . Sidra, I swear. I didn't know." He took a few uncertain steps toward her. "I didn't know he was listening."

She stood numb, slapped. Curtis would cool off, eventually, she thought—he always did. But she'd felt a finality in his gaze, as if he were taking his last look at her. "He left," she said.

"I'll stop him. I'll fix it." Paul spoke as if he knew exactly where Curtis had gone. He moved past her, bolted down the stairs.

She followed, past her mother's questioning look from the living room, out the front door, onto the porch, and Paul was rushing into the garage. Of course. Curtis would want his bass. He was packing his things. She moved across the dark lawn to the yellow light of the first window. Under the naked bulb inside, Curtis was snapping his case shut. Paul stood half inside the open doorway, pleading, "Curtis—Curtis, listen," his voice plaintive with desperation. "What do you want? I'll do it, I swear. I won't see him. I'll stop. Whatever you want, just tell me. Just say—" As Curtis pushed past him, out the door, Paul latched onto his arm with a two-handed grip, and Curtis didn't turn his eyes or take a swing but simply kept walking, pulling loose from the restraint, as if Paul didn't exist. Paul collapsed to his knees outside the shed door. Curtis walked out to the driveway and set the bass in the front seat of his truck.

"I'm coming back for the amp," he shouted. "No one touches it." He got into the driver's seat and slammed the door, revved the engine.

It took Sidra a moment to notice that Paul was sobbing, not loudly but bereft, like an abandoned child, still on his knees and watching the taillights of Curtis's pickup bump down the driveway. She went to him after a minute, knelt in the grass in front of him. "Stop it," she said. Taking hold of his upper arms, she forced his hands away from his face, which was wet and rawly contorted. He gasped, pulled loose with a shiver of sudden control, one palm out to hold her back.

"Don't, okay?" His voice was almost a growl, clogged and harsh. "I'm fine."

She shook her head, too furious to speak. She wanted to blame him, but it was her own fault as well—she had seen this coming, hadn't she? Paul hugged himself, eyes averted. She leaned close and said, "He doesn't want you. He's never going to want you. Do you understand that?"

Paul swallowed, didn't answer. Sidra felt a twinge of remorse under her anger, but knew there was no way to comfort him, no way to reason, and she couldn't stand to look at him anymore. She rose and went past her mother into the house.

vertigo

They had dinner in a dim restaurant called The Last Resort, their small table candlelit, near the back. Kent sat facing the open kitchen, his eyes flicking toward the periodic orange flames that burst from the grills and thickened the air with the greasy smoke of seared meat. *Nude at the gates of hell* lingered unpleasantly in his head. He ordered a glass of wine, then poured ice water from a carafe spiked with translucent wheels of lemon, drank it and poured another.

"I don't think Sidra's too mad," Paul was saying, "or mad at us, at least. We talked. Curtis won't even take her calls—just took his toys and went home. But honestly, you didn't know he was listening, did you?"

"No. I didn't."

"I guess you haven't talked to him either, huh?"

Kent shook his head.

"I just wonder what he's up to, if he's—" Paul smiled uneasily—
"you know, plotting revenge or whatever, over there in his shitty little
apartment." Kent's face must have raised the question, because Paul
said, "Oh, I haven't been there. Sidra said it was shitty. And I can
just picture it." He shrugged one shoulder, pumped the straw up and
down through the ice of his cherry Coke. "I'm sorry this is such a mess.
I know you might not think this is worth losing your band over.
Whatever this is."

Paul was subdued tonight, tentative. He fidgeted with the sugar
packets and his napkin and picked at the edge of the table until Kent
wanted to take hold of his hand. "I'm not really worried about the
band right now," he said, trying to be reassuring. "Hey." From a daze,
Paul blinked up at him, and for the first time Kent sensed, with some
pleasure, that he might have more control over their situation than
Paul did. "What I do—what we do—is none of his business in the
first place."

Paul nodded, but seemed so preoccupied that Kent instantly lost
his confidence. "You're right," Paul murmured. "It's not. I need to
stop thinking about it. Just fucking stop."

Twirling the straw between his fingers, he straightened his shoulders, lifted his chin with faintly pursed lips to examine the people
at the other tables. Kent sipped his wine, not daring to glance
around much while Paul offered him sly, random tidbits about the
sex lives of people he recognized, or the ones he could at least make
amusing guesses about. In a simple black shirt, the silver and amethyst necklace under the open collar, his bright hair elegantly
gelled, he was an eye-catching glimmer, a presence in their back
corner. Kent wondered if other people found their eyes as drawn
to that light as he did. He was still waiting for the crisis to hit,
when he would finally wake to the realization that he was openly

pursuing someone who was not a girl. But Paul hadn't fully resolved for him into a gender. He was simply a fascination. A beautiful person.

Their salads arrived with a basket of bread, and Paul glanced up to thank the waiter. He dug into the bread basket and tore off a hunk. "Can I ask you something?" Kent said.

Paul buttered the bread thickly. "Anything."

But Kent hesitated. "Never mind." Paul bit into his bread, making a "come on" gesture with his curled hand. "I was just wondering, I guess," Kent said, "why you're here. Or why we're doing this. Or, maybe, what all of this has to do with Curtis."

He half expected Paul to blink with surprise, to launch into protest. But he only tipped his head and went on sorting through his salad with his fork. "You feel him too? Between us somehow. I know. He's there. We're both . . . attached to him in some way. I know you two are close." He glanced up. "At least I've heard how he talks about you. He practically worships you, like you're some kind of god. Like, the *god* of music. He talks about you a lot. Not to me, of course, but I hear things." He took a bite of salad and chewed it, smiling. "He could be in love with you."

Kent laughed. "Bullshit. In your fantasy world, maybe."

Their food arrived—Kent had the filet, Paul the house special: salmon and grits—and Kent tried to remember, as they tasted their entrees, that Paul hadn't quite answered his question. When he glanced up again, Paul's lynx eyes were fixed on him as if they had been that way for some time, the doubled candle flames glowing at their centers.

"I'm having a little fantasy about you right now," he admitted softly. "Curtis isn't in it."

⌣

From the beginning of the evening, until they had moved word-less back to Kent's apartment—Paul's mouth on Kent's throat and fingers tugging at his belt buckle before they were fully inside the door—the night had been no more than a movement toward the bedroom. They knew this, knew that sex would be a test, a hurdle to pass. And there was nothing, Kent found, to resist in the boy's body, nothing he didn't want, and what began at the door and progressed to the sofa and the floor and then on to the bedroom was better than he remembered from before. Maybe from his entire life before.

It wasn't until after—both of them on their backs on the still-made bed, under the faint bluish light of the alley window, stargazing, stu-pefied, reduced to the mere process of breathing. He turned to look at the boy beside him, to reach toward him, a back-fallen hand brush-ing lightly along Paul's cheek. "Come here," Kent said, urgent sud-denly, and Paul smiled, rolled in snug to his right side, head on Kent's shoulder—a jigsaw creature, he seemed, never at a loss for pieces that fit. But it wasn't close enough. A chill cut and spread through Kent's chest, and he held on harder, though Paul didn't seem to notice the grip. He began making lazy curlicues of Kent's chest hair and telling him how great he was.

Kent tried to remember now what he'd done—the mechanics of sex. What was *great* supposed to mean anyway, to Paul, whose stake in this remained so unclear? Or was it just a ritual lie? Suddenly he was sure of it—Paul was lying, saying what he said to anyone. So soon, still languid in the bed, and Kent couldn't stop him from drifting away into a history, a future, so many others it dizzied him. He gasped, a flash of panic in which he recognized the very sensation he had felt when, at age twelve, climbing the main mast of his father's boat, he'd been knocked loose with a change of the wind—the way time had slowed to show him the moment before his loosened fingers closed on air, the moment just beyond reversal and before surrender to the implacable thing that was happening.

His breath came in short bursts, and Paul raised himself to study Kent's upturned face. "No, babe," he coaxed. "Easy. Don't you yack on me, not now."

And then Kent was indeed nauseated, couldn't deny it—all that vast air between the mast and the deck had opened below him. His fingers dug at Paul's shoulders. He tried to will himself out of it, out of the rocking sea to solid, level ground.

Paul's eyes narrowed. "You'd better not move. I'm warning you. You better stay put." He pressed his face to Kent's chest. Kent lay huffing at the ceiling for a minute and then eased himself out of the bed, the floor tilting a little under his bare feet. He crept away to the bathroom and closed the door.

Paul was dressed by the time he emerged, and was staring fixedly at the TV, stabbing the arrow button on the remote. Kent sat softly on the opposite end of the couch. Paul went on flipping channels, pausing here and there without interest, stopped finally on cooking show—beaten eggs hissing in a skillet—and snuck a spiteful, sidelong glance. But Kent only gazed into the space in front of his knees with acute misery. Paul flicked off the set and turned to face him, his look unsoftened, angelic, without pity.

"You like the lights off, don't you?"

Kent blinked, stunned and uncomprehending. He couldn't think past the fact of his sickness, his need for sympathy. A girl would have at least felt sorry for him.

"So tell me." Paul's jaw twitched. "You were fine the first time, in the hayloft. Was that because it was just a blow job, you can handle that? Or because it was so dark you couldn't see me."

"No." Kent shook his head carefully. "That's not it."

"It's not, huh?" Paul stood, arms folded, though Kent could see he was shaking. "Look, we ain't gonna play this. If fucking me makes you want to puke—"

"It's not *fucking* you that's the problem," Kent said firmly, with extreme effort, though he felt how the evidence weighed there and couldn't be entirely sure himself. Another wave of nausea passed over him. He desperately fought it down. "I don't know, okay? I don't know what's wrong with me."

Paul glared, but under the surface heat of his fury passed a visible welter of hurt and fear, and Kent saw how the boy tried to marshal his defenses—against compassion, understanding, forgiveness. Kent winced at it. He reached a hand across the space between them, though Paul was too far away to touch. "Don't be mad," he said, his voice strained with desperation, too weighted. "Please. Please. I—"

Paul stiffened presciently, moving as if by reflex to catch something fragile about to be dropped. "You need to relax," he said. He sat beside Kent, sliding up close. "Take it easy, you know? We're just messing around. It's nothing to get all . . . whatever, freaked out about." He smiled and reached for the back of Kent's neck, caressing along the hairline.

The relenting gesture did nothing to soothe Kent, who looked down at his knees and nodded. "I'll be okay. I mean, I'll get over this. It's a phase or something."

"Sure you will." Paul looked at his watch, and his tone turned brisk and business-like. "Mother Mary, look at the time! I gotta run. Call me, okay?" He rose, bending to kiss Kent's forehead.

"Don't go," Kent said.

"I got plans." He touched Kent's goatee, brave enough for a direct look. "It's nothing personal. I promise. Call me later."

magic eye

Band practice was canceled indefinitely. Early Friday evening, in the second week of the hiatus, Lyle stopped at Kent's apartment. He knocked, then let himself in—Kent was curled on the sofa with a beer in his lap, Hank Williams and Patsy Cline taking turns softly on the CD changer. On the soundless TV, a muddle of colors, unidentifiable images, flickered in slant.

Lyle tilted his head and squinted at the set. From the scramble, he caught what looked like a flash of skin. "Is that porno?"

"Playboy Channel."

"Bud, you don't get the Playboy Channel." Lyle strained to identify body parts from the dominant flesh tones, picked out what might have been a thigh. But it stretched thin and tumbled away, lost before it was clear. "Man, that's worse than that Magic Eye shit. Doesn't that drive you nuts?"

"Watch it for a while. I think it's actually better like this."

Kent didn't seem to be watching though. He flicked the remote at the stereo to double back on "Walking After Midnight." "This is just a good one," he explained, his voice nearly cracking as if the song affected him deeply.

Lyle sat beside him. "Let's you and me go grab a beer or something."

"I'm stocked. Help yourself."

Lyle's mouth pursed and twisted. He patted Kent's foot, left his hand there in a rough hold. "Look, bud. This is all going to work out eventually. I mean, no one really knows which end is which right now."

Kent nodded. They sat in silence for a moment, and Lyle went to get a beer from the kitchen, Patsy's clear tones climbing in the background. Kent hit the remote again. "Listen how the fiddle picks up on this one, right at the beginning." He closed his eyes, made a soft gesture toward the stereo, his hand like a bird's wing balanced on a stiff current of air.

Lyle returned to his seat. He sipped the beer and listened for an interval that seemed polite. "I mean, face it, man. We don't have a band without you. The three of us are useless." He laughed nervously. "You could do a lot better than us anyway. Shit, it's obvious, we know it. Not that I mean—"

"Please. Don't talk about it. I'm in the middle of losing my mind."

Lyle sighed, looked helplessly around the dimly lit room. "Is it Paul?"

"It's me."

"You, uh, you seeing him?"

Kent made ambiguous, shruglike movements. "Paul sees a lot of people."

Lyle raised his eyebrows, said, "Oh," but soundlessly, hoping Kent would say something else. The thing didn't make a whole lot of sense, as far as Lyle could see. Not that he was the expert on guys, but Paul didn't strike him as all that special—certainly not special enough to be seeing a lot of people. And hardly worth the headache if he did.

"He's—" Kent grimaced faintly, waved a hand in the air as if sorting among adjectives for something that would pin the boy like a butterfly, and Lyle waited. But the hand dropped. "Gone home for the weekend, I guess."

Hank's "Ramblin' Man" started up. Lyle tried to think of a casual way to get Kent out of the apartment, out into the normal world for a beer with people, but nothing came to him. Kent said, "If you want to know the truth, I'm sitting here thinking about that sailboat. You know, that thirty-footer I found down at Tybee? I think I could use a boat in my life about now."

Lyle recalled it only vaguely—a beach trip two years before, a bunch of them kicking around the marina one day, when Kent had become infatuated with a junk heap parked under a "for sale" sign. At first they had all laughed at the boat's lofty name, the *Rapture*, while Kent critiqued the age and neglect revealed in pale, damaged wood. The owner, once Kent tracked him down, admitted further blemishes—busted forestay, shaft out of alignment—but added that "she'd go anywhere," once the work was done; she was seaworthy at least for the Caribbean. And Kent lit up. Since then, he'd been stealing off on solitary trips to visit the *Rapture*, as if it were his own or soon would be.

"You can't afford a boat," Lyle said, now starting to wonder if his friend might have meant it about losing his mind. "Even that piece of crap."

"I could if I lived on it."

"Are you serious? Live on a boat. What would you do for a job?" Lyle tried to keep the tone light but felt a creeping anxiety. It wasn't hard to imagine Kent casting off, *bon voyage*, into his own high-flung perverse notion—to hell with reason and anyone else.

"I'd find something," Kent said. But he was slumped and dull, sipping his beer. "I mean, what's to keep me here? I could set off south along the islands, maybe play guitar in some of those little marina bars. Anchor out in the bay at night. Start clean."

the one that got away

Sidra met her father, Jimmy Ballard, for lunch once a week, usually at East-West so they could make use of Sidra's employee discount. They ordered tapas and margaritas rimmed in salt, sat in the white light of the front window, their colors drained against the bright noon traffic of Broad Street. Today, as always, they talked about horses, less about the ragged herd they jointly owned—four at present, all

young—than about the ones they would buy next. The real invest-
ment to come.

"Eddie's got a line on some mares out in Winder," Jimmy said,
wonder-eyed and boyish still, despite thinning hair. He chewed on-
ion flatbread. "I wouldn't mind a test run for old Cicero, you know?
See what we got?"

The plan—to breed painted sport horses—was Sidra's idea. A week
after she'd first floated it, some years back, Jimmy had snapped up a
weanling paint colt, now coming three and solid black but with genes
that promised to show spots in the next generation. If only, now, they
had some mares. Good mares, Sidra stressed, at least half warmblood.
We don't need any scrappy babies on our hands. But her father had
connections in every sale barn and bargain lot in the state, knew
where he could get him a nice little quarter-type filly dirt cheap—
same way he'd acquired the colt. Can't beat that price, it's once in a
lifetime. Her father, Sidra was only now beginning to realize, was
incorrigible.

"That colt's gonna be something special in a year or two," Jimmy
said. "I'd wager my best hat."

"Nobody wants any of your hats, Daddy." Sidra grinned, dipping
a sweet potato chip in blue cheese. Truth be told, the colt was ma-
turing a little weedy, but her father didn't want to hear a word spoken against their dreams. Maybe they'd luck out with the babies—lots
of studs that didn't look like much themselves threw exceptional foals.
"It'll just be hard to find the right mares," she said, "And expensive.
I mean really expensive."

Jimmy sighed, looked out the window toward the distant campus,
his eyes transparent in the light. Something in his expression depressed
Sidra, made him seem suddenly old. This man had been the best friend
of her childhood, always waiting just past her mother's stern shoulder

with a private wink that said *Don't listen to her*. Late at night, if there was ever anything good happening, like fireworks or something about horses on TV, he was sure to sneak into her room and get her up for it. Caught hell the night he rousted her from bed and carried her to a dog track over the state line—"She'll have nightmares!" Florie had said. But Sidra slept soundly every night, sure in the knowledge that she would never miss anything, because her father would wake her.

Now it seemed all they talked about were their horses, this dream that was going nowhere. They didn't have the money to keep the horses they had, let alone buy more. But they stumbled along through this same conversation every week, the phrases familiar with repetition, as if they were casting a desperate spell to hold the dream in place. Sidra didn't have the heart this time to continue.

"Mama's going nuts with Paul," she said brightly, to change the subject. "You should see her. You know how she is—has to be in control of everything."

"Paul—that boy you've got on the side?" her father teased. "It's no wonder Curtis is jealous."

"Daddy!"

"He's too cute to be gay, I say." He winked over a spoonful of corn chowder.

"Oh, a lot you know!" she sneered, their ritual joust over her love life. "He's all 'yes-ma'am' with Mama, but he's out running wild every night."

Despite her efforts, she saw her father's eyes turning dull, his attention slipping away out the window somewhere, and her story, all on its own, strained higher into gross exaggeration. "God knows what he's doing, who he's with. And Mama, you should just see her. In a tizzy over it."

"I'm sure," he muttered, chewing.

"Of course she thinks she can mother him. Preaching abstinence and safe sex. Meanwhile he doesn't even want to get tested. He's showed *her*. And it's just what she deserves after all. I don't feel one bit sorry for her."

She nearly cringed against her own words, her chest tight and airless at the summit of all she could say. But his eyes were off toward the campus, refusing to spark. More and more, she caught him in these distant reveries, as if he weren't listening. If she didn't know better, she might have worried he was trailing some thought of his own that didn't include her.

not even touching you

Lights on, this time, to appease him, and now he lay sleeping on Kent's chest, the fingers of one hand still thatched in the hair of Kent's belly, for luck or maybe solidarity, or for an alarm, should Kent feel the need to rise. *You feeling okay?* Paul had murmured, and Kent had said "Yes, fine," though he lay awake for some time afterward propped on pillows, monitoring the state of his body and asking himself the same tentative question. *Still feeling okay?* Hoping, if the answer became no, that Paul would prove a deep sleeper. Then sleep caught him too and he dozed for an hour, awoke again under the lights, in complete ease.

Maybe it was Paul's exhaustion that made the difference—he was so deeply asleep—or the fact that he had guided them this time so they were facing each other, a position that Kent somehow hadn't thought possible. But it was easy, a revelation that filled him with wonder and calmed him, facing Paul's unguarded eyes—the small shock of union. Later, when he thought to look again, those eyes were rolled back in lacquered crescents, his lip curled and twitching above clenched teeth, like some fierce little animal in a dream. More wonder. He wanted to keep him that way and to call him back, both at once, and he watched the shifting sands of the boy's responses. Pain, it looked like. Did it truly hurt? He needed to know. A flood of pity made him push harder, drive toward the center of this other body as if by sheer effort he could break through and become the other, see through those eyes, feel what he felt.

All such mystery to him, Paul's appetites. Kent didn't see the appeal in anything he did—going down, playing the girl for sex—saying when asked *I like it,* as if pleasure were just that simple. Kent wondered if it was only someone else's pleasure Paul craved. Or if maybe Paul was different, more demanding, with other men.

Tonight, in the moment afterward, while Kent was still unready to move even to break apart, Paul had asked without words that he stay a little longer where he was. Gazing up as if to apologize or ask permission, he stroked himself slowly. Kent felt an urge to give him privacy, had fallen into behaving generally as if Paul harbored a small space of invisibility between the legs, like an endearing defect, and he knew that Paul helped him in this, denying himself—the spell of attraction so fragile. It was the apprehension in Paul's eyes now that made Kent take over, without another thought, and soon Paul's pleasure erased any memory of what might have been lost.

Now Paul slept, head heavy, mouth parted, his breath feathering along Kent's chest. His pale hair stuck damply in several directions and even his eyelashes were tousled fringing lids that ticked through a dream. His forehead puckered once, smoothed again, and Kent felt a wave of tenderness for the way Paul slept. Like a child, in spite of all his efforts.

At some point this night, Kent had said *love,* not intending, not meaning anything by it. He couldn't remember now what made it slip out, remembered only the word itself and then what Paul had said—so much later in the murmur of peaceful aftermath that it might have had no connection.

"I figured out the whole love thing a while ago," he said. "The truth about it. It's not like they say. See, there are people you want to have sex with, once. Twice, maybe. That's it. And then there are people you want to keep on having sex with. That's all anyone means when they say love. They mean 'I want to keep doing this.'"

Kent mouthed the words now, testing the shape of them. He studied a pale spray of freckles along Paul's hairline, stroked back a tuft of stuck hair to kiss him there, very lightly. Wishing him asleep and awake, both at once. *I want to keep . . .*

Paul had said, to explain, "Those other men, men in bars, you know, it's just sex. It's only once. It's not like this. Not at all like this."

Outside a storm was rising, wind gusting down Clayton Street, moaning in the leaky panes of the alley window behind his head. A nice sound to hear from the bed, cozy and safe. But it made him anxious too, that reasonless, feral howling. Any shelter seemed hopelessly temporary, as flimsy as the boy's sleep. It occurred to him that maybe he and Paul had reached the only true balance, the perfect state, this moment with Paul asleep in his arms, and it couldn't last.

Paul rubbed his nose roughly with the flat of a palm. "What are you doing?"

"Watching you sleep," Kent admitted.

Paul shuddered, hid his face. "God, don't do that. I'm probably ugly or drooling or something." He rolled over to check the clock, settled back on his stomach beside Kent, propped on his elbows. "Not sick?"

"Nope."

"So. You want to mess around or what?"

Kent blinked at him. "You can't be serious."

"No?" Paul chuckled. "You don't pay much attention, do you?"

"You think you just, what, push a button?" he said, amused, as Paul dipped to kiss his stomach and up along his ribs, caught a nipple between the tip of his tongue and teeth, and Kent's breath shuddered in spite of himself. Maybe he could after all, this body of his like some borrowed vehicle running on its own unaccountable drives. He wondered vaguely if Paul was right, if all of his chaotic feelings could be reduced to the physical.

"Enough," he groaned, joking but weary, faintly disgusted with himself and Paul too. He seized Paul at the ribcage. Paul shrieked, bucked, and doubled convulsively against him. "You're ticklish!" Kent said, with a predatory thrill.

Paul begged him, "No, I'm not, actually, please," as Kent turned him easily onto his back and pinned his legs and arms to the mattress. Under his fingers the ribs heaved, straining in and out against the skin, a washboard he couldn't resist playing. Wild, streaming tears, Paul laughed and went on laughing long after Kent let up, though he still held him prone, fascinated by the way hysteria wracked him with little seizures, one after another. Whenever he seemed about to calm, Kent goosed him again, set him reeling anew like a windup toy.

"Stop," was all Paul could say, and his entreaties turned to squeals at no more than the sight of Kent's hand moving toward him.

"What was that?" Kent asked, grinning—he could keep this up for hours. "I can't understand you. Can you speak more clearly? Look, I'm not even touching you."

Eventually, when Paul seemed overheated, at the edge of heart failure, Kent let up. He reached past the head of the bed to the alley window to raise the blind and the sash. The wind that entered was pleasantly cool and still rainless, and Kent propped himself a little so the air could pass between their bodies. "There. Better? You feel the storm coming?" He stroked Paul's flushed face, moved by his helplessness—it seemed a state worth cultivating.

Paul inched on his back toward the window as if it were the only source of air, tipped his head over the edge of the mattress, whimpering and slack. He stretched an arm back to graze the screen with his fingers. "I can smell it too," he said, let out a wounded moan. "God, you're so mean. The evil brother I never had." His breathing slowed by degrees. The center of his chest was flushed in a diamond pattern, a deep purply red, and Kent kissed him there, felt the feverish burn of the skin on his lips.

"Tell me something," Kent said, "about Greene County."

"Like what?" Paul grinned playfully. Out on Clayton, the streetlights blinked in and out as the trees lashed over them. "I gotta go."

"Not yet. One story about when you were little. Back home."

so much unfinished

At Christmas, Curtis had four days off from work, nowhere to go but Greene County. Sidra would be home, of course, but he was avoiding her, and his friends too, for the most part. "No," he assured Sidra, assured the band, when they called him exasperated, when he was in the mood to pick up the phone, "we're not breaking up." To whatever they urged him toward—drinks, a movie, band practice, dinner, just come over for a while and talk, Curtis—he answered, "I don't feel like it right now."

So he went home to Greene County—or, more precisely, to Dan Foster's house, which would never feel like his, never entirely home. A pitiful, shit-ass, depressing little place, he thought of it, the plain white ranch house hardly a step up in class from a double-wide, with low ceilings, cramped bedrooms down a shotgun hall. When the time came, he'd damn sure have something better to offer his own new wife. If he owned the land Dan Foster did—a reasonable two-acre slope on the highway with cows for neighbors—he'd at least manage to put something better on it for a house.

His mother had put up a plastic tree, decorated to the last twig, but draped real fir garlands over doorways and around table tops, "for the smell." Cinnamon sticks simmered continuously on the stove. There were stockings for all four of them over the fireplace, cartoon reindeer and Santas praying over baby Jesus everywhere he looked. Muriel baked continually, and he stationed himself close by in the kitchen, waiting for the opportunity to list his grievances against everyone—starting with his stepbrother, his mother's sweetie-pie, cloistered now in his room at the back of the house but otherwise busy doing everything in his power to systematically ruin Curtis's life.

The lawn frosted each night, as near to snow as they were likely to get, and when Curtis woke late on the mornings before Christmas, the kitchen windows would already be steamed with the heat of the oven and the early cookies set out to cool. These would be arranged later in mixed sets, topped in tinfoil and bows, for the neighbors and, apparently, every member of the Baptist church. He nursed a cup of coffee at the table while Muriel, with a HoHoHo apron tied over her Christmas-sweatshirt-of-the-day, shifted the overflowing racks of cookies from the counters to the table in front of him. "Try those," she urged. "I just found the recipe in the *Ladies' Home Journal*. Aren't they yummy?"

He sampled and offered opinions. They discussed doneness and the relative amounts of various ingredients. Muriel's cheer, full of warm smiles and peppermint sugar and brief touches of Curtis's arm or his head, was impenetrable; it never allowed him an opening for his mood. He was content, though, just to have someone to talk to, about anything. He clung to this alliance.

"Maybe I could make something too," he offered. "We could use some eggnog to go with all this."

"Oh, you know none of us around here're much on drinking," she said.

"Paul would drink it," he said, before he could stop himself with a flinch against whatever impulse in him couldn't help counting heads, counting Paul among the human. He scowled, added, "He's always stealing my beers. I'm sure he drinks plenty, the way he runs around."

"Paul don't need any," Muriel said casually. "But you go right ahead and make eggnog if you got a craving."

The impulse died quickly though, before Curtis had even hunted down a recipe. It didn't seem worth the effort, after all, for only one person.

Dan was usually in the next room reading the paper, or else somewhere nearby, with his holiday air of makeshift industry, inspecting the house. Once he enlisted Curtis's help in replacing a leaky pipe under the bathroom sink. "I don't know where Paul's got to," he murmured, as if his fruity son was generally the one to be handing him wrenches. As if Paul would even know what a wrench was.

Paul was hiding, it seemed, keeping to his room for Curtis's few days home with the excuse that he was working on college admissions essays. Every so often, Muriel would arrange a plate of the most recent cookies, pour a glass of milk, and carry them back to him as if he were a shut-in. It was strange, Curtis discovered, not to see him more, not to have the slinky little creep brushing up under his nose as usual. He'd been expecting something—a confrontation, maybe. Who would have guessed that Paul could show this much restraint?

When Paul did appear, often not until suppertime, Curtis's chest went tight, his mind echoing a jumble of tangled phrases—*what you did to me . . . what you've done . . . no mercy, no forgiveness.* Paul heaped his plate with green beans and crescent rolls, glazed ham with rings of pineapple, bowed his head belatedly for the prayer, and Curtis watched him covertly, the angle where his shoulder notched into his back. *There was what Kent wanted, what he touched, the clothes he re-moved, the body beneath.* No telling why the mind played these sick games with itself, envisioning what it least wanted to see. But he could not look Paul in the face, threateningly or otherwise. Simply couldn't make himself do it, even as he felt Paul's glance passing over him, Paul the Chatty Cathy of the meal—on and on about colleges up north and holiday bellringers and a commercial for soup and some joker's theory of something Curtis had never heard of. No mention of Kent.

He rose to clear dishes when Paul did, though he knew his mother and Dan were exchanging glances across the table. "So nice to have help," Muriel called out, her singsong tone somewhere between pleased and alarmed.

Their shoulders nearly brushed, passing back and forth between the table and the refrigerator, except that Paul stepped delicately out of the way. "That doesn't go there," Curtis said. He removed the honey bear with a jerk from the cabinet over the stove. "Are you planning to rinse that?" Paul glanced up with that cowed, girlish look from under his lashes, silent beside the sink, absolutely still. Dan by now had moved to the den; Muriel was making the rounds of the other rooms to draw the drapes closed.

Paul lowered his eyes, sidestepping. He moved to wipe the crumbs from the table, but in broad, careless swipes that missed half the mess—Curtis could see it clearly. "God, give me the sponge, if that's the best you can do."

"You finish," Paul said, not looking at him, leaving the sponge on the table. *Yeah, you better hide,* Curtis thought, as Paul slipped away down the hall.

So that's how it was now. But Curtis couldn't feel the relief of fi-nally being left alone, not with so much out of balance between them.

It seemed there was no way to bring Paul back into his orbit. Up past midnight, Curtis wandered along the hall past the darkened bedrooms, into the den, touched the stockings and the fir garlands and the fake snow, listening for stirring in the house. He felt he would either explode or cry if he couldn't find a way to reveal the extent of Paul's crimes, of his own injuries. He didn't want much—just the chance to show him, to grab him by the throat and make him look. To hold him down.

bigger man

January, morning, a chill mist over the green Ballard pastures. From across the field, Curtis could hear the suck and slosh of a horse's hooves—Paul in the saddle—cantering in wet grass, and Sidra's voice as well, just the sound of it breaking against the cold, damp air. Not the words. Her hair was loose. She sat her black colt bareback, turning it at a walk to follow the wider circle of the other horse around her, a horse he didn't recognize. It was almost as dark as the colt but bigger, fancier. They were up on the flat of the ridge, the field unfenced, Paul's mount steaming forward with nose tucked, knees snapping high—was it straining to bolt? With each triple beat, there was an audible rattle of horse breath. He imagined the horse slipping past Paul's control, leaving the circle to fly toward the woods, hell-bent, white-eyed, unstoppable. He imagined a hoof slipping, the animal crashing down.

But the gait remained steady, slowed to a neat trot, then a walk. The horse halted with his neck bowed, restlessly mouthing the bit. Sidra nudged Cicero forward and the two horses stretched their muzzles to greet each other, the colt chewing in submission as if he had a wad of gum the size of a baseball. With a jolt, Curtis recognized the other horse—Simon, Sidra's retired show horse, the very bastard that not long ago had kicked him square in the back.

From the saddle, Paul was looking at him fixedly now. Then Sidra. They stood that way for a moment, frozen in the mist like a pair of alerted deer. Paul lowered his face, moved the horse off. Sidra turned the colt toward Curtis and ambled across the grass to meet him.

"Hey," she said from above. At a halt, the colt weaved drunkenly, stretched his narrow mouth on the snaffle and received a smack on the neck with the flat of Sidra's hand. "Cut it out, idjit."

Curtis stood shoulders hunched, fists in the pockets of his coat, his eyes on her muck shoes that hung loose below the colt's belly. She slid off, took the reins over the colt's head. In the distance, Paul walked his horse and from time to time looked toward them, looked away.

"You're riding with him now?" Curtis tried to sound casual.

"You weren't available."

"I told you I was coming over."

"You haven't been available for a long time, Curtis. My life hasn't stopped. What do you think, I just sit it in my room and mope? Just wait for you?"

His throat clenched, and he felt a little pang of desperation, as if cornered. "You could try maybe having a little compassion, maybe?"

She scoffed. "Oh, for what?"

"You could try not throwing that—" he gestured sharply at Paul with an upturned hand—"in my face, every time I turn around." He caught himself, tried to calm down—*be the reasonable one. Make her understand.* "I can put up with a lot, you know. I can try to be tolerant of . . . of—" He waved his hand vaguely.

"Paul?" she prodded.

He looked at the ground. "But you ask too much. There are limits."

"I want you to say his name."

He stared at her placid face, a little glimmer at the back of her eye. His fists tightened and he jammed them deeper into his pockets. "This is funny to you, isn't it? You don't even know—" His voice broke, but she wasn't paying attention—the horse fidgeting, nipping her, so she had to wrestle him into behaving with the reins caught tight under his jaw. Curtis turned away to pace.

"Act right, you little jerk," she growled at the horse. Head lifted high, the colt danced a few steps sideways, his expression horrified beyond any logical cause. "Curtis, let me tie him, okay? I can't talk this way."

She led the horse into the barn, and Curtis followed, glancing once at Paul out in the field, walking his horse in circles—still watching them and pretending not to. He was glad to get Sidra alone inside the barn walls. She slid a halter over the colt's bridle and cross-tied him.

Curtis tried again. "All I cared about in my whole life was that stupid band."

"And me," she reminded him blandly.

"Well, yeah, of course you. Sid, you know that. I hope I don't have to say *that*."

She raised her eyebrows, tilted her head, waited. He forged ahead. "But I made up my mind, I want you to know. I've been thinking, and I thought about it for a long time and I came to a decision." He had her full attention now, and he looked at her defiantly. "So we're gonna have a band practice. Tonight. In case you care."

She nodded. "So you talked to Kent?"

He shrugged. "I will. I can do that."

"Good for you." The sarcasm seemed absent from her voice, though he strained to hear it.

"I mean, I'm willing to be the big man here, be the one to make the effort, which should be enough. That should be as much as anyone can ask of me." He looked at her so hard that he shook a little. She remained impassive. "So is that it, Sidra? Is that enough?"

Her eyes softened, which was all he had been waiting for—for her to step toward him and put her arms around him and say it was finished, that he had won, completed his Herculean task and now everything fucked with the world would go back to normal and they could all go back to how they had been before. And she did put her arms around him; she kissed his razor-stubbled face and cuddled up with her head under his chin. "Poor Curtis," she said. "We're all so hard on you, I know."

He held her, his cheek against the top of her head. The urge to cry into her hair passed almost immediately into the warm, soothing calm of her body against his, a complete ease and safety like nothing else he had ever known. What a bizarre and hellish way to discover once again what this woman was worth. *Anything,* he would do anything. He held her tighter, knowing he couldn't afford to say that out loud.

"You're doing good, baby," she said. "But there's a ways to go yet."

who you're with

Kent sat at the edge of their low, makeshift stage in the trainyard warehouse, which was theirs once again for practices. With his electric guitar across his knees, he belted out a random montage of current radio songs—U2, Pearl Jam, R. E. M., snippets of each in exaggerated imitation of the vocalists: the sexual throes of Bono's breath stops; Vedder's deep, head-twitching moans; Stipe's wiry, incomprehensible verses. Nearby, Lyle and Jeff listened in fascination, laughed and shook their heads at each agile shift, the new voice instantly recognizable. They were certain that if Kent ever dropped the joke and really tried, he could be as good as any of the originals. But Kent preferred the joke of it.

"He's not coming," Jeff said during a pause, watching the door.

"He's coming," Lyle insisted.

Jeff said, "Let's start without him."

"He'll be here." Lyle looked at Kent, caught his eyes, and Kent looked back down to strum the guitar, wishing he were quicker on the draw with a song to cut Lyle off. "I know this has been pretty rough on you, man, but I gotta admire the hell out of him if he shows up tonight."

"Enough with the pity parade for Curtis," Jeff snapped. "No one's asking him to join the Moonies. It's a fuckin' *band*, for Chrissakes! It's like a job, a responsibility. You do it, it gets done. Grow up!"

Lyle shook his head. "Yeah, and it's a lame-ass band too. Let's get realistic—there's no reason to bother with shit one in the name of this band."

Jeff bristled. "Hey—first off, you don't know that. And I'll tell you another thing, Curtis sure don't. He's married to this band, man." He laughed. "Fuckin' married to it. There's his whole problem right there. He's married to *you*, my friend." He pointed at Kent, laughed louder until he was howling at his own joke and slapping his thigh.

Kent smiled—maybe it was a little funny. He shifted keys, C to F, but had lost the thread of his montage. Impatient for music and craving the chance to play, the sole reason he had come tonight, he was stuck instead in this conversation and waiting, as usual, for Curtis. He felt raw at the thought of Curtis, but his fingers slid back into a U2ish chord and he followed it into a song, wailed plaintively, "*With or without you-ou-ah-ah. I can't live . . . with or without you.*"

When he dropped the parody, Lyle sat beside him in slack-jawed awe. "Man, why do you waste your time with us? Really, I'm curious. You could be something. You're the real thing." He looked at Jeff. "Tell him, man."

Jeff only raised his eyebrows pointedly, as if Lyle were letting loose a secret they should keep to themselves. Kent's fingers slid effortlessly into "The Real Thing," and Jeff laughed. "There you go, that's it."

"I'm serious," Lyle persisted. "Why are you with us in the first place?"

"Never really thought about it that way, I guess." Kent shrugged, the chords progressing but slower and softer. "God, I don't know. You're my friends. You wanted me."

They were quiet for a moment. When Jeff and Lyle took up the topic of Curtis again, Kent wasn't listening. He was thinking of Paul, who had been striking that same note lately: *Why are you with me?* It wasn't a fight exactly, no particular conflict to call it forth, except maybe Kent's near-despair at Paul's social calendar, what Paul called "seeing other people"—his euphemism, as Kent could only imagine, for fucking strangers.

Kent knew the score, understood from the beginning, when they'd started. He would do nothing more, in fact, than be quiet for a few seconds too long, and Paul would tear into him. About how he'd never asked for a relationship, how it was obvious they didn't belong together in the first place. He insisted that Kent had no business being attracted this way, didn't even know his own market value so Paul would fill him in: "You could have someone like *you*," he'd said, a strange, wild light in his eyes as if he were invoking the holy grail.

This news meant nothing to Kent. He couldn't make himself picture Paul's phantom man: someone meaty and rugged, Kent's own age, a member of his own brotherhood. Paul had it all figured out. How Kent should sit around laughing with this man on park benches, like the men in magazine ads. They could lift weights together, go camping together, and then, then Kent would see what it meant to be happy.

"And you'll just laugh," Paul informed him smugly. "One day, you'll look back and laugh to think you ever got involved, ever thought twice about some little jailbait piece of trash." Pacing the room, he pivoted, chin raised in haughty confidence. "You'll see. It'll be hysterical."

As if to illustrate, he began laughing, hysterically, until Kent, still bewildered, had to take him into his arms and soothe him, ask, "Why do you want to say things like that?"

"It's the truth, that's all."

"Shut up, Paul. Just shut up."

Curtis arrived. He came through the metal door with a draft of night air and walked more or less directly across the box-strewn warehouse to the stage where they were gathered. Stopping before Kent, he glanced at Jeff and Lyle. "Let me talk a minute."

Jeff and Lyle moved off. Kent wanted another minute of his own to finish thinking about Paul, wished Curtis would leave him alone. He closed his eyes over the guitar, touched the frets. A line of a song he hadn't written yet came to him full blown, seized him, *You deserve to know . . .* and faded just as suddenly, vanished. He fingered a chord that might chase it.

"Look," Curtis said. He waited for Kent to raise his eyes, then drew himself up straight to make a speech. "I don't guess I care for your lifestyle choice, or whatever."

Kent was surprised by the words. Lifestyle? Choice? Neither seemed to apply even remotely, but he said, "I don't ask you to," without thinking, as if he had rehearsed it.

Curtis took a breath, and whatever he had planned to say slipped from his grasp. "Why?" he asked, his voice so full that one word was ten questions at once, and the only question that mattered. "Kent," he said. "*Why?*"

Suddenly this was Curtis standing before him, his friend of ten years running. They had connected over the music, understood each other in ways other people didn't seem able to, and did it easily. They had come to count on each other for that.

Kent shrugged, shook his head. "I don't know, man. I'd tell you if I could. I didn't . . . mean it. You know?"

Curtis crossed his arms, blinking, trying to process.

"It just happened."

He raised a hand to stop him, shut his eyes and held silence. After a while, he said, "You're gonna keep this up, I guess?"

It was the same question he'd been asking himself, asking Paul, wanting to know in his own mind for months now, and he just wanted an answer, any answer to put it to rest. But it was hardly Curtis's business.

"It shouldn't matter," he said quietly. "Am I right?"

"It shouldn't."

Kent focused on his face for the first time. It was red with emotion, with a sort of trauma as if Kent had physically battered him and Curtis didn't know, now, how to find level ground between them and meet his eyes like a man. Kent felt sorry for him, then knew exactly how he felt. He hadn't clearly seen it before, this imbalance between them—that he mattered just a little more to Curtis than Curtis had ever mattered to him. Since high school, Kent had been the abstracted one, their group's resident loner. And Curtis had understood that.

"Curtis," he said gently, "let's just try to forget about this. Okay? Let's just have practice." He wanted to put an arm around him but knew that Curtis would not be touched. Maybe not ever again. So he held out a hand instead, waited for Curtis to shake.

brain fever

The question remains: how Paul spends his time that goes unaccounted for. They can all guess the how and the why of it. They can picture the way he waits outside the club, half in light, against the brick wall of the wide entranceway, looking aloof, bored. One slim leg bends up, the silver-tipped alligator boot resting heel to the wall. Hands palm-flat against the brick or tucked into his back pockets or hooked languorously into the waistband of his jeans, he bounces a little, lets his head loll loose on his neck, eyes half closed, his face edged in a blue glow of neon. As a child, he wanted nothing more than permission to look at a man openly without punishment, so now when they pass in and out of the club, he looks. Someone walks by, lingers, receives his appraisal, but fails to pass inspection—he wouldn't go off with just anyone, would he? Not this blue-eyed boy, this tender, gold-headed immortal. He can afford to be selective, to wait on something better. But he won't wait long.

Or maybe he waits inside, because they don't always card him. Hell, it's a business—can't leave the pretty ones out in the cold. Just don't serve him. The bartender offers a weary stare when, just to see what will happen, Paul asks for a rum and Coke. He'd like to get a little drunk—it's all better that way. "Fine," Paul says, rolling his eyes, flashing his warmest smile. "Coke, then." Later, he'll find someone to buy him drinks. Later, the drinks will appear like magic.

The bartender, whose name is something like Bull, draws the Coke with massive arms, and Paul takes a good look from behind, the shaved, thick-skinned head down to the linebacker thighs; his knees go wobbly. Bull turns, crosses his arms—not tonight, not ever, no skinny chicken for this man's man. You want Bull, you better look like Bull.

So Paul isn't everyone's ideal. No matter. He's someone's. He moves to the dance floor, under the wicked strobe. Up into the high ceilings, the air throbs with a machine beat, haunted with a dance track's female voices, the lower reaches full of watching men. How many want him? He's dancing now at the center of the floor, alone, waiting, the revolving center of so many eyes, so much potential. He is naked in the temple of men, a sun god with the burnished skin of an idol, and all want to touch him, enter him, enter God through him and they know, as he knows, that this is his function. It's all he wants. It's what he does.

But, then again, it's a weeknight in Athens, Georgia, and early, so maybe there are only one or two others lurking in the dim reaches, at the bar or along the edges of the floor—the ones who are always here. He's bored with these by now.

Not even Paul makes men appear out of thin air, but he knows the tricks. He's a smart boy—a prodigy, after all—knows how glances are passed in the street, knows the language of certain restrooms, certain parks and woods, and the signals hidden in the angle of a parked car. He answers personal ads, the ones listed under "Variations." He holds his fingertip to a vast, pulsing network, men upon men interlinked, an endless procession of men who want him. He gives over his body in restroom stalls and woods—not cars, not anymore—but the restrooms, sure, maybe even nice ones, that coded glance exchanged up and down the very stacks of the public library, where he often reads in the afternoon. And there are hotel rooms, apartments, suburban homes—the list must go on because the boy is insatiable, wants more than is possible, more than he can survive, sex with ten men in a week, ten a day, sex with a hundred men in a single day, no time to ask names and he only glimpses their faces but they will let him look—oh, yes, they will meet his eyes and let him look all he wants.

But these days, there is so little time. The world is a carnival, open, waiting. He chooses the rides that spin to a blur.

graceland

Late one Friday afternoon, after Paul had left for Greene County, Florie Ballard climbed the stairs to Kent McKutcheon's second-floor apartment. As she rose, stair by stair, she was thinking, oddly, of Graceland. She kept a postcard of Graceland's musical gates in the top drawer of her dresser, where it absorbed the scent of the floral sachet, and every so often she took it out and held its smoothness against her face for a second or two, before she put it back.

One day, she would see Graceland for herself, and she kept this planned journey private, in reserve, continually delayed. She was, perhaps, a little afraid to go—the one misty place on all the map that she could put her finger on and know for certain that Marcy had been. *This place is the biggest ripoff*, the postcard in her drawer read. *I went. Aren't you proud I'm seeing the world?* She had signed her full name and added across the bottom in block capitals: DON'T WORRY I'M FINE.

One day she would get up the nerve to make the trip. It seemed important to see something Marcy had once seen. She thought it might satisfy her to glimpse the darkened side of her daughter's round and complete life, complete as a moon in the night heavens. Of course there were craters darker than Graceland, places she could never see. Places she wouldn't want to see.

She found the right door, knocked. Kent opened it, betraying little of the surprise she had expected. She remembered this friend of Curtis's, whose self-effacing smile when he played requests on the guitar had appealed to her. A dark, good-looking boy—but as masculine, as normal-looking as could be. No one would have guessed with this one, not like Paul.

"Mrs. Ballard." He stepped back for her to enter, lowered his eyes. She surveyed the tall, graceful sweep of the room, the lit alcove of the kitchen, the sofa before the TV. There, the sofa. She tried to place Paul on it the way he sat on her own, maybe tucked into one corner with a knee drawn up to his chin. That was enough visualizing, she thought—*stop there*. Funny, though, if only she could sustain him that way, in her mind, seated safely in this room, then she would be content enough.

"I wanted to speak with you," she said. He made an awkward gesture toward the furniture. "Thanks, but I don't care to sit."

"Can I get you something? A drink?"

The boy was fairly blushing, wanting somehow to please her, poor thing. She took pity on his predicament—not entirely fair of her, after all, to catch him unawares like this. "No, no, I'll just say my piece and be going. Paul came home the other night with liquor on his breath."

A reasonable pretense for a visit, she thought, though Kent was clearly thrown by it. He opened his mouth, shut it again. She had expected as much. He wasn't about to let it slip that Paul still ran loose on certain nights, that he wasn't always under Kent's watch.

"He's a minor, you realize," she went on. "I allow him to come here, to see you. I made that decision. That's on me. So I'd think that under the circumstances, this one thing would be a fair request."

"Yes, ma'am." He was deeper red now, mortified. "He . . . it won't happen again."

"That's fine. There's only so much I can do, after all, from where I stand. I tell myself it's better he's with you than, well, out there somewhere. I trust that you won't hurt him, like he could be hurt. There's so much that could happen to him in this life, I don't even know where to begin."

"Yes, ma'am," he said, his eyes shifting low. She didn't think he could take much more, and she was sorry. But Kent was their best hope, and he needed to hear this.

"He makes it easy, I know," she said, more gently, "to forget how young he is. He's got a sort of maturity about him. Doesn't he? Like he knows what he's doing, everything's peachy."

He looked at her, nodded warily.

"It's an act. Remember that. You need to keep track. Be responsible for him."

She stepped toward the door, and her eyes made a last pass over the room. She breathed the air, took the measure of this dwelling, the space of another life connected to hers in such a tenuous, accidental way. "Well," she said with a smile, "I mostly just wanted to stop in and see this place for myself. I don't know what that helps. But I thought it would."

alternate lives

Saturday night, the band played a frat house gig—standard fare. But Kent wasn't concentrating, and the first set staggered along as he dropped lines, lost his place. Twice they scrapped the song and started over. All he could think of was Paul, paired with shadow after shadow, a faceless cast of thousands, and of the weight of the life Florie Ballard had placed in his hands. He couldn't stop thinking, hopelessly, and he filled his cup at the keg several times, until finally he could get through a reasonable-sounding song. Their second set improved.

He stayed late, after they had loaded the equipment into Jeff's van. Three girls had been trailing him all night: Amy, Lisa, and something with a J or a G, but he kept confusing them anyway, giving them new names that amused him. Their presence was a welcome relief, or maybe being drunk was the relief. He was very drunk, no other reason he would have stayed to talk without a guitar in his hands. The night faded into oblivion. In the morning he woke in his own bed with a raging thirst, a headache like a scythe blade. And one of the girls, naked, beside him.

He looked at her, asleep on her stomach with her face sideways on the mattress, a little drool glossing her parted lips. She was honey blond, small and soft-looking, not much older than Paul. Well, there you go, he thought. A neat solution. But he was empty of relief. He knew they'd had sex, of some ordinary kind, or he'd dreamed it— little flashes, neutral in tone. Had he liked it? He wasn't in the mood to test desire now. He lifted himself carefully from the bed, went to the bathroom, stared at himself in the mirror for a long time without registering an image.

An hour later she dressed and departed. She'd done this before, it seemed, knew the dance of the one-night stand, left her phone number on a torn scrap of paper as a matter of form. Ginger. He studied the slip for a while, thought of throwing it away, but then set it next to the phone, where the ragged white curl caught his eye every time he passed.

"*Ginger?*" Paul waved the scrap, his voice teasing in mock recrimination—he found it almost immediately.

"She's this girl I met." He sat down on the sofa, met Paul's eyes steadily. "You know, that frat gig Saturday night."

"Yeah, and?"

"And I kind of picked her up." A warmth climbed his neck—but there was no reason, not a reason on earth he should feel guilty about this or let Paul imagine that he did, not for a second. "I slept with her."

"You what?" The question sounded simple enough, but the look on Paul's face made Kent seize up with foreboding.

"I slept with her." He enunciated each word.

Paul closed his mouth and nodded. Arms folded tight, he paced along the end of the sofa. "So. How'd it feel? Good?"

"I was drinking. I don't much remember it, to tell you the truth. You're upset." Kent rubbed his hands over his face. "I guess that's because you're allowed to fuck around and I'm not. Why am I surprised?"

Paul stopped, agape, struggling with apparent shock. "There's a difference!"

"Oh? Well, I'm glad you know the rules to this game, Paul. I wish you'd give me a copy, so I could maybe have a chance to keep up."

"What I do—" Paul paced, his cheeks burning. "That's different and you know it. Don't play dumb. They don't mean anything to me."

Kent shook his head as if to clear the reception. "I never said that girl meant anything—"

"Don't you lie to me, I've never lied to you. Of course she meant something. You went to her for *something*."

"Wait. You—"

"Why couldn't you just pick up some other guy? You could do that—I'd almost be happy if you did that. But no. A girl." He swallowed hard, in tears now. Kent, mystified, rose toward him, and Paul drew back. "Don't you fucking touch me."

He laughed gently. "Paul. You're not making sense."

"*Ginger*." He pushed the tears back, hardened his face. "I was wondering how long your little exploration would last. When you'd get tired of being daring and shocking everyone. Time of your life, wasn't it? Well, it was fun while it lasted."

He was at the door, hand on the knob, and Kent, following, took hold of his shoulders, turned him back against the wall. "Stop it."

The rage in Paul's face had ebbed back to a raw misery, so that all Kent's pretense crumbled away in an instant. "I'm sorry, okay?" Kent said. "God, I had no idea. I wanted to hurt you, I guess, if I could, if there was any way to get through to you, to show you—"

Paul only blinked, expectant and half-hopeful, as if waiting for a puzzle to solve itself. Kent sighed. "I thought we were seeing other people. That's all."

"A girl?" His voice caught on the word.

"I don't know, Paul, don't ask me. She was there. So maybe I'm not gay—I never said I was. Is that so awful, if I'm attracted to *people?*"

"*Yes.* It's the worst possible—"

Kent rolled his eyes. "I used to date girls, remember?"

"Yeah, girls who will marry you and give you children." His forehead dropped against Kent's collar, his voice a mumble near incoherence; Kent had to strain to understand. "And give your parents grandchildren, and give you a normal life."

"Stop it. You're talking crazy." Baffled and touched, he braced Paul back by his limp shoulders. "Look. If I knew who it was okay to be attracted to, you and me never would have gotten together in the first place. Right?"

Paul nodded, eyes down. "So I guess you'll keep seeing her."

"What?"

"Well, you kept her phone number, so—"

Kent laughed wearily. "God, you're impossible. Don't you get it yet? I don't want to see anyone else. I don't want you to see anyone else. I don't want *us* to see anyone else."

Paul went slack against the wall and gazed toward the window. "Kent, you know, emotional monogamy, that's one thing, but sexual . . . I don't think it works. It's an unnatural way of thinking."

Kent backed away, jaw clenched. "You got some convenient philosophies. Whatever gets you off, I guess."

Paul's hands went to his hips. "Look, if I want to experience things, not close myself off from the rest of life, it's not about you. Or us."

He tried to move past, but Kent blocked him, pushed him back. "It's dangerous. You don't think about that, do you? Not to mention the danger you put me in."

"*You're* not in danger!" Paul snapped. He looked down at the fist full of his shirt that now pinned him to the wall, and his eyes narrowed on Kent's face. "It really bothers you, doesn't it, that you don't own me? Congratulations, Kent, you're a hetero after all! Look at you—don't even have the balls to come out of the closet, and still, the idea that some other man is fucking what you're fucking, whatever that—"

"Shut up!" Kent seized hold and slammed him back against the wall, hard enough that Paul's head bounced. Paul fell silent, eyes round and wary. In the sudden stillness, Kent became aware of the force of his fingers still clamped into Paul's arms, pressure enough to leave prints. He was ready to hit him. Hard. He wanted to keep hitting, until Paul relented, until he was transformed.

He released his hold in a spasm. They eyed each other across a little distance, while Kent's anger simmered, restrained but not cooling, and from deep underneath rose the strained fear of an animal. Somehow his life had cornered him here, chained him to this infuriating, irresistible being who would never change, who would never understand him, who would never make sense to him. It was clear to him now, how they would be stuck this way, forever.

"Get out," he said.

Paul's eyebrows lifted. "Excuse me?"

"You heard me." Kent's voice came thick and low. He felt as if someone else, more clearheaded, were speaking for him. But he knew this was right, because he was seconds away from putting a fist in Paul's face, and there stood Paul, still sparring with sarcasm—not the first notion of how to protect himself. "Leave," Kent said. "Before you get hurt." The words brightened for him like the small glow of a candle, and he added calmly, "I don't want to see you. Any more. Ever."

Paul's cocky expression dissolved. "You don't mean that."

"Really?" Kent brought his face close to Paul's, the breath shallow through his nostrils. "Get out. And don't come back." Paul's mouth hung open. "Now."

Paul blinked several times, stunned. "Right," he said, with an almost casual lilt. He turned and walked out, and Kent closed the door behind him, shaking.

As if Paul might try to force his way back in, he remained leaning against the door, while relief seeped through his limbs—relief that it was over, finally, that he was free—even if he did have to stop himself from running out, calling him back, because surely Paul was safer here than he was out there. But no longer his concern. And Paul, with his cast-iron pride, would never come back, not unless Kent went to his knees and begged.

After a while, he sat on the sofa and told himself—lips moving—that it was better this way, that he had finally done the right thing. And he felt something he hadn't expected, the quiet presence of his own life returning to him. He began to think of the next day, the future, without Paul, and it wasn't bleak.

Two hours later, before Kent had thought to move from his position on the sofa, Paul came back. Kent answered his knock, let him in before he could think of what he needed to say. There was something. It had come more than once to the surface of his tumbling thoughts of the past two hours, so that he had shaped scenes of Paul's return out of longing, even in the midst of buoyant relief that Paul was not there.

"What are you doing here?" he asked. Nothing remained of his anger. His two deepest desires, wanting Paul back and wanting him gone, had canceled each other perfectly so that now, faced with Paul in the flesh, it was hard to feel much of anything, even surprise.

Paul sat on the sofa. He met Kent's eyes once and turned away again without a word. One hand still on the knob of the open door, Kent watched him, waiting for him to leave, to make a speech, something. He had never seen that butterfly fastened so firmly to one spot.

"Do I need to pick you up and throw you out?" Kent approached the sofa, still so lightened from their breaking that his voice carried no weight. So light that he began to laugh in slight spasms of breath. He sat down beside Paul, exhausted, laughing. *In a minute*, he thought, *when I have the energy, I'll have to pitch him into the hall*. Paul gave him a hurt glance but remained in place, as if to say he wasn't going anywhere, wasn't planning to move an inch, no matter what Kent said.

"So," Kent said after a minute. "Tell me a story."

"With you I get scared."

Kent blinked, examined Paul's profile. "That's actually not a bad story."

"I don't want to leave," he said flatly. His breath came quicker. "I don't want to leave. I don't want to leave."

"Okay." He spoke now into Paul's hair, and Paul began kissing his neck with energy. "But, hold on. We have to talk about this." It seemed worth a shot, though they were already beyond talk, and he didn't remember anymore what the topic was.

"Later," Paul said, and Kent thought, *Later, that's good, later we'll get this straight, sort it out, do it right*.

pda

Muriel came into town one day in February to have lunch with Sidra at East-West, partly to get the report on Paul. "He spends time with this friend of Curtis's, still?" was as much, once they had covered school work, as she knew how to ask. And Sidra answered yes, he spent a lot of time with Kent. So much she hardly saw him anymore.

"He's been asking to spend more of his weekends with you," Muriel confided, stirring lemon into her tea while they waited for their salads. "The whole discussion, it's upset his father. Like you wouldn't imagine."

"Really?" Sidra couldn't help reacting with interest. In Paul's eyes, he was hardly his father's son any longer—more like a disturbing but politely tolerated distant relation, one gladly handed off to other caretakers.

"I *know*," Muriel said, as if to confirm Paul's view of it. "But I think he's been telling himself all along that Paul still lives at home with us." She laughed a little and caught herself with one hand. "Oh, Lord, it's not funny. It's hard, is what it is—hard to let them go, to live their own lives. And Dan loved that boy. Still does—more than he knows how to show."

Sidra nodded in sympathy, not knowing what to say except *Men aren't always fixable*. But you try, she thought. You try, and maybe they even try, and by small steps, if you're lucky, they come around.

"It's been good for Paul, being with you and your mom," Muriel said. "So, what do you think? You mind keeping him the weekends too?"

"Fine by me. But what about Dan? He won't mind?"

She smiled, her eyes wrinkling sadly. "Honey, it's about time he minded something in all this." She brightened. "But let's talk about this wedding of yours. I want to hear every detail."

‸

That night Sidra was summoned to attend band rehearsal, since they were getting ready for a gig at Picola's, one of the snazzier clubs in town. Their hopes were modest—just a chance to move up a tier in the quality of local clubs that would hire them—but still, it was enough to get them excited. She found herself, though, tiring of the band altogether, of her assigned role as audience. The endless farce of faking enthusiasm for the same old songs, over and over—her duty as girlfriend.

She thought it was about time Paul joined the groupie pool, as a distraction for her, if nothing else. He had never been more than a lurker in the garage, never ventured at all to the trainyard. "You think so?" he asked, hesitant, when she caught up with him after school. He dropped his books on his desk, collapsed backward on the bed, arms outstretched. "Kent wanted me to come. But I thought it would be too weird, you know?"

"What, weird!" she scoffed, before the image of it came to her—a boy perched amid the adoring girls, some of whom had spent years quietly pursuing Kent. "Well, so what if it is?" she amended with a shrug. "The question is, do you want to come?"

His grin, the light in his eyes, answered for him. "You're coming," she said. "Be ready at eight."

In the warehouse, Paul sat quietly beside her—behind her, really—their tall, shared crate angled so that he could almost use her as a shield from the other groupies and from the makeshift stage, where the band worked methodically through the playlist. Two of the regulars, Robin and Tiff, sat together near the front; they had each slept with a band member or two over the years but never achieved girlfriend status. Lyle had brought a girl named Mimi, who sat off by herself, fidgeting on her crate as if it were giving her splinters. She was big-boned, with black curls snugged back in a ponytail and glittery, wary eyes. She returned Sidra's smile of greeting and looked away again.

Paul sat close, his shoulder, thigh, and ankle brushing against hers. Their heels, a foot off the ground, bounced lightly against the crate. She turned now and then to speak in his ear, provide liner notes for the songs, and he nodded, concentrating; he clapped when she clapped. Robin caught her eye from across the room, mouthed *"That's him?"* pointing toward Paul behind the shielding palm of her hand. When Sidra nodded, Robin rounded her eyes. Those two, Robin and Tiff, knew everything. In the next few lulls, Sidra hooked her arm around Paul's neck, whispered all the dirt she knew about Robin and Tiff. Paul stifled giggles in her shoulder. And if anyone wondered before, they had a clearer picture now—Paul was with her.

Toward the end of the first set, Kent broke a string. It would take several minutes to fix. Jeff slipped off his guitar, reached for his cigarettes. The girls hopped down from their crates and stretched with studied indifference, keeping apart, but ready in an instant to edge up to the first boy who offered an opening. Lyle tightened and tapped at the snare, and Sidra knew that after a measured, casual interval, he would wander toward the dark-haired girl. Curtis had nothing to do but pretend to tune, pretend his amp needed adjusting. On any other night, he would have come down from the stage to spend a minute with Sidra—not tonight, she was sure.

But to her surprise, he laid the bass down. She heard Paul exhale once, sharply, and he became very still—Curtis was approaching, wending through the corridor of crates. Kent, kneeling on stage, raised his eyes. He couldn't intervene. But it was okay. *It's okay,* she wanted to say, to Kent, to everyone. She didn't know why, but she trusted Curtis.

He stopped before her, met her eyes sternly. She gave him a little smile and looked away. Paul sat with hands clamped over the edge of the crate at either side of his thighs, looking prepared for flight if necessary. But he didn't move, and when Curtis turned to face him, their eyes almost on a level, Paul was gazing back with a stilled, soft intensity.

Curtis raised his eyebrows casually—a sort of greeting, an invitation. Paul took it, said, "Y'all are really good." He tipped his head, not quite smiling, his studious gaze locked and rapt. He considered a moment and added, "You play really well."

Diffident, Curtis shifted his shoulders but wouldn't look down, wouldn't smile. "We're a little rough," he said.

"No, I mean you," Paul clarified, with an air of pleased precision. "The bass."

Curtis stared, eyebrows arched, quizzical. "You don't really hear the bass." He glanced at Sidra. "*She* doesn't hear it. It's like you only really notice it when it's not there."

"I hear it fine," Paul insisted. "You're good."

"Thanks." He met Paul's eyes again, then looked back toward the stage; at the same moment Kent turned his face away, the guitar slung over his shoulders again. "Well. Better get back." Like a soldier in the queen's service, he silently petitioned Sidra for release. She smiled. He left.

Paul flicked his eyes at her, checking, a little sheepish, saying nothing. But the preparations at the stage area—thwang of guitar, roll of drum, in random bursts—took longer than he might have expected to grow into obliterating noise. He cleared his throat. "I didn't expect that. I mean—" He sighed, distressed, blinking toward the stage. "I just came to see Kent. I guess I wasn't . . . prepared."

"You did great," Sidra said, and added, "He'll get better."

He shivered. "God, darlin', that was good enough."

⤳

In the dim red light beneath the exit sign, in the back corridor of Picola's, Paul and Kent were making out—a stolen moment in a slim privacy. Vigorous as puppies, their hands in each others' clothes, their mouths slipping and seeking and unashamed. Like bad children. Like children who had been good for too long, suddenly released from rules. There was no audience, other than Sidra's accidental glimpse. And yet, they were so close to one—the band busy with setup just around the corner. Sidra kept walking, resumed her work. By the time she glanced up again some minutes later, Paul and Kent had returned to the stage.

Paul had joined their flock, the girlfriends and assorted others who could be counted on to arrive for setup. Here, they were the roadies of incidentals: move this, plug that, find duct tape, but mainly stay out of the way: The Boys were busy. Curtis was always so keyed up close to a show that Sidra didn't crave his company anyway, was glad to be banished from the stage area and his presence. But Paul and Kent, it seemed, had made their own arrangements. Though they worked at separate tasks and barely made eye contact, their awareness of each other remained palpable, almost visible. Sidra imagined she could see beams of energy crossing the space between them, felt jealous and implicated and thrilled with her secret.

When they were nearly finished with setup, Lyle wandered over toward her with hands jammed in his pockets, singling her out with a smile.

"Where's Mimi?" she asked, feeling giddy. She nudged his shoulder with hers.

"Who? Oh, yeah. She's—" He shrugged. "She might come tonight, I guess. She's got a kid, so it's tricky."

She studied him, the unreadable trouble of love in his eyes. So much like her own recent shiftings, perhaps. Except that she was happy now, wanted everyone else happy.

She said, "I like her. She seems nice."

"Yeah." He made an ambiguous twist with his mouth, looked off toward the stage, where Paul perched on an amp with his face tipped back to bask in the newly rigged spots. Kent leaned close over his shoulder to whisper something that made Paul laugh brightly. Lyle shuddered. "Jeez, I wish they'd cut out that PDA shit."

Surprised, Sidra wondered what he had seen to count as a public display, or what she herself had missed. She played it casual. "Oh, come on. What's wrong with a little open affection?"

"It's embarrassing, that's what."

She put her hands on her hips, cocked her head. "And here I thought you were so open-minded!"

"Hey, I'm fine with them. Just, get a room, is all I'm saying."

"But you don't mind when me and Curtis do that."

He raised an eyebrow, unsmiling. "Yeah, I do."

She couldn't help it, found Curtis where she knew he would be, fiddling with the light board in the back of the room. There was nothing left to hold his attention now, nothing he could claim, and she went to him and fit her body against his in the circle of his arms. "Kiss me," she said, and he did, deeply, turned her back against the wall and kissed her again.

"Poor Lyle." She giggled, as Curtis's mouth moved down her neck. "He hates this PDA shit."

Curtis grunted. "He's just jealous. You realize that."

"Well, then he's jealous of Kent and Paul too because he said the same thing about them."

Curtis stiffened, mouth at her collar bone, hands on her hips. "Sid. Not while I'm kissing you, all right? That's a rule."

"Oh, listen to Mister Rule Man, laying down the law! Who says you make the rules anyhow?"

Grinning, he pinned her wrists gently to the wall above her head. "How about that paper that's gonna say Mrs. Sidra Cantrell?"

"Oh, well, that. I wouldn't count on that for much. Especially since I'm keeping my own name."

Curtis drew back, frowning, waiting for her placid face to reveal the joke. "We'll talk," he said finally.

"Sorry, babe, but there's really nothing to talk about."

He squinted at her, and she could tell by the grinding of his teeth that he was trying to decide how mad he ought to be. "Why, Sidra?" he asked, his tone no more exasperated than usual. "Why is it always something with you? I mean, we're getting married, and we can't have two minutes of just—" He smoothed a hand flat across the air, horizontal, as if to invoke a calm sea.

She smiled, half-apologetic. "You didn't think things were going to change, did you?"

in the coming days

Kent wanted to go away for a weekend, down to Tybee, but it never seemed to work out. Though Paul now spent most weekends in Athens, with extended curfews, he was hesitant to ask for more. "What's it going to take to get you on a boat?" Kent asked.

"Ah, the *Rapture*. That thing you insist on calling a she. Still planning to run off with her?"

"Yeah, one day." He told Paul often of his dream to buy the boat, to loose the slips of the world, fully and forever.

"So romantic," Paul said with a sidelong look, his shifty mix of sincerity and irony. "But alone?"

"Why?" Kent challenged. "You want to go with me?"

Paul grinned, sidled close, tugged back. "Why? You want me to go?"

Of course, Paul would never go, Kent knew, not if the *Rapture* were the ark and all the world flooded around him. But what a perfect island, to have Paul on a boat. So Kent smiled and didn't answer, wanting to hold that fleeting moment of balance for as long as he could, the two brilliant, contrary dreams like a pair of birds perched on a single hand, both at once.

⤳

They went to a local park instead, walked along the banks of the Oconee River, and Paul told Kent about turning a few tricks in these very woods when he had first come to town. Still plenty of action out here, he claimed. It was the first week of March and warm for the season, the river a dull metallic, rushing and broken over its full width with unseen stones. Trash hung in the trees at Kent's eye level, deposits of a recent flood. Though elsewhere in Athens the peach and pear trees were in bloom, daffodils and a pale carpet of violets, here there were no flowers yet, the trees still bare but for colorless strips of plastic and other flood detritus.

It was what he most wanted to escape, this waste of humanity. Sometimes the AM radio fundamentalists started making sense to him, with their extremist talk of salvation, damnation, of separating oneself from the evils of the world. He tuned in sometimes on car trips, once paid attention on a drive to Tybee because a woman mentioned the Rapture. In the coming days, she'd explained, the true believers—the saved—and the chosen of God would be taken up as if on a great whirlwind and they would ascend into heaven, not as spirits but as living things. Those buried in the earth would be exhumed, their bodies restored for the journey. To the people left behind, it would appear as a great vanishing of bodies, from cars and streets and houses, from stores and schools, from places of business, from churches everywhere, and not one would know in advance the hour or the day. For those who remained, there would be no second chance. She urged her listeners to look to their souls and prepare.

Beyond the fact that it amused him to think of his boat as such a vehicle—he had always thought of the name as having more to do with earthly love—he didn't know what to make of the woman's words. He wasn't sure how to consider his soul. It was the bodies that intrigued him more. What use would they all have for bodies in the afterlife?

He and Paul sat on a table of stone at the river's edge, Paul farther out with his arms around his knees, his profile gilt-edged before the sun of afternoon. "It's nice here," Paul said. "All this water—it's reassuring. Flows straight home to Greene County, to the lake. This river saved me, for years and years." He kissed his fingers, trailed them into the water that churned past the rock. Lowering one sneaker, he scooped up a little spray. Then he felt his way farther out, moved without warning until both shoes were submerged, and he stood in water above his ankles, feet braced below the surface and the water tugging fat cuffs on his jeans.

Kent laughed. "What the hell—? That's got to be freezing."

"It's a little cold." He stepped farther out on rickety steps, and the water rose to his knees. "I'm not recommending it."

Paul stood in the river with his back to the shore, hands on his hips, as if taking stock of his own private kingdom. The water dragged against his legs, nudging, coaxing, and he stood with his feet planted somewhere in the unseen bottom, somewhere among the rocks and algae and all that slid and tumbled beneath the surface. Kent didn't trust the footing in that current. He fought a crazy urge to go pick Paul up, carry him back onto the shore.

"You're going to stink," Kent said. "You know that water's polluted, don't you?" Paul turned to face him, approached on steps so wobbling that Kent cringed. "Don't fall. Please."

"Would you come in after me, if I fell?"

"No."

Paul pretended to lose his balance, pitched forward and caught himself with his hands on the rock where Kent sat. Kent didn't react, held still and met the boy's eyes, his long, deep, omniscient gaze. "Yes, you would," Paul said. He tipped his head as if puzzled by his own pronouncement, leaned closer and kissed Kent softly. In the next minute, he bent and caught a handful of water. Before Kent could move, Paul dribbled the water onto Kent's head, stroked it into his hair; it drizzled cold down his forehead.

He grunted in disgust and went to back away, but Paul held a firm, steadying hand at the back of his head, his face close and intent. "That's just your christening," he said. "What you need is full-immersion baptism, so you know you been down and back." He let go, stood straight again in the water.

Kent smiled ruefully. "Were you baptized that way?"

"Oh, hell, yeah. Weren't you?"

"I'm Episcopalian."

"Lord, look down," Paul said. "A lost one in our midst. A sinner, and unrepentant. I'm gonna have to get to work on you."

Kent shook his head, unamused, suddenly tired. "I'd say you've done enough already."

"Oh, baby. Life's hard."

"Fuck you," he said mildly. He gazed upstream. "If I'm lost, you're the reason."

Paul laughed, impressed. "Hey, easy now. I'm just playing."

"Yeah, what else is new?" He picked up a pine cone and began ripping off pieces, tossing them past Paul's legs into the water. "I wouldn't be too sure I'd come in there after you. Not if you were drowning."

Paul was silent, studying him with a calm that made Kent's heartbeat deepen and slow in spite of himself.

"You want me to come out now?"

"Yes."

"It's cold," Paul admitted, looking into the water that turned around his legs, looking at Kent, weighing his options. "My legs are going numb. You gonna take care of me?" He leaned over the rock, held Kent's ankles for balance.

Kent cupped his hands over Paul's, which were icy and wet with the river. "You know so much—what am I thinking now?"

Paul grinned. "Something dirty?"

"Wrong."

⤶

They went home and peeled off Paul's wet clothes and made love in long rectangles of sunlight that quartered Kent's bed. For long afterward, they lay dazed and torpid, half-asleep in the sun, facing each other. Paul's arm was propped along Kent's neck, fingers playing in his hair. "Do you wish I was a girl?" he murmured.

"No." Kent's fingers traveled down the boy's ribs and belly, knuckles curling to brush the shallow basin inside his hip. "Do you wish I was Curtis?"

"No. Do you wish I was a boy with a cunt?"

"No. Do you wish . . . what is it that you want from them anyway? Those other men."

"Nothing you can give me."

"How do you know? Try me."

Paul blinked into the sun, his eyes pooled with light. "Newness.

The endless first time. And that look in their eyes—pure desire, like
you can only feel for something that's not yours."

"I can do that."

"No, you can't. You already know I belong to you."

Kent closed his eyes, so peaceful that he was almost ready to accept that offering. Just now it seemed enough. His fingers traced slow
circles on Paul's back. "Do you wish I was one of them?"

"No. But—"

"But what?"

"I like the chase, you know? The conquest. I like the surrender. I
like to see them naked. That's about it. After that, I just close my
eyes and pretend they're you."

"Really?"

"Always. But, you know, I don't do it as much as you like to think."

"What makes you think you know what I think?"

Paul smiled and closed his eyes. Kent drifted off kissing the tender inside of his forearm, woke again bathed in a redder light, approaching sunset.

"You awake?" Paul murmured. "Guess what? Guess when my birthday is?"

Kent opened his eyes, found Paul's before him, sleepy and calm,
shadowed in the fading light. "When?"

"Three weeks. March twenty-ninth."

"It is?" He didn't say *you'll be eighteen,* though it struck him instantly, a surprise. It had never really occurred to him that Paul would
eventually age. He barely dared to think, yet, how eighteen meant
the end of curfews, the beginning of Paul's freedom to live where and
how he pleased.

Kent smiled. "What do you want for your birthday?"

"Oh . . . the possibilities!"

〜

Kent woke again in the dark, and Paul was gone. The scramble of his dream made him struggle for a moment to recall if Paul had ever been there, or if he had been alone all along, naked in the dark. He sat bolt upright in the bed, touched on the reality of tangled bedsheets, the stark light from the hall. He couldn't think straight enough to find his clothes.

There was a noise from the kitchen, a curse. Paul's voice. Kent breathed in relief. "Paul," he called. "What are you doing?"

"Oh, you're up. Good. I thought you were going to sleep straight through dinner." He appeared in the doorway. "I'm cooking. Don't faint."

"That's a little scary." Kent rubbed his eyes, rubbed his scalp vigorously. "Cooking what?"

"A surprise." He vanished again.

"Don't," Kent called. "Come here."

He returned. "What, babe?"

"Come here."

Paul came to the bed and Kent reached for his hand, pulled him down beside him. He kissed the orbits of the boy's eyes, his chin, his mouth, and Paul's mouth smiled against his, arms tendriled and folding around Kent's neck. They kissed for a long while before Paul laughed, breaking away. "You're gonna burn it."

"I don't care."

"I do." He gave Kent a smack on the lips. "Wait here."

He left and returned a minute later, the bowl of a wooden spoon balanced carefully over his open palm. "You have to taste this."

"Oh, Jesus. What is it?"

"You'll see."

"You're gonna have to tell me what it is."

"Nope. It's a surprise. Don't you trust me?"

"No."

"Yes, you do." Paul held the spoon to Kent's lips. "You think maybe it's poison? Maybe it's a little bite of heaven. You're about to find out. Open."

the elixir

Monday morning, another one. I'm finished with the feeding and am fetching a wheelbarrow to start mucking stalls, when I feel my boot roll something as soft and little as a mouse. It tumbles a few feet along the brick-lined hall, spinning dust and cobwebs and horsehair and specks of wood shavings about itself as it goes. When I pick it up, it's grown into a grayish cocoon wrapped around a pulse of life. I know it's alive—the way you know a cocoon has life in it, despite the fact that I just kicked it half across the floor—but it's so entangled it can't move. I hold it as gently as I can and worry some of the grime away with my fingernails. A black reed of a beak appears, like a grain of wild rice, then a glimmer of green feathers, a pumping iridescent breast the size of my thumb. Another damned hummingbird.

They come in here after the fluorescent lights. Maybe a thing with a brain the size of a needle's eye can't tell the difference between a gladiolus and a tube full of electricity—I don't know—but they'll fly in here sometimes and just bounce off the lights like moths. I saw one doing that for a good ten minutes, until I scootched it out the door with a broom; then it flew away. If I don't catch them in time, they'll exhaust themselves and wind up on the floor, like this one. Their metabolism's so fast they just short out after a while.

Once I've uncovered her white throat, I know it's a female. Maybe she's the same one I chased out yesterday. "Stubborn," I tell her. "See where it got you." But you can't reason with a bird as if she were your teenage daughter. Then again, teenagers don't necessarily listen any better than birds—they're bound to go zinging off their own bright lights, deaf to common sense.

With Marcy, it was cities. First Atlanta, then Jacksonville, then Memphis—three times home in the back of a police car. Between those, and after, I never knew her destinations or what drew her one place or another. Something about a city. She'd show you with her glass-hard eyes and the set of her chin which way she was oriented, as if she were picking up a distant signal other people couldn't hear. As if the whole time you were trying to talk to her, she was listening to something else.

The truth was, I didn't understand that girl. I wanted reasons. Sometimes I blamed her dad for not paying any attention to her. "She's not easy to love," Jimmy would inform me like it was news, like I ought to be outraged with him that she wasn't the older one made over again, and I'd holler back, *She's thirteen. You're right she ain't Sidra. But she's your daughter.* We would fall to silence, and later Marcy might pass through to get a Pop-Tart and go back to her room, without ever looking, as if she walked in another reality and Jimmy and I were just a background flutter, characters on her TV.

After Atlanta, she returned armored in the proof that she could take care of herself. "It's not about you," she would say. "It's not about him, either." But I wanted a cause, and when she took off for Memphis I settled on Jimmy. He came home one day hauling the trailer, another horse he'd got for a bargain to make Sidra light up, and I said, "No, sir. You are not putting another horse in my barn, not at a time like this." He said, fine, they'd pasture it over at Ernie's place, and I said, fine, and he could go with it. I meant it too. After that, it was me and Sidra, she barely sixteen and hating me on her father's account, old enough to keep clear of me so it got to be like living alone, except for those brief times when Marcy was home.

The last time I saw her the way I think of her now, she was fourteen—round, pretty face, long brown hair I used to wash and comb. I didn't see her again until she was nineteen and sick, too weak to stand. "I'm dying, Mama," is what she told me over the phone, as if there would be no use arguing. "I need a place to stay for a while."

She came off the plane in a wheelchair. A flight attendant rolled her through a dazzle of sun that flooded the glass walls of the terminal, so that she all but vanished in light. Then she was before me, my daughter—wide blue eyes and crooked smile—wanting to know, would I have recognized her.

She was true to her word, about the dying, though at times her body argued otherwise. Miracle drugs—first one, then another—briefly lifted her strength, and for a time she would feel well. But eventually I had to quit my job to look after her, to feed her and clean the vomit and try, during the bad spells, to keep her in bed. She wandered. Even after she lost her sight, I'd find her bumping around the house, disoriented, looking for a door.

Once in winter at midnight, I found her outside in nothing but a nightgown, barefoot in the garden, out of her wits. "Come inside, love," I begged, tugging her chilled arm, but she persisted toward the west, chin thrust before her as if it knew the way. "Why are you so stubborn? Look where it's gotten you." Instructive, forgetting her blindness, I pointed to the coiled hose where her feet were tangled, the naked, frost-crusted vines climbing the trellis. But she didn't know me. She had somewhere to go, it seemed, and it took me a time to turn her face, to coax her back indoors. From then on, I put her down each night in my own bed, between my body and the wall.

Nine times in fourteen months I carried her to the emergency room—vomiting, diarrhea, pneumonia, blindness, dementia—words I didn't know how to attach to my daughter. An IV went directly into her chest. A tube served her last meals. I cleaned her as I had when she was a baby—never, never in all my prayers, did I imagine a child returned this way. Forty-four different medications, and each one wore itself out, or wore her out, and no sooner one horror banished than another rooted in a new spot, resisting the drugs or caused by the drugs, the internal functions in chaos and shutdown and revolt.

It seemed wrong, after all that, that the one to end it would be a strain of tuberculosis only birds get. The doctor thought she'd carried it for some time, that she'd probably picked it up from pigeon droppings. In a city, he said, she could hardly have avoided exposure. It was in the air that everyone breathed.

⌒

This spring, five years after her death, with Sidra off married and Paul out on his own, the hummingbirds started showing up. I find them buzzing along the walls a few inches from the ground or panting in the horses' bedding, their little feet rimed with cobwebs. One I found actually caught in a new web, suspended from a crossbeam like some spider's lunch, with its miniature wings outspread. I looked up, and it blinked—I swear I saw it blink at me with its black pin eyes.

After Marcy died the way she did, I never wanted to touch a bird, any bird. Dirty things, they seemed. And these minute visitors so often arrive coated in a filth denser than their own bodies. But I can't just leave them to die. Hummingbirds never touch the earth if they can help it, so once they're down they must have no capacity to cast off the lint of the world. Perhaps their bodies even attract it somehow. But underneath the matted debris, they're like jewels still; just lift it off and they shimmer again.

I admit it's a trial to clean a thing so delicate, always feeling that one unfortunate twitch of your finger could crush it beyond repair. But I always try. I know some magic too. This little female I carry up to the house this morning—she's weaker than most, still partly cocooned, won't even lift her head to give me a defiant look like some of them do. On the back porch, I drop two sugar cubes in a coffee mug, add some water, pop the mug into the microwave. While it warms I use a pair of tweezers, still out here from last time, to remove the remaining cobwebs and one long dark horsetail hair that has the bird bound like a package. When she's free, she lies on her side in my palm, breathing five breaths for every second.

"You're going to use up your life awful fast at that rate," I tell her. They never listen. "Sorry about kicking you," I add. "That probably didn't help."

I take the mug out of the microwave and stir the water, then scoop out a teaspoonful. Specks of sugar are still visible in the spoon's silver bowl, but I hold it up to the bird anyway, submerge the tip of her reedlike beak. At first she doesn't move. Then her black lash of a tongue flicks out once, experimentally. Pretty soon the tongue is going like the needle of a sewing machine, ravenous. I'm freshly amazed. Even caged in my loose-curled fingers—surely she's terrified of this giant— the bird knows sugar when she tastes it, knows her body needs it, and she drinks.

For a full minute she drinks, then seems to tire. She looks at me. Her stiff matchstick wings are spread against my palm like little flippers, propping her upright—what intricate mechanisms of the body must be required to beat those wings into a blur, to zip quick as a bee to a flower cup and then hover, poised there in startling visibility. What strength. I've never kicked one across a floor before, can't imagine the damage. But I go outside onto the step and open my hand.

There is no moment of waiting, hoping. Like magic, she rises. Her wings hum with effort, and her leaving is slow, gradual, as if her body is heavier than she remembers. But still, she rises, over the barn and past it. To the limits of vision, she is a dark seed lofted into the morning, and I clap my hands to my face, forgetting the dirtiness of birds.

All I wanted, in the end, was one last drug. Marcy lay in a hospital bed, her long, clean hair spread on the pillow around her upturned face. She weighed eighty-two pounds. She didn't know me, didn't know where her body lay, spoke urgently in words—as clear as daylight—that made no human sense. There has to be another drug, I insisted. Someone's lab must hold a cure, newly cooked, experimental, untested. I'll take anything.

What a slap from God to see these exhausted birds revived, again and again, with a single spoonful of kitchen sugar. But I never get tired of it.

acknowledgments

I'd like to thank all those whose encouragement has been essential to the growth of this book. First, my parents—I couldn't have done anything without their continuous support in my life. Jim Kilgo was the first writer to believe in my work. His confidence has kept me going for years. Stan Lindberg took a chance on publishing my first story and then cared enough to engage with it on a sentence level until it was right. His influence on the literary world will be sadly missed.

Thanks to Elisabeth Schmitz, my editor at Grove/Atlantic, for her insight, instinct, and unflagging attention to detail in helping this book reach its final form. I'm also indebted to my many readers over the years whose response helped me shape revisions, especially to Lauren Cobb, my indispensable one, and to Lorraine Lopez. Buck Butler has a sharp editorial eye, and his support has been a daily source of energy. I'm also grateful for the friendship, advice, and optimism of many more along the way, especially Karen McElmurray, Ed Hohlbein, Bonni Huff, Marie Bruce, Liz Mandrell, John Allison, Steve Almond, and Lara JK Wilson.

Special heartfelt thanks to my agent, Jay Acton, whose belief in the book has been its strongest advocate, and to Amy Bagwell, without whom I and the book would be nowhere. Along with Karen Schwenk, another fine reader, Amy has shepherded this book toward publication with amazing generosity, sensitivity, and enthusiasm, and I really can't thank her enough for all she's done.